Thomas Hugo

The Bewick Collector

a supplement to a descriptive catalogue of the works of Thomas and John Bewick -

consisting of additions to the various divisions of cuts, wood blocks, etc.

Thomas Hugo

The Bewick Collector
a supplement to a descriptive catalogue of the works of Thomas and John Bewick - consisting of additions to the various divisions of cuts, wood blocks, etc.

ISBN/EAN: 9783337368692

Printed in Europe, USA, Canada, Australia, Japan

Cover: Foto ©Andreas Hilbeck / pixelio.de

More available books at **www.hansebooks.com**

The Bewick Collector.

A

SUPPLEMENT

TO

A DESCRIPTIVE CATALOGUE

OF THE WORKS OF

THOMAS AND JOHN BEWICK;

CONSISTING OF

ADDITIONS TO THE VARIOUS DIVISIONS OF CUTS,
WOOD BLOCKS, ETC.,

ENUMERATED IN THAT WORK.

The whole described from the Originals

CONTAINED IN THE LARGEST AND MOST PERFECT COLLECTION
EVER FORMED,

AND ILLUSTRATED WITH A HUNDRED AND EIGHTY CUTS.

BY

THOMAS HUGO, M.A., F.R.S.L., F.S.A., ETC.,

Vice-President of the London and Middlesex Archæological Society;
Honorary Fellow and Honorary Member of various other Literary and Archæological Societies;
Rector of All Saints, Bishopsgate;
etc. etc. etc.

THE POSSESSOR OF THE COLLECTION.

LONDON:

L. REEVE AND CO., 5, HENRIETTA STREET,

COVENT GARDEN.

MDCCCLXVIII.

J. E. TAYLOR AND CO., PRINTERS,
LITTLE QUEEN STREET, LINCOLN'S INN FIELDS.

PREFACE.

Although but a space of little more than two years
has elapsed since the appearance of 'The Bewick
Collector,' and the interval may accordingly be considered more than ordinarily brief between the issue
of that work and of the present Supplement to it,
there are exceptional circumstances which will be held,
I think, more than sufficient to justify me in adopting
the course which I am now taking.

The book was hardly published before I was well-
nigh inundated by consignments from all quarters
far and near, including two from America, of parcels
of greater or less magnitude, whose owners solicited
my judgment of their multifarious and too often un-
interesting contents. Some of these were gifts, a few
were for inspection only—the rest were for sale.
Books, Pamphlets, Miscellaneous Engravings, Wood
Blocks, crowded on each other. For many months I
positively lived—so far as important duties would
allow me, and frequently at a considerable outlay of
labour, patience, and self-denial—among old woodcuts

and their impressions. Gradually the storm cleared, the influx of boxes and parcels became less and less, and finally ceased, so that during the last few months I have had sufficient leisure to arrange and describe the result, and in this manner to make the various treasures, thus strangely yet most happily brought together from so many and distant quarters, available for the use and enjoyment of others as well as of their more immediate owner.

From an inventory which I have kept of the subjects of examination, I find that I have had before me about seven thousand Books and upwards of fifty thousand Wood Blocks. A large proportion of the latter, however, came under my notice during three journeys which I have made in various parts of England, especially the five northernmost counties, in the course of the last two years. Many scores—I might truly say hundreds—of old printing offices have I ransacked— not only in Newcastle and the neighbourhood, but in London and various other and distant places where books were published with Illustrations by Thomas Bewick—hundreds of booksellers visited and corresponded with. If, therefore, the result be inadequate or unsatisfactory, which few, I think, will allege, it is owing neither to want of zeal in the pursuit nor to stint in the employment of means.

It may not be without interest for some of my readers if I remark that the additions to my Books and to my Wood Blocks have almost invariably been made from different localities. Hardly a tenth part of the former—the additions to my Books—have been obtained from Northumberland, Durham, Cumberland, and Westmoreland; while, on the other hand, with the exception of some interesting London purchases, very few Wood Blocks of Bewick's execution have been discovered beyond the limits of those four counties. The reason lies apparently in the fact that in the search for Books illustrated by Thomas and John Bewick the extreme north of England had been thoroughly examined and exhausted; while Blocks engraved by the former, especially those for miscellaneous purposes, were done almost exclusively for his immediate neighbours, and consequently were not to be found at a distance from their several localities. The great majority of his most celebrated works for remote employers were already included in my Collection, and I have now done my best to make his own neighbourhood even more bare of his Blocks than it previously was of Books illustrated by him.

These, then, are the reasons which induce me to offer the present Supplement to all who feel interested in the Artists and their labours. Circumstances have crowded into weeks and months what is ordinarily the result of the successful labours of many and long years. And the repose which has followed the pressure of the throng, if it have not added to the result, has at least gone far to impart the certainty that little if aught more remains to be effected, and to make me feel that I shall do well, without a delay which would now be unproductive and consequently useless, to present those who have already testified their approbation of my work with the Additions which I may not unreasonably hope will supplement and complete it.

Touching the former volume, I have in the first place to tender my best acknowledgments for the very flattering reception with which it has been honoured by the public press at large. Not only has it received the hearty approbation of various of our London critics, but a goodly number of the provincial journals, including more than one in Bewick's own noble town, have been pleased to comment most favourably and handsomely on my labours. I have heard, indeed, but a single adverse criticism, and that from but one or two private objectors. It is to the effect that I have created an unnecessary labour and inflicted a gratuitous weariness on my reader by the enumeration of " another " and yet " another " duplicate of many of the articles. I beg in reply to remind such a critic that my book is professedly and designedly not only a Catalogue of the Works of the Artists but of my own Collection, and that the mention of each article is, accordingly, a very important and indeed necessary feature in such a work. And, further, I take leave to add that it is rather hard, when I have spread so rich and varied an entertainment for my guests, that I should be grudged a single and homely dish for my own special gratification.

There is, however, a further reason which will hereafter in all probability impart a public value to what is now, I own, but a private advantage. The feeling is strong within me, daily increasing in intensity, and all but arrived, if it have not quite done so, at the certainty of a fixed determination, that either the British Museum, or some other National Art Collection, shall hereafter be, as it ought, the depository of this host of artistic treasures. There the multitude of unique articles, which not only impart to it an unapproachable precedence, but remove it from even distant comparison,—the wonderful series of Books and Pamphlets, many apparently unknown beyond its limits, others of hardly less rarity, including a goodly number of volumes either the property of Thomas Bewick himself, or presented by or to other celebrated persons, or for some other reason possessed of special interest, —the matchless collection of Proofs in various states, —the immense aggregate of Miscellaneous Cuts done for public purposes and private persons, the fruits of the life-long gatherings of well-known Collectors,—and, perhaps above all, as, if possible, more than all unique and incomparable, the priceless assemblage of Wood Blocks, as well of many of the most celebrated books illustrated by Thomas and John Bewick, as of a multitude of the best performances of the elder brother for all kinds of purposes of business and amusement— would be in their rightful place, secure from casualties which in their case would be an irreparable loss to Art in general, and safely preserved for the study and admiration of generations yet to come. In the event of my Collection being deposited in such an Institution, where the possession of duplicates for careful comparison would be estimated as it deserves, the present Catalogue would acquire a greatly increased value, as not only an enumeration of the results of private and long-pursued research, and a guide to Collectors desirous of following, so far at least as possible, in the same track, but a ready key to the contents of a great Public Department of Art. So that what now appears a blemish to the critics just referred to may ultimately become a thing of special utility to them and multitudes besides.

Let me add that a far more serious objection—which, however, I have not met with—might have been advanced against my work, and for which I should have had humbly to solicit forgiveness. I am sorrowfully conscious that among the Books and Pamphlets there are more than a few—upwards of forty at least—which should never have been admitted to a place in the list. My reader, however, if he have carefully perused the notes appended to many of the articles, will not fail to recollect that I have in numerous instances expressed my doubt, and sometimes more than that, of the correctness of their attribution to either of the Artists. These doubts are now increased to certainties. I am quite sure that neither Thomas nor John Bewick had any hand in the productions referred to. And the same must be affirmed of a very large number of other publications, especially those of the London press, with which their names have of late been most improperly associated, but in which not a single line of their work is to be found.

This should be well understood, for Collectors are pertinaciously beset, and now more than ever, by all kinds of specious pretences. In various Book Catalogues, for example, I have been considerably amused by the note affixed to a number of worthless volumes —"Not in The Bewick Collector," "Not in Hugo," "Unknown to Hugo," etc. etc. Many of them were indeed "known" to me so well as to be intentionally excluded. They were certainly "not in ' The Bewick Collector,'" and it would have been simply a blunder in the book and a disgrace to its author if they had been. For they were mere pretenders to that to which they had not the shadow of a rightful claim.

I feel, accordingly, that I shall be doing the Collector a very important service, if I endeavour to prevent him from being cajoled by the practices referred to by enumerating some of the classes of books the illustrations of which are thus—to speak mildly—erroneously attributed to the Brothers Bewick. There are, indeed, hundreds of volumes which nothing but the most profound ignorance or the most shameless indifference to honest dealing can ever attempt to identify with either of the great Newcastle Masters. Disgraceful, I must say, and utterly unworthy of English tradesmen, has been the late traffick in such commodities. I warn my readers against the deception. The remedy, however, after all lies with themselves. For so long, I must be allowed to add, as Collectors are willing to be victimized, so long will worthless books "with charming engravings by Bewick"—such is the phrase

—be offered for their purchase. Ready, indeed, and thoughtless must many of them be, to be so impudently, clumsily, and absurdly duped.

Passing these, however, as unworthy of further remark, I would direct my reader's attention to other works, which have, in good faith but ignorantly, been assigned to the Artists :—

1. The publications in general of Vernor and Hood. For example :—The Letters of Junius, No. (98.); Marmontel's Tales, No. (136.); Bloomfield's Farmer's Boy, Nos. (155.), etc.; Britton's Beauties of Wiltshire, No. (166.); Rural Tales, Nos. (182.), etc.; Holloway's Scenes of Youth, No. (189.); Zimmerman, No. (195.); Bloomfield's Wild Flowers, No. (245.); Bloomfield's May Day with the Muses, No. (448.); Hudibras, No. (3803.); and others mentioned in Appendix, No. V., which I have compiled with the special intention of guarding the Collector against deception. Many of the illustrations in these volumes, indeed, are of considerable excellence. They are in some cases the work of Anderson, and in others that of Austin and Charlton Nesbit. Nor, it is right to add, are Vernor and Hood to be held accountable for the error into which modern students have fallen as to the attribution of these engravings. While, whenever they could do so, they expressly stated the fact of the illustrations of their books being the work of Bewick, *e. g.*, Dodd's Beauties of History, No. (88.); Scripture Illustrated, No. (225.), etc., they never attempted to impart a fictitious value to their property by the dishonest use

of the Artist's name. This cannot be affirmed of all their brethren.

2. A large majority of the publications of J. Carnan, of St. Paul's Churchyard, of E. Newbery, also of St. Paul's Churchyard, and of J. Harris, his successor. Among others, evidently by the same artist, are the cuts in Youthful Portraits, No. (89.); Pity's Gift, No. (122.); Mrs. Pilkington's Historical Beauties, No. (123.); The Crested Wren, No. (129.); Paternal Present, No. (176.); Triumph of Goodnature, No. (177.); False Alarms, No. (3779.); and others noticed in Appendix, No. V. Most of the Cuts in these publications of Newbery and Harris exhibit very minute care in their execution, but have little or nothing of the boldness and freedom of the Artists' genuine works.

A word, before proceeding further, to some who may imagine that too much attention has been devoted to works of a trifling nature and by-gone interest. "The world is probably not aware," says Washington Irving, in his 'Biography of Oliver Goldsmith,' "of the ingenuity, humour, good sense, and sly satire, contained in many of the Old English Nursery Tales. They have evidently been the sportive productions of able writers, who would not trust their names to productions that might be considered beneath their dignity. The ponderous works on which they relied for immortality have, perhaps, sunk into oblivion, and carried their names down with them; while their unacknowledged offspring, 'Jack the Giant Killer,' 'Giles Gingerbread,' and 'Tom Thumb,' flourish in wide-spreading and never-ceasing popularity."

3. The publications of John Marshall, Aldermary Church Yard. Among many others are Life and Perambulation of a Mouse, No. (56.) ; Jemima Placid, No. (279.) ; Memoirs of a Peg Top, No. (280.) ; Adventures of a Pincushion, No. (334.) ; Life and Adventures of a Fly, No. (3767.), and others in Appendix, No. V.

The engravings in this Division are very peculiar. They appear to be the work of the same artist, and in their tasteless want of meaning can hardly be said to illustrate the books in which they occur. They consist usually of figures, in hard outline, of immoderately tall and thin personages, whose action and employment it is difficult so much as to guess. The following is a favourable example, bad as it unquestionably is,

by the same hand, and its inspection will make my meaning clearer. I selected it some time since from a large and worthless stock of old Wood Blocks in London, where there can be no doubt that it was executed, and for one of the volumes of this publisher.

4. In addition to these are a number of books issued

by various Houses. Among them :—Riley's Historical Pocket Library, No. (57.); Musical Budget, No. (145.); Zion's Pilgrim, No. (170.); Life of Peden, No. (171.); The Nurse, by Tansillo, No. (197.); Miss Owenson's Irish Harp, No. (226.); The Painter's Budget, No. (329.); Burdekin's Publications, Nos. (339.), (340.), (341.), (461.), etc. ; Brown's Poems, No. (433.); Tom Bragwell, No. (437.); Irish Family, No. (447.); Foote's Works, No. (3778.); Misfortunes of Love, No. (3781.); Life of Turpin, No. (3782.); Rowe's Fables, No. (3801.); Evans's Juvenile Tourist, No. (3802.); Week at Harrogate, No. (3808.); and others in Appendix, No. V.

As I have previously remarked, most of those to which numbers are attached have been already mentioned in terms of suspicion, so that I would fain hope the Collector has not been seriously misled by finding them admitted to a place to which they had no well-grounded pretensions.

With a view, however, of affording him a better idea of the extent of the field which he will find himself compelled to investigate, and still more of putting him on his guard against its dangers, I have added an Appendix of several numbers, a frequent reference to which I feel assured will prove very useful and profitable.

I. A List of Books printed for T. Carnan, in St. Paul's Churchyard.

I know of but one of his publications, No. (22.), which contains any specimen of Bewick's powers.

b

Their illustrations appear to be older than any of his productions. The list, however, is necessarily valuable to those who are interested in this species of all but obsolete literature. Like those which follow, it has been compiled from a number of the publisher's own catalogues.

II. A List of Books printed for E. Newbery, and for J. Harris, successor to E. Newbery, at the Corner of St. Paul's Churchyard.

Only a few of these contain illustrations by either of the Brothers Bewick, some of which, however, are among the choicest productions of the younger of the two. All will be found in the Collection.

III. A List of Books printed and sold by John Marshall, Aldermary Churchyard.

I am not aware that any of these contain illustrations by Bewick, though many are popularly considered so to do, and, like those before mentioned, attempted to be sold as such.

IV. A List of Books printed and published by T. Wilson and R. Spence (and afterwards Thomas Wilson and Son), High-Ousegate, York.

A considerable number of the books in this List are not included in the 'Bewick Collector,' from the fact of their containing no examples of the Artists' work. Of a large number, containing such examples, careful descriptions have been given in that volume and the present Supplement. It should be distinctly remembered, however, that none of these cuts were done by Bewick for the York publishers, but that they were purchased by them from Messrs. Hall and Elliot, of Newcastle, and were used as occasion required for the productions of their office. In many instances, the cuts originally done for one book were forced by their subsequent owners to illustrate others, and are consequently more or less unsuitable for the purpose to which they were compelled to minister.

It will be perceived that the titles of many of the York books are identical with those of Carnan, Newbery, Marshall, and others. The illustrations, however, of the latter are different, and the work of other hands. Hence the admission of the one, and the rejection of the other.

V. A Century of Books, of various publishers, places, and dates, which have been offered to me among the multitudes referred to at the commencement of this Preface, selected from the rest for their plausible appearance and consequent ability of deceiving the Collector, but which I hold to be as really undeserving of a place in this Catalogue as other and less artistic productions. Of course the articles in this Division—this specimen list of pretenders—might have been added to largely and without difficulty. But enough, and perhaps more than enough, are given to enable the Collector to perceive the kind of books which he will certainly do well to reject. If he will carefully compare the illustrations of these volumes with those about which there is no question, executed and published at the selfsame time, he will see without difficulty how impossible it is that productions

so entirely dissimilar could be the work of the same
hand. The style of Thomas Bewick is always to be de-
tected even in his most trivial performances. It is not
always equal, but it is always individual. And it is at
once absurd and dishonest to attribute to him works
which detract from his well-earned fame, not from any
desire to increase his celebrity, or to evidençe the ver-
satility of his powers, but—if the truth must be said—
only with a studied intent to deceive the unwary, and
dishonestly to give a fictitious value to articles which
would otherwise be deservedly without a purchaser.

I may add that not only is there no sign of un-
willingness to give high prices for genuine articles,
but that the value of such is still rising. One of the
copies, for example, of the Chillingham Bull on parch-
ment, which I mentioned as being in private hands,
has been sold within the last year for fifty guineas.
Other instances hardly less conspicuous have been re-
ported to me.

The process by which I have been enabled during
the last two years to examine so many and distant
productions, while it has proved by lack of results in
various Divisions how complete were my previous
acquisitions in such, has been the means of bringing
before my notice many relics of singular interest un-
connected with, or but distantly allied to, the subject
before us. This is not the place, nor have I time at
my present command, to enter into details. But, as
specimens of the class of additions to which I refer,
I annex impressions from two original Blocks which

I doubt not will be duly valued. The first illustrates the old and well-known poem of 'The Friar and the Boy,' while the latter represents the Morris Dance which was so great a favourite in the olden days of 'merry England.' I am well aware—and indeed it ought to be strongly insisted on—that rudeness of execution is no certain criterion of the antiquity of a Wood Block. Many which appear to be the oldest, used in the Chap Books printed at Newcastle at various times, are known to have been engraved by the printers' apprentices in that town between the years 1770 and 1780. While a knowledge of this fact will reconcile the critic to my attribution of some in the following pages to the apparently late date to which I assign them, the primitive state of the Blocks whereof impressions have just been given is conclusive of their real and genuine antiquity.

As I may, further, presume that my reader is more than ordinarily interested in the works of the old Northern engravers and printers, I give him the benefit of another of my acquisitions which unites each of these two specialities. It is an impression *(see the next page)* from an original Wood Block by the celebrated Thomas Gent, printer, of York, with which he was so far contented as to annex his name to his work. The Block has been much injured by being employed as a "bearer," and otherwise maltreated. I also possess a Cut of Pontefract Castle, with "T. Gent York." engraved on the back, used at page 122 of his 'History of the Great Eastern Window in York Min-

ster,' 8vo. York, 1757–1760; and an impression of his Book Plate, the only one that I have ever seen, in a copy of Conybeare's 'Defence of Revealed Religion,' Third Edition, 8vo. Dublin, 1732, which was formerly "e Lib. Tho. Gent, Civ. Lond. Ebor. &c.", as appears by his autograph on the title. It consists of an oval border of roughly executed foliage, enclosing the printed inscription "A.C. MDCCLXXII. Mr. Thomas Gent. Printer, Æt. 80."

I have, in the last place, the pleasing duty of expressing my grateful acknowledgments for the many kindnesses and courtesies with which I have been favoured in the course of these investigations. Numerous friends have either enriched my Collection with gifts of rare or unique treasures, or have aided me with their introduction and influence, apart from whose assistance the acquisition of many of the articles would have been simply impossible. Their names, where I have been authorized to give them, are annexed to the notices of the various objects. I have omitted them, indeed, in some instances, for the reason stated in my previous volume. But such donors, although unmentioned, will be pleased to accept this poor memorial of my gratitude, which a desire to comply with their wishes makes so inadequate and to me unsatisfactory.

In concluding a work to which from the nature of things it is absolutely impossible to make any additions of more than very secondary importance, I feel that I am bidding a partial farewell to a pursuit, which, although rightly subservient to other and much beloved yet very different subjects of study, has long possessed for me a delightful fascination, and could almost wish, for the pleasure of acquiring, that the acquisitions themselves were less complete. Of course, as I have stated elsewhere, it would be folly to pretend that such a result has been attained without a long period of very large and unhesitating disbursement. This was necessary at all times—for the objects were possessed of great interest and value from the very moment of their production—and still more so for a number of years last past, partly through the reverential regard felt by their possessors for many of them as the sole surviving relics of old and celebrated Houses, and partly through the daily increasing avidity with which every thing connected with the subject is seized upon by Collectors, oftentimes more desirous of acquiring than intelligent in the selection of the ob-

jects submitted to them.   Added to which have been
various rare opportunities past and over, invaluable
and beyond recall, long intimacy with deceased friends
and business connections of the Artists themselves, and
the successive dispersion of the other famous Collections made during the lifetime of both,—precious evidences of which are thickly strewn in the former and
the present volume. And, lastly, the aid of living friends,
able as well as willing to help, whose influence towards
the conclusion has been equally propitious.   Fortunate accident and designed kindness have thus com-
bined to aid the powerful adjunct of long and liberal
expenditure.   And the result is that to which I have
now the pleasure of welcoming my reader, with the
concluding assurance to him that it is one which no
zeal to acquire, no desire to oblige, nor any amount
of pecuniary outlay can ever again purchase or pro-
cure.

THOMAS HUGO.

The Chestnuts, Clapton, London, N.E.,
Whit Monday, 1868.

CONTENTS OF SUPPLEMENT.

LIST OF CUTS IN SUPPLEMENT.

ADDITIONS

TO

BOOKS AND PAMPHLETS.

THE observations prefixed to the similar Division of
the former volume—as to the mode of description,
degree of rarity, monetary value, and necessary care in
selection, of the several articles—are equally applicable
to the present, and to them the reader is referred.

As to their uncommon occurrence, however, it may
be repeated, that many of the following articles, especially those which appear to be of least importance,
are, as may indeed be inferred by the reader of the
foregoing Preface, of the very highest degree of rarity;
while, as to the prices demanded and paid for such of
these as now and then find their way into the market
(though it may be observed that few of the rarest ever
do so), there would really appear to be no limit to the
extravagance of either. The reader will find examples
of this in many of the following pages.

B

I would merely add the explanation already given, that the first number (in brackets) is the running number of the entire Collection; the second, that of the particular Division; and the third, where there is any, that of the separate Copies or Impressions. This mode of enumeration has been found so useful, both in presenting as perfect a view as possible of the Collection itself, and in enabling Collectors to identify articles at a distance without the need of lengthened description, that any change would appear to be as objectionable as it is unnecessary.

(4026.) 1. 1. A New Lottery Book Of Birds and Beasts. No. (4.).

Another very fine copy, in its original Dutch paper boards.

(4027.) 1. 2. Another similar.

(4028.) 2. Impressions From Wood Cuts In the Possession Of Thomas Saint.

Newcastle : Pilgrim Street, MCCLXXII.

Small 4to. Consisting of a title and nine leaves. There is one cut on the title, and the others, fifty-three in number, are printed on each side of the leaves. Fifteen of them had already appeared in the ' New Lottery Book of Birds and Beasts,' just referred to, published by Saint the year before. Among the rest, fourteen appear to bear evidences of the hand of Thomas Bewick, while the remainder are older than his time.

Almost as fresh as when published, in its original gilt and flowered paper cover.

Of the utmost rarity. Formerly purchased for £3. 3s.

(4029.) 3. The New English Tutor: Or, Modern Preceptor. This Work is beautified with elegant Cuts, representing such Vices as Children are most addicted to, and such Virtues as should be first inculcated: Likewise several Fable Cuts, with striking Lessons, referring to each particular Passion, &c. The Third Edition. Much Improved and Enlarged. By A. Fisher, Author of the New English Grammar with Exercises of bad English.

Newcastle: Printed for the Author, and sold by L. Hawes and Co. G. Robinson, and W. Nicoll, in London; T. Slack in Newcastle, and all other Booksellers in Town and Country. M.DCC.LXXIV.

18mo. Pp. viii, 164. With ten cuts, which I believe to be older than Thomas Bewick, although generally claimed for him, and by very high authority. The original Blocks are in my possession, No. (3755.), and the following are specimens of the impressions.

(4030.) 4. 1. Moral Instructions Of a Father to his Son, Comprehending the Whole System of Morality. [etc.]   The Third Edition.

Newcastle : Printed by and for T. Saint. MDCCLXXV.

12mo.   Pp. 168.   With thirty-four fable cuts, some of which are very similar in style of execution to those in the ' Youth's Instructive and Entertaining Story Teller,' ' Hastie's Reading Easy,' and other of Saint's publications illustrated by Thomas Bewick.

" The cuts [some of them] were engraved by Thomas Bewick in the first year of his apprenticeship, except that of a ship at sea, p. 167,—which was engraved by Bewick's fellow apprentice, David Martin,—Bewick at that time disliking to represent water."   Miss Bewick.

Very fine copy, in old calf.

(4031.) 4. 2. Another beautiful copy, in sheep.

(4032.) 5. Select Fables, In Three Parts.   Part I. After the Manner of Dodsleys.   Part II. Fables with Reflections.   Part III. Fables in Verse.   To which are prefixed, The Life of Æsop; And An Essay upon Fable.

Newcastle: Printed by T. Saint.   MDCCLXXVI.

12mo. Pp. 211, ii. With a copperplate frontispiece by Ralph Beilby, and one hundred and fourteen cuts, some, at least, of which are by Thomas Bewick.

Good copy, in old calf.

(4033.) 6. A New Epitome Of the Annals Of Great-Britain: Or, a succinct, impartial History of England, From the remotest Period of Intelligence, to the Conclusion of the last War. [etc.]   The Second Edition, Enlarged and Corrected.   By G. Grey.

Newcastle: Printed for the Author, and sold by T. Slack. MDCCLXXVII.

18mo. Pp. xviii, 284. With whole length portraits of the Kings and Queens, drawn by " R. P.," though generally considered to be engraved by Thomas Bewick, the original Blocks of which are in my possession. The following are those of Stephen and James I.

Fine copy, in half russia. It belonged to Mr. Thomas Bell, and has his book-plate.

(4034.) 7. A New Years Gift For Little Masters & Misses.

Newcastle: Printed by T. Saint, for W. Charnley, 1777.

Square 18mo. It consists of thirty-one cuts, enclosed in borders, most of them printed singly, and all on one page only of each leaf, without letterpress.

Among the cuts are six illustrations of the ' History of Little Red Riding Hood,' of which I possess the original Blocks. The following are specimens.

Very beautiful copy, in tree-marbled calf, gilt.

(4035.) 8. The Oxford Sausage: Or, Select Poetical Pieces, Written by the most Celebrated Wits Of The University of Oxford. A New Edition. Adorned with Cuts, Engraved in a New Taste, and Designed by the Best Masters.

Oxford: Printed for G. Robinson, in Pater-noster-Row, and F. Newbery, the Corner of St. Paul's Church-Yard, London; W. Jackson and J. Lister, in Oxford; and sold by the Booksellers of Oxford and Cambridge. M.DCC.LXXVII. [Price Two Shillings, sewed.]

12mo. Pp. x, 224. With cuts, some of which have much to
recommend them as the early work of Thomas Bewick.
Beautiful copy, in old calf, from the Fenwick Library.

(4036.) 9. Youth's Instructive and Entertaining
Story-Teller; Being A Choice Collection Of Moral
Tales, [etc.] The Third Edition.

Newcastle upon Tyne: Printed by T. Saint, For
W. Charnley; and M. Vesey and J. Whitfield.
MDCCLXXVIII.   [Printed in error MVCCLXXVIII.]

Sm. 8vo. Pp. xii, 246. With cuts differing from those in the
former editions at pp. 1, 48, 130 (a reversed copy), 135, 138,
207, and 245. That at p. 207 is a large cut of a Monk seated
on the Seashore, and heads "The Epistle of Abelard to Eloisa."
It is mentioned under No. (3468.).
Fine copy, in old calf.

(4037.) 10. Wood Engravings From A Pretty Book
of Pictures For Little Masters and Misses, Or Tommy
Trip's History of Beasts and Birds, Dog Jowler, Giant
Woglog, &c. &c.

Newcastle: Printed by T. Saint.   1779.

Sm. 8vo. A title and twenty-seven leaves, containing eighty
cuts, printed three on the recto of each leaf, except in a single
instance, where two cuts, one of them representing the Giant
and Tommy Trip, occupy the page.
"The proofs from Tommy Trip in this state must be excessively
rare, if not unique. I have never seen or heard of a copy in
any collection of Bewick's works." Letter of Bookseller.
A matchless copy, fair as when printed, in old tree-marbled calf,
gilt and tooled, with marbled fly-leaves. It cost a former possessor £7. 7s.

(4038.) 11. [A Series of Cuts, for some Toy Book,
published about the year 1779.]

They are forty-three in number, and are printed, with one exception, two on the recto page of a leaf, without title or letter-press, in an 8vo volume of twenty-two leaves.

Some of them were used many years afterwards in 'Tommy Tagg's Poems,' published by Wilson and Spence, York, 1800. See under the publications of that year.

Fine copy, in old half-calf binding. It was formerly priced £3. 3s.

(4039.) 12. The Mirror; Or A Looking-Glass For Young People of both Sexes; To make them Wise, Good, and Happy. Consisting of A Choice Collection of Fairy Tales. By Mother Goose. A New Edition. Newcastle Upon Tyne: Printed by and for T. Saint. [n. d.]

18mo. Pp. iv, 186. With cuts at pp. 1, 21, 44, 59, 73, 80, 90, and 102, by "R. J.," and at pp. 109, 118, 149, 158, and 173, by Thomas Bewick. Those by Bewick are truly beautiful, and equal to his very best in the 'Tommy Trip' and other works of the period. That at p. 173 is signed "T. B. *Newcastle*."

Beautiful copy, in old calf.

At the end is the following catalogue of "Books printed for, and sold by, T. Saint, in Newcastle."

> Youth's Instructive and Entertaining Story-Teller. Second Edition.
>
> Moral Instructions of a Father to his Son. The Third Edition.
>
> The Modern Cook; and Frugal Housewife's Complete Guide.
>
> The Prettiest Book for Children: being the History of the Enchanted Castle. By Don Stephano Bunyano.
>
> Fables of Æsop, and Others. By S. Croxall, D.D. The Seventh Edition.
>
> A Choice Collection of Hymns and Moral Songs.
>
> The Sugar Plumb; or Sweet Amusement for Leisure Hours.
>
> A Pretty Book of Pictures for Little Masters and Misses; or Thomas Trip's History of Beasts and Birds.

Christmas Tales. By Solomon Sobersides.
" And a great variety of little Books for Children."

(4040.) 13. Robinson Crusoe. [Published apparently by Saint, and about the year 1780.]

A set of six large cuts for this work, printed each on the recto page of a 12mo leaf, without letterpress or title.

They were formerly in the possession of Mr. Thomas Bell, and were purchased at his sale by Mr. Lynch, of Newcastle.

The first cut is the Figure of Robinson Crusoe, which was afterwards the frontispiece of ' A Supplement to the History of Robinson Crusoe,' Nos. (19.) and (20.).

A History of Robinson Crusoe, with the same series of cuts, was subsequently published by Wilson and Spence, of York. See under the publications of the year 1802.

Fine copy, in its original blue wrapper.

(4041.) 14. Be Merry and Wise; [etc.] By Tommy Trapwit, Esq. Adorned with Cuts.

London. Printed for the Author, and sold by T. Carnan, In St. Paul's Church Yard, 1781. (Price Six Pence.)

24mo. Pp. vi, 128. The cuts in this little book are older than Bewick, but that on the outside of each leaf of the cover, which in the present copy happily remains, is a most beautiful specimen of his skill. Each represents children at play,—one, a game of blind-man's-buff, the other, of battledore and shuttlecock,—surrounded by a border of foliage and flowers. These borders were evidently engraved on separate blocks, pierced so as to receive any kind of insertion, similar to the famous Barber's Cut, Nos. (2326.), (2327.), (3645.), etc., of this Collection, engraved about the time that this book was published, and the execution of which they most closely resemble.

(4042.) 15. A Choice Collection Of Hymns, And

Moral Songs; Adapted to the Capacities of Young
People, on the several Duties and Incidents of Life.
Adorned with elegant Wood-Cuts, to impress more
lasting Ideas of each Subject upon the Mind, than can
be attained by those in common Use. To which is
added, Specimens Of Divine Poetry. By several Authors.

Newcastle : Printed by and for T. Saint ; and Sold
by W. Charnley; and J. Whitfield. MDCCLXXXI.

> 18mo. Pp. iv, 177, iii. With seventy-one very beautiful cuts,
> some of which are used in others of Saint's publications. Those
> at pp. 96, 102, 104, 110, 120, 129, 139, and 145, are particu-
> larly excellent, and clearly indicate that the skill of Thomas
> Bewick was fast arriving at perfection.
>
> Very fine copy, in old calf.

(4043.) 16. The Real Reading-Made-Easy : Or,
Foreigners' and grown Persons' Pleasing Introductor
To Reading English, Whereby all Persons, of what-
ever Age or Nation, may soon be taught, with Ease
and Pleasure, to read the English Language.

Newcastle : Printed and sold by T. Saint. 1782.
Price One-Shilling.

> 18mo. Pp. x. Followed by "A S'upl'im'int Too thi Histire
> ov Robinsin Kruzo," No. (20.).
>
> This singular book consists of Lessons in Reading on the phonetic
> principle. At the end are " Propozils for printing bi Sub-
> skripshin A Nu Edishin ov thi Hole Bibil," etc.
>
> Good copy, in old calf.

(4044). 17. Moral Instructions Of a Father to his
Son, [etc. as in No. (4030.).]

Newcastle : [etc. as before.] MDCCLXXXII.

12mo. A reprint of the article referred to.
Good copy, in old calf.

(4045.) 18. A Curious Hieroglyphick Bible; Or, Select Passages In the Old and New Testament, Represented with near Five Hundred Emblematical Figures, For the Amusement of Youth: Designed Chiefly To familiarize tender Age, in a pleasing and diverting Manner, with easy Ideas of the Holy Scriptures. To which is added, A short Account of the Lives of the Evangelists; and other Pieces, illustrated with Cuts.

London: Printed by and for T. Hodgson, in George's-Court, St. John's-Lane, Clerkenwell. MDCCLXXXIII. [Price One Shilling bound.] Entered at Stationers-Hall agreeable to Act of Parliament.

18mo. Pp. vi, 128. With a large number of cuts, some of which are most admirable, and the work, no doubt, of Thomas Bewick during his short residence in London. The frontispiece, and most of the animals,—as the "Flock" at p. 8, "Sheep" and "Oxen," "Camels" and "Asses" at p. 13, "Ass" at p. 30, "Apes" and "Peacocks" at p. 35, "Lions" at p. 52, and "Beasts" at p. 53,—are excellent specimens of the Artist's skill; and Samson and the "thousand Men" at p. 30, "Woman" and "House" at p. 31, "Children" at p. 32, "Horsemen" at p. 60, "Men" at p. 62, and "Doomsday" at p. 125, are hardly less beautiful.

"There is every reason to believe that Bewick, when in London, was chiefly employed by T. Hodgson. It is, at any rate, certain that several cuts engraved by Bewick appeared in a little work entitled 'A Curious Hieroglyphic Bible,' printed by and for T. Hodgson, in George's Court, St. John's Lane, Clerkenwell." Chatto, in Jackson's 'History of Wood Engraving,' pp. 565, 566.

Good copy, in old calf.

(4046.) 19. Union Association Articles for the Insurance of Their Ships.

North Shields: 1783.

8vo, with cut on the title.
Good copy, in its original wrapper.

(4047.) 20. The New English Tutor: Or, Modern Preceptor. [etc.]   The Sixth Edition: With the Author's last Corrections.   By A. Fisher, Author of the English Grammar with Exercises of bad English.

Newcastle: Printed for T. Slack, in Newcastle; and sold by G. Robinson, in London; and all other Booksellers in Town and Country.   MDCCLXXXIV.

12mo.   Pp. vi, 144.   With the ten Cuts previously noticed.
    See No. (4029.).
Fine copy, in old calf.

(4048.) 21. The Newcastle Magazine: Or, Monthly Journal.   For [1785, etc.]

Newcastle: Printed by Brown and Thompson. And sold by all Booksellers in Town and Country.

8vo.   With the Arms of Newcastle on the cover, by Thomas Bewick.
Good copy, half-bound in calf.

(4049.) 22. An Introduction to Spelling and Reading: Containing Lessons for Children, Historical and Practical; [etc.]   By the Rev. Francis Fox, M.A. Rector of Reading in Berks.   The Twelfth Edition, Corrected and Improved.

London: Printed for J. F. and C. Rivington, Booksellers to the Society for Promoting Christian Knowledge, in St. Paul's Church-Yard.   1785.

12mo. Pp. v, 107. With an alphabet and ten Scripture cuts, the former and some of the latter of considerable excellence. I am in doubt, however, whether all of them are not older than Bewick.

Good copy, in its original calf binding.

(4050.) 23. Fables Of Æsop, And Others. Newly done into English. With an Application to each Fable. Illustrated with Cuts. By S. Croxall, D.D. The Eighth Edition.

Newcastle upon Tyne: Printed by and for T. Saint. MDCCLXXXV.

18mo. Pp. iv, 184. With cuts, some of which are older than Thomas Bewick, and others in which I feel little hesitation in expressing my belief that I see the work of his earliest years. This edition must not be confounded with those printed and published in London at and about the same period.

Good copy, in old calf.

(4051.) 24. The School Companion, Or Youth's Pleasing Instructor.

Newcastle: Printed for the [Booksellers.]

Small square 8vo. Pp. xviii, 129. With Fable Cuts at pp. 3, 4, 6, 8, 9, 12, 14.

My copy is unfortunately imperfect, the title itself being partly supplied in MS. I have never seen or heard of another.

(4052.) 25. Account of Newcastle Upon Tyne. No. (29.).

Another very fine copy, in half russia. It belonged to " E. Edwards, 1788."

(4053.) 26. The Habitable World Described, Or The Present State of the People in All Parts Of the

Globe, from North to South; [etc.]   By the Rev.
Dr. John Trusler.   Part. I.
London.   Printed for the Author, at the Literary
Press, No. 14, Red-Lion-Street, Clerkenwell; and Sold
by all Booksellers.   M DCC LXXXVII.

> 8vo.   In twenty volumes, published from the year already men-
> tioned to 1797, the date of the twentieth volume. The second,
> dated 1788, the eighth, 1790, the ninth and tenth, 1791, and
> the eleventh, 1792, contain cuts by John Bewick. That at
> vol. ii. p. 96 is signed " J. Bewick Sculp."
> Fine copy, in old calf gilt.

(4054.) 27. The Death Of Abel.   In Five Books.
Translated from the German of Mr. Gessner, By Mrs.
Collier.   The Second Edition.
Newcastle: Printed by M. Brown, At the Bible, In
the Flesh-Market.   M.DCC.LXXXVIII.

> 8vo.   Pp. xi, 143.   With a copperplate frontispiece, which,
> though very indifferent, I believe to be by Thomas Bewick.
> Fair copy, in half calf.

(4055.) 28. Fox against Fox!!!   Or Political Blossoms Of the Right Hon. Charles James Fox: [etc.]
London: Printed for John Stockdale, opposite Bur-
lington House, Piccadilly, 1788.   Price One Shilling
and Sixpence.

> 8vo.   Pp. xvii, 74.   With a frontispiece, and cut of " The Revo-
> lution Pillar," at p. 68, doubtless by John Bewick.
> Very fine copy, in half calf.

(4056.) 29. Fables By the late Mr· Gay.   In One
Volume Complete.
London: Printed for J. Buckland, J. F. and C.

Rivington, B. and B. White, T. Longman, B. Law,
T. Carnan, G. G. J. and J. Robinson, T. Cadell, S.
Bladon, R. Baldwin, J. Sewell, J. Johnson, H. L. Gard-
ner, J. Bew, W. Goldsmith, J. Murray, W. Lowndes,
J. Scatcherd and J. Whitaker, G. and T. Wilkie, and
E. Newbery. M DCC LXXXVIII.

> 12mo. Pp. viii, 232. With a frontispiece, representing a Tragic
> Mask, and sixty-eight cuts, by John Bewick.
> The first edition of this celebrated book. The second is No.
> (63.). Few volumes can show such an array of celebrated
> publishers as that which decorates the title-page of this.
> Fine copy, in old calf.

(4057.) 30. The New Robinson Crusoe; An In-
structive and Entertaining History, For the Use of
Children of Both Sexes. Translated from the French.
Embellished with Thirty-two beautiful Cuts. Second
Edition.

London: Printed for John Stockdale, opposite Bur-
lington House, Piccadilly. M DCC LXXXIX. Entered
at Stationers' Hall.

> 12mo. In four volumes. Vol. I. pp. 173. Vol. II. pp. 156.
> Vol. III. pp. 137. Vol. IV. pp. 177. Most of the cuts, if
> not all, are by John Bewick, and many of them bear his name.
> The work was a mere reprint of the edition of the previous
> year.
> Very fine copy, bound in two vols. in old calf.

(4058.) 31. The Life Of John Howard, Esquire;
LL.D. and F.R.S.

Newcastle Upon Tyne: Printed By W. Thompson.
M,DCC,XC.

8vo. Pp. 186. With a most beautiful vignette on the title,—the " W. T." of the printer, surrounded by flowers, palms, etc.,—by Thomas Bewick.

Good copy, in its original boards.

(4059.) 32. [A Hieroglyphic Bible. Published about the year 1790?]

18mo. Pp. 136.

The title is wanting. The cuts are generally similar to those in No. (4044.).

(4060.) 33. 1. A Battledore. [Without printer, place, or date; but probably printed at York, and about the year 1790.]

12mo. With eighteen cuts, some of which—" Flowers," " Ox," " Chrystal Stream," and " Thrush,"—are similar in style to the early and undoubted works of Thomas Bewick, in ' Hastie's Reading Easy,' and similar publications.

(4061.) 33. 2. Another copy.

(4062.) 34. Ancient Songs. No. (54.).

Another very beautiful copy, in old calf.

(4063.) 35. The Bee, Or Literary Weekly Intelligencer, [etc.] By James Anderson, LLD, [etc.]

Edinburgh: Printed by Mundell and Son, Parliament Stairs. MDCCXCI.

Sm. 8vo. Eighteen vols. A periodical, containing various cuts of animals, plants, etc., by Thomas Bewick, published from 1791 to 1794.

Fine copy, in old calf.

(4064.) 36. Pieces Of Ancient Popular Poetry. No. (58.).

Another beautiful copy, in half russia.

(4065.) 37. The Looking-Glass For the Mind; Or, Intellectual Mirror. A New Edition, With Seventy-four Cuts, Designed and Engraved on Wood By Bewick. No. (66.).

Another good copy, in old calf.

(4066.) 38. A List of Books, Published By the Rev. Dr. Trusler, At the Literary-Press, No. 62, Wardour-Street, Soho. 1792.

12mo. Pp. 12. With a specimen of the cuts in his ' Proverbs,' and two leaves from the ' Progress of Man and Society,' with cuts by John Bewick.

Good copy. Taken from the end of a copy of one of Dr. Trus-ler's publications.

(4067.) 39. The Vanity and Vain Glory Of Mortals; Or The Pride and Folly Of Man; Explained in the Six Several Stages of his Life. Printed & Sold by T. Evans, 79, Long-Lane. [n. d.]

12mo. Pp. 8. With eight cuts, five of which have much of the appearance of John Bewick's early work.

Good copy, in paper cover.

(4068.) 40. The Works Of Aristotle, In Four Parts. [etc.] A New Edition. London: Printed for, and sold by all the Booksellers. 1792.

18mo. Pp. 491. With cuts at pp. 94, 95, 96, and 97, by Thomas Bewick.

Fine copy, in old calf.

(4069.) 41. Fables By the late Mr. Gay. In One Volume Complete. The Plates beautifully cut in Wood, by T. Bewick of Newcastle.

Edinburgh: Printed for W. Coke, Leith. M DCC XCII.

12mo. Pp. viii, 252. With a copperplate engraving of Gay's monument, by Ralph Beilby; and sixty-seven Fable cuts and thirty-five vignettes, the latter frequently repeated throughout the volume, by Thomas Bewick.

A re-issue of Saint's edition of Gay's Fables, 1789,—No. (14.) of this Catalogue,—with a new title.

A poor, but perfect, copy, with excellent impressions of the cuts, in old calf.

(4070.) 42. Select Fables of Æsop And other Fabulists, In Three Books. By R. Dodsley. A New Edition. London. Printed for Willm. Osborne & J. & H. Mozley, Gainsborough. [n. d.]

12mo. Pp. xlviii, 228, 12.

The Fable cuts are older than Bewick, but the vignettes, especially that at p. 228, are most probably by him.

Good copy, in old calf.

(4071.) 43. The New Whole Duty of Man, Containing The Faith as well as Practice Of A Christian: [etc.]

Newcastle Upon Tyne: Printed by M. Brown. M.DCC.XCIII.

8vo. Pp. x, 550, 38. With a copperplate frontispiece, representing the Law and the Gospel, "Engraved by Beilby & Bewick."

Very fine copy, in old calf.

(4072.) 44. Tales for Youth. No. (72.).

Another copy, in its original calf.

(4073.) 45. General View Of the Agriculture Of the County of Northumberland, With Observations On the Means of its Improvement. By Mr. John Bailey, of Chillingham, And Mr. George Culley, of Fenton, in Northumberland.

London: Printed by C. Macrae. M DCC XCIV.

> 4to. Pp. 63. With a ground plan, on wood, of Farm Build-
> ings at p. 13, which is attributed to Thomas Bewick.
> Good copy, in its original boards.

(4074.) 46. The Universal Spelling-Book; Or, A New and Easy Guide To the English Language. [etc.] By Daniel Fenning. A New Edition, Carefully Corrected.

London: Printed for A. Millar, W. Law, and R. Cater; and for Wilson, Spence, and Mawman, York. M.DCC.XCIV.

> 12mo. Pp. xii, 156. With a frontispiece and a number of cuts,
> of the correctness of the attribution of which to Thomas Bewick
> I entertain considerable doubt.
> Good copy, in old calf.

(4075.) 47. The Florist's Companion. No. (74.).

> Another fine copy, in old calf.
> It formerly belonged to T. E. Headlam, Esq., M.D., of New-
> castle, and has his book-plate.

(4076.) 48. 1. The Poetical Works Of Oliver Goldsmith, M.B. [etc. as in No. (79.).]

Hereford: [etc. as before.] 1794.

> 12mo. Pp. 95. With six cuts. Exactly similar to the article
> referred to, except that it bears the imprint of the previous year.
> Fine copy, in its original marbled paper cover.

(4077.) 48. 2. Another very fine copy, in old calf.

(4078.) 49. Kings of England. Characters Of the Kings and Queens of England; Selected from The Best Historians. To which is added, A Table of the Succession of each, from Alfred to the present Time. With Heads, by T. Bewick, Newcastle.

London: Printed for E. Newbury, St. Paul's Church-yard; and Vernor and Hood, Birchin Lane, Cornhill. 1795.

> 18mo. Pp. viii, 204. I believe that in this little volume the cuts were used for the first time, which were afterwards, on the removal of their plain line borders, continually employed in the various editions of Dr. Goldsmith's Abridgment of English History.
>
> Good copy, in old calf.

(4079.) 50. The Cries of York. For the Amusement Of Little Children. In Twenty-three Elegant Cuts.

Stockton: Printed by Christopher and Jennett. [n. d. but about 1795.]

> Square 18mo. Without letterpress. The cuts are printed on both sides of the leaves.
>
> Excellent copy, in its original paper cover, as it left the publishers.

(4080.) 51. The Hive Of Modern Literature: A Collection of Essays, Narratives, Allegories, and In-structive Compositions; Calculated to instil into the Youthful Mind the Principles of Morality, Friend-ship, Honour, Truth, Justice, and the other Virtuous Dispositions, Which fortify it against the Allurements Of Vice and Youthful Propensities, too Apt to grow into Incurable Habits.

Newcastle: Printed for S. Hodgson, and G. G. and J. Robinson, Paternoster-Row, London.   [n. d.]

12mo. Pp. viii, 287. With the celebrated cut of the Hive—already given at p. 371—on the title, and others at pp. iv, 83, and 90, the original Blocks of which are in my possession.

The first edition of this well-known book, afterwards published with a large number of illustrations by Bewick and Clennell.

Fine copy, in calf gilt.

(4081.) 52. The Picture Book; Or, York Toy. York; High Ousegate.   [n. d. about 1795].

Square 18mo. Pp. 30. With an oval, surrounded with palm, bay, and flowers, bearing the letters "W S M" (for Wilson, Spence, and Mawman) in ornamented capitals, on the title; and thirty-two cuts, in broad borders which edge each of the pages.

Fine copy, in its original Dutch paper cover.

The following was its description in a bookseller's catalogue, in March, 1867, where it was priced £3. 3s.

"This is a *charming* little Toy Book, with 32 very pretty cuts within borders, which are beautiful specimens of JOHN BEWICK's early, distinct, and truthful style of engraving. I have not seen a copy of this choice little gem in any of the numerous and varied BEWICK COLLECTIONS which I have had the gratifying pleasure to inspect."

(4082.) 53. Poems By Goldsmith And Parnell. No. (78.).

Another very beautiful copy, in its original boards, with edges uncut.

(4083.) 54. A Curious Hieroglyphick Bible; Or, Select Passages In the Old and New Testaments, [etc.] The Thirteenth Edition.

London: Printed and Sold by Robert Bassam, No. 53. St. John's-Street, West-Smithfield: (by Assignment, from the Executors of T. Hodgson,) H. D. Symonds, Paternoster-Row, Scatcherd and Whitaker, Ave-Maria-Lane, and may be had of all the Booksellers. MDCCXCVI. (Price One Shilling bound.) Entered at Stationers-Hall agreeable to Act of Parliament.

> 18mo. Pp. vi, 136. With a very beautiful frontispiece and a large number of admirable cuts. See No. (4045.), of which it is a reprint.
> Good copy, in its original half calf binding.

(4084.) 55. The Death of Abel.
York: Printed by Wilson, Spence, and Mawman. 1796.

> 18mo. Pp. 160. With twelve cuts.
> Good copy, in its original cover.

(4085.) 56. Nixon's Cheshire Prophecy, At large. [etc.] Also his Life.
J. Ferraby, Printer, Market-Place, Hull. [n. d.]

> 18mo. Pp. 24. With cut on the title, which appears to be the work of Thomas Bewick.
> Good copy, in its original cover.

(4086.) 57. Cinderilla.
J. Ferraby, Printer, Market-Place, Hull. [n. d.]

> 24mo. Pp. 31. With eight cuts, which resemble the early works of Thomas Bewick. Most of them are included in the miscellaneous collection which constitutes the " New Year's Gift," No. (4034.).
> Good copy, in its original cover.

(4087.) 58. The Pleasant and Delightful History Of Jack and the Giants. Part the First.

Printed by J. Ferraby, Market-Place, Hull. [n. d. but about 1796.]

18mo. Pp. 24. With a cut on the title and six others, four of which appear to be early works by Thomas Bewick.

Fair copy, in old paper cover.

J. Ferraby was a noted printer of ballads, chap books, and children's books, at Hull. I possess a number of his publications, and some of the Blocks with which he embellished them, but cannot attribute any to Bewick, except the three described above.

(4088.) 59. The Sugar-Plumb; Or, Sweet Amusement For Leisure Hours: Being an Entertaining and Instructive Collection of Stories. [etc.] Embellished with Curious Cuts.

London: Printed for the Booksellers in Town and Country. (Price Six Pence.) [n. d.]

18mo. Pp. viii, —. With the same series of cuts as that afterwards used by Wilson and Spence in their edition of this book, of which a subsequent notice will be found.

Imperfect copy.

(4089.) 60. General View Of the Agriculture Of the County of Northumberland, With Observations On the Means of its Improvement; Drawn up for the Consideration of the Board of Agriculture And Internal Improvement, By J. Bailey and G. Culley.

Newcastle: Printed by Sol. Hodgson; And Sold by Mess. Robinson, Paternoster-Row, and G. Nicol, Pall-Mall, London. 1797.

8vo. Pp. viii, 168. With a wood-cut Plan of Farm Buildings, at p. 27, said to be by Thomas Bewick.

Fine copy, in half calf. In the same volume are bound the

'Agricultural Surveys of Cumberland and Westmorland,' and Bailey's ' Essay on the Construction of the Plough,' 8vo, Newcastle, 1795.

(4090.) 61. The Children's Miscellany: In which is included The History of Little Jack; By Thomas Day, Esq., Author of The History of Sandford and Merton.   A New Edition, Embellished with Twenty-eight Cuts, by Bewick, And a Frontispiece.

London : Printed for John Stockdale, Piccadilly. 1797.   [Price 3s. 6d. bound.]

12mo.   Pp. v, 325.
Good copy, in old calf.

(4091.) 62. The British Champion: Or, Honour Rewarded.

York : Printed by Wilson, Spence, and Mawman. 1797.

18mo.   Pp. 95.   With forty-four cuts.
Good copy, in its original paper boards.

(4092.) 63. Mother Shipton's Prophetic Legacy : Or, A Favourite Fortune-Book.

York : Printed by Wilson, Spence, and Mawman. 1797.

18mo.   With fifty-four cuts.
Good copy, in its original paper boards.

(4093.) 64. The Fables Of Mr. John Gay.   Complete in Two Parts.   With Cuts by T. Bewicke, of Newcastle.

York : Printed by Wilson, Spence, and Mawman. Anno 1797.

18mo. Pp. vii, 252. The precursor of the various editions published by this firm and their successors, and described in the present Catalogue, which were little else but simple reprints.
Fine copy, in old calf.

(4094.) 65. The Seasons. By James Thomson.
York: Printed by Wilson, Spence, and Mawman. 1797.

18mo.
Imperfect copy.

(4095). 66. Poems by John Gay: [etc.]
Manchester, Printed and sold at the Office of G. Nicholson, 9, Spring-gardens. Sold also by T. Knott, 47, Lombard-street; and Champante & Whitrow, Jewry-street, London. Anno 1797.

Sm. 18mo. Pp. 56. With cut on the title, used in articles subsequently described, of the authenticity of which I am very far from certain.

I have " Poems of Thomas Parnell, D.D.," "An Essay on Man. By Alexander Pope, Esq.," "The Grave. By Robert Blair.," "Moral Tales.," "The Economy of Human Life. By Robert Dodsley.," and others, issued by the same firms, and illustrated with cuts on their titles; but I do not believe any of them to be the work of either Thomas or John Bewick.

(4096.) 67. Holy Bible. With Notes by Matthew Henry.
Newcastle: Printed by M. Angus. [n. d.]

Folio. With Portrait of "The Rev^d. Matthew Henry, V.D.M.," " Engraved by Beilby & Bewick."
The First Number only, in paper cover.

(4097.) 68. Specimens Of Wood Engraving By Thomas and John Bewick.

Newcastle: Printed by M. Angus. Side. MDCCXCVIII.

4to. Consisting of a title and eleven leaves. On the former is
  Mrs. Angus's beautiful cut described under No. (93.) ; and the
  leaves, which are printed on one side only, contain twenty-two
  cuts. The twentieth also has already been mentioned, No.
  (3539.), the original Block of which is in my possession.
Fine copy, in its original bronze paper cover. I have known but
  one copy for sale, which was priced £3. 3s.

(4098.) 69. The Looking-Glass For the Mind;
[etc. as in No. (66.)] The Seventh Edition.
London: Printed by J. Crowder, For E. Newbery,
the Corner of St. Paul's Church-Yard. M,DCC,XCVIII.
(Price Three Shillings and Sixpence.)

12mo. Pp. viii, 271. A reprint of the article referred to above.
Beautiful copy, in tree-marbled calf.

(4099.) 70. A Tour Through The Island of Mann
In 1797 and 1798; [etc.] By John Feltham. Em-
bellished with a Map of the Island and other Plates.
Bath, Printed by R. Cruttwell ; And Sold by C. Dilly,
Poultry, London ; Jones, Liverpool ; Brown, Bristol ;
Ware, Whitehaven ; Woolmer, Exeter, &c. 1798.
[Price Seven Shillings.]

8vo. Pp. viii, 294. The cuts on the title and on page 93 are
  possibly, but not probably, by Thomas Bewick.
Fine copy, in its original boards.

(4100.) 71. Sotheran's York Guide; Including A
Description Of the Public Buildings, Antiquities, &c.
&c. In and about That Ancient City. Illustrated with
Nine Copperplates.
York : Printed by Wilson, Spence, and Mawman,

For H. Sotheran and Son, St. Helen's-Square : Sold
by R. Baldwin, Paternoster Row, London ; II. Hargrove, Knaresborough ; and by All the Booksellers in
Town and Country. Anno 1799. (Price Two Shillings.)

> 8vo. Pp. 80. With a beautiful cut of the Arms of the City of
> York, with flowers, bay, palm, etc., on the title, by Thomas
> Bewick.
> Fine copy, half-bound.

(4101.) 72. The Picture Book. [On the cover is
added, Containing upwards of Six Hundred Engravings On Wood.]

Stockton : Printed by Christopher and Jennett. [On
the cover, Price One Shilling.] [n. d. but about 1799.]

> Small 8vo. Pp. 80. Containing a most extraordinary assem-
> blage of cuts, many of which are by Thomas Bewick, and ex-
> tremely beautiful.
> A bookseller, who in 1866 priced it £7. 7s., thus describes this
> pamphlet :—
> "The MOST INTERESTING BEWICK GEM *I ever saw or possessed.*
> *It contains* 600 *of the* MOST CHARMING LITTLE CUTS *by*
> THOMAS BEWICK, *including* FABLE CUTS, TRADESMEN'S CUTS,
> *the* LARGE CUT *of the* EXECUTION, ORNAMENTAL ALPHABETS,
> VERY SMALL CUTS *of* ANIMALS *and* TREES, *about the size of a*
> *shilling,* PORTRAIT *of* OLD JENKINS *the* YORKSHIRE MISER,
> RACING CUTS, ELEGANT BORDERS *of* FLOWERS, COATS *of*
> ARMS, BIBLE CUTS, *etc. Some few in the volume are by*
> *Green,* but the others are by THOS. BEWICK, with his signa-
> ture. *This is the* ONLY COPY known ever to have occurred for
> public sale. It is unknown to, I believe, all Bewick Collectors,
> and was given by the hands of Mr. Jennett, the publisher,
> many years ago, to the gentleman from whom I had it."

I have lately had the good fortune to secure some of the most beautiful of the original Blocks, of which the following impressions are characteristic specimens.

Others will be found in the Division " Wood-Blocks."
Good copy, as new, in its original paper cover.

(4102.) 73. Cato, A Tragedy, By Joseph Addison. Manchester, Printed and Sold by R. & W. Dean, 9, Spring-gardens. Sold also by Sael & Co., 192, Strand, and T. Knott, Lombard-street, London; and all other Booksellers. 1799.

18mo. Pp. iv, 58. With cut on the title, " T. Bewick, sculp." Good copy, half-bound in calf.

(4103.) 74. The Pleasing Instructor, Or Entertaining Moralist, Consisting of Select Essays, Relations, Visions, and Allegories, Collected from The most Eminent English Authors. To which are prefixed New Thoughts on Education. A New Edition, With Additions and Improvements. [By A. Fisher.]

Penrith: Printed by A. Soulby, And Sold by Crosby and Letterman, No. 4, Stationer's Court, Ludgate-Street, London. [n. d. but about 1800.]

12mo. Pp. xii, 372. With a frontispiece and four other cuts, which, from a comparison with some of his acknowledged works, appear to be by John Bewick.
Good copy, in its original calf.

(4104.) 75. The Beauties of History; Or, Pictures of Virtue and Vice; [etc.] By the late W. Dodd, LL.D. The Third Edition.

London: Printed by T. Maiden, Sherbourne Lane, For Vernor and Hood, E. Newbery, J. Cuthell, Darton and Harvey, J. Scatcherd, Lackington, Allen & Co. and J. Walker. 1800.

12mo. Pp. xxiv, 288. A reprint of No. (88.).

Fine copy, in old calf.

(4105.) 76. The History Of the Family at Smiledale, Presented To all little Boys and Girls Who wish to be Good, And make their Friends Happy.

London: Printed for E. Newbery, at the Corner of St. Paul's Church Yard. (Price Six-Pence.) [n. d.]

18mo. Pp. 128. With ten cuts. Of those at pp. 36 and 124 I possess the original Blocks. An impression of the former is given at page 485, and one of the latter here follows.

Good copy, in its original coloured boards.

(4106.) 77. The Triumph of Goodnature, Exhi-
bited in the History of Master Harry Fairborn and
Master Trueworth.   Interspersed with Tales and Fables, and Ornamented with Cuts.

London: Printed for E. Newbery, The Corner of
St. Paul's Church-Yard.   Price Six-pence.   [n. d.]

24mo.   Pp. 110.   With twelve cuts.
Fair copy, in its original boards.

(4107.) 78. Youthful Recreations; Or, The Amusements of A Day.

London: Printed for E. Newbery, at the Corner of
St. Paul's Church Yard.   (Price Six-Pence.)   [n. d.]

18mo.   Pp. 128.   With twelve cuts, several if not all of which
    I believe to be by John Bewick.   I possess the original Blocks
    of those at pp. 23, 70, and 94.   An impression follows of the
    second.

Good copy, in its original cover.

(4108.) 79. Elmina; Or, The Flower that never
Fades.   A Tale for Young People.

London : Printed for E. Newbery, at the Corner of St. Paul's Church Yard. 1800. By J. Crowder, Warwick-square. (Price Two Pence.)

24mo. Pp. 60. With a frontispiece and eight cuts, most if not all of which I am inclined to attribute to Lee. Of those at pp. 41 and 53 I possess the original Blocks. An impression of the former is here given.

Fine copy, in its original cover.

(4109.) 8o. The Life And Adventures Of A Fly. Supposed to have been written by Himself. Illustrated with Cuts.

London : Printed for E. Newbery, At the Corner of St. Paul's Church-yard, By G. Woodfall, No. 22, Paternoster-Row. (Price 6d.) [n. d.]

18mo. Pp. 121. With a frontispiece, signed " J. Bwk.," and eleven cuts. I possess the original Blocks of those at pp. 28 and 73, an impression of the former of which is annexed.

Fine copy, in its original coloured boards.

(4110.) 81. The Happy Family : Or, Winter Evenings' Employment.　Consisting of Readings and Conversations, In Seven Parts.　By a Friend of Youth. With Cuts by Bewick.

York : Printed by and for T. Wilson and R. Spence, High-Ousegate.　1800.　Price One Shilling.

18mo.　Pp. vii, 151.　With a frontispiece and seven cuts.
Most beautiful copy of this rare little book, in its original Dutch
    paper boards.

(4111.) 82. The Forsaken Infant ; Or, Entertaining History Of Little Jack.　Embellished with Cuts.

Derby : Printed by and for Henry Mozley, Brook Street.　(Price Sixpence.)　[n. d.]

18mo.　Pp. 72.　With a frontispiece and eight large cuts by
    John Bewick, of which I possess the original Blocks.
Good copy, in old calf.

(4112.) 83. Divine Songs, Attempted in Easy Language For the Use of Children, by I. Watts, DD.

Adorned with Appropriate Wood-Cuts by Thomas Bewick, of Newcastle, To impress more lasting Ideas of each Subject on the mind than can be attained by those in common use.

York: Printed by and for Thomas Wilson & Son, High Ousegate. 1800.

18mo. Pp. 72. With thirty-eight cuts.

Good copy, in its original boards.

For some remarks on the Illustrations to Wilson and Spence's publications, see the Preface to this volume.

(4113.) 84. A Collection of Pretty Poems for Children. By Tommy Tagg.

York: 1800.

24mo. With sixty cuts.

Imperfect copy.

(4114.) 85. Dermody's Poems. No. (156.).

Another copy, in old calf.

(4115.) 86. 1. Poems On Several Occasions. By The Late Rev. Thomas Browne, Of Kingston-upon-Hull.

Printed for Vernor & Hood, London, by R. & W. Dean, Spring-gardens, Manchester; And Sold by Merritt and Wright, Liverpool, and Thomas Browne, Hull. 1800.

12mo. Pp. xxviii, 179. With vignette on the title, which occurs in Nos. (4095.), and (4173.), and to which I accord the benefit of a doubt.

Good copy, in its original cover.

(4116.) 86. 2. Another very fine copy, half-bound in calf.

D

(4117.) 87. The English Minstrel. No. (142.).
Another very fine copy, in its original boards.

(4118.) 88. The Scottish Minstrel. No. (143.).
Another fine copy, in half-calf.

(4119.) 89. The Scottish Minstrel; Containing the Choice Songs of Caledonia, With Music Adapted to the Voice, Violin, or German Flute.
Edinburgh: Printed by and for Oliver & Boyd, Netherbow. [n. d.]
12mo. Pp. vi, 216. With the cuts of the other edition.
Very fine copy, in its original boards, and uncut.

(4120.) 90. Streanshall Abbey: Or, The Danish Invasion. A Play of Five Acts: As first performed at The Theatre in Whitby, Dec. 2d. 1799. Written by Francis Gibson, Esq:
Whitby, Printed by Thomas Webster. Sold by G. G. and J. Robinson, Paternoster-Row, London. 1800.
8vo. Pp. 108. With a view of Streanshall Abbey on the title, apparently by Thomas Bewick.
Good copy, in its original cover.

(4121.) 91. The Grecian Daughter. A Tragedy, By Arthur Murphy, Esq.
Manchester, Printed and Sold by R. & W. Dean, 9, Spring-gardens. Sold also by Sael & Co. 192, Strand, and T. Knott, Lombard-street, London; and all other Booksellers. 1800.
18mo. Pp. iv, 60. With a cut on the title, to which is appended " T. Bewick, sculp."
Good copy, in its original cover.

(4122.) 92. Douglas, A Tragedy, By John Home. Manchester, Printed and Sold by R. & W. Dean, 9, Spring-gardens. Sold also by Sael & Co. 192, Strand, and T. Knott, Lombard-street, London; and all other Booksellers. 1800.

18mo. Pp. 49. With cut on the title, "T. Bewick, sculp." Fine copy, half-bound in calf.

(4123.) 93. George Barnwell. A Tragedy, By George Lillo. Manchester, Printed and Sold by R. & W. Dean & Co., Corner of New Cannon-street, Market-street-lane. Sold also by Sael & Co., Strand; and Crosby and Letterman, Stationers'-Court, London; and all other Booksellers. 1800.

18mo. Pp. iv, 62. With a cut on the title, which, as so many of those in the same series of volumes are by him, may be attributed to Thomas Bewick. Fine copy, half-bound in calf.

(4124.) 94. Kay's New Preceptor. No. (167.). Another fine copy, in half-morocco.

(4125.) 95. The History of England & Scotland, [etc.] Abridged, from Hume, Smollet, Robertson, Heron, And Other Continuators. In Four Volumes. Newcastle upon Tyne: Printed by and for M. Angus and Son, in the Side. 1801.

8vo. With vignette on the title, which I believe to be by Thomas Bewick. Good copy, in old calf.

(4126.) 96. The Blossoms Of Morality. [etc.] With

Forty-Seven Cuts. Designed and Engraved by I. Bewick. The Third Edition.

London : Printed by J. Crowder, Warwick-square ; For E. Newbery, the Corner of St. Paul's Church-yard. 1801.

12mo. Pp. x, iv, 221.

A very beautiful copy of this rare edition, in its original calf binding.

(4127.) 97. Pathetic & Sentimental Pieces.

Wolkmar and his Dog, by Drake. The Captive Mother, by Miss Williams. Story of Lady Harriet Auckland. The American Farmer.

Poetry. The Soldier's Return, by Miss Blamire. Elegy, by Burns. The Emigrant, by Henry Erskine.

Newcastle on Tyne, Printed and sold by J. Mitchell. Sold also by West and Hughes, No. 40, Paternoster-Row, London. 1801.

18mo. Pp. 36. With frontispiece of " Wolkmar and his Dog."

" Bewick fecit." and cut on the title, by Thomas Bewick.

Fine copy, in half-morocco.

(4128.) 98. Pathetic & Sentimental Pieces.

Story of Dr Clement, from the Philanthrope. The Death of Rousseau. The Patriotic Clergyman. The Victim of Dishonour, a true Story.

Poetry. The Lass of Fair Wone, by Buerger. Mortality, by Southey. The Downhill of Life, by Collins.

Newcastle on Tyne, Printed and sold by J. Mitchell. Sold also by West and Hughes, No. 40, Paternoster-Row, London. 1801.

18mo. Pp. 36. With frontispiece of " The Death of Rousseau."
" Bewick fecit." and cuts on the title and p. 27.
Fine copy, in half-morocco.

(4129.) 99. Humorous Pieces, Consisting of
Prose. The Life of Mr George Harvest. The
Strolling Player.
Poetry. Tam O'Shanter. The Pilgrims and the
Peas.
Newcastle on Tyne, Printed and Sold by J. Mitchell;
Sold also by West & Hughes, No. 40, Paternoster-
Row, London. 1801.

18mo. Pp. 28, 8. With cut of ribbons, masks, and flowers,
" Bewick fecit." on the title, and a charming vignette of a
Water Mill, at p. 28, by Thomas Bewick.
Fine copy, in half-morocco.

(4130.) 100. Humorous Pieces.
Epistle on Marriage, and the Cheese Present, by
Burns. The Newspaper Editor, by Peter Pindar.
The Auctioneer, &c.
Poetry. Watty and Meg, Monsieur Tonson, Epi-
grams, by Anderson, &c.
Newcastle on Tyne, Printed and sold by J. Mitchell.
Sold also by West and Hughes, No. 40, Paternoster-
Row, London. 1801.

18mo. Pp. 24, 12. With frontispiece of " Watty and Meg."
" Bewick fecit." and cut on the title, by Thomas Bewick.
Fine copy, in half-morocco.
The four foregoing articles are more generally known in their
subsequent form, where they appear incorporated in one vo-
lume, under the general title of " The Charms of Literature."

(4131.) 101. The Happy Family: Or, Winter Evenings' Employment. [etc.]　With Cuts by Bewick.

York : Printed by and for T. Wilson and R. Spence,
High-Ousegate.　1801.　(Price One Shilling.)

18mo.　Pp. vi, 105.　With a frontispiece and seven cuts.　A reprint, for the most part, of No. (4110.).

Very fine copy, in its original Dutch paper boards.

(4132.) 102. Dodsley in Miniature ; Or, The Polite
Fabulist.　With Cuts by Bewick.

York : Printed by and for T. Wilson and R. Spence,
High-Ousegate.　1801.　Price One Shilling.

18mo.　Pp. 106.　With many admirable cuts, used in the Select
Fables of 1784.

Fine copy, in its original boards.

(4133.) 103. Elegiac. Shaw's Monody ; Pratt's
Elegy Of A Nightingale ; Jago's Goldfinches ; &c. &c.

Printed and sold by G. Nicholson, Poughnill, near
Ludlow.　Sold also, in London, by Champante &
Whitrow, 4, Jewry-st., Aldgate ; R. Bickerstaff, 210,
Strand ; T. Conder, 20, Bucklersbury ; and all other
Booksellers.　Anno 1801.

18mo.　Pp. 40.　With vignette on the title, " designed from
Dr. Wolcot's ' Elegy on my dying Ass, Peter,' by Mr. M. W.
Craig, and engraved on wood by Mr. T. Bewick."

Good copy, in its original paper cover.

(4134.) 104. Fisher's Grammar Improved ; [etc.]
The Thirty-Third Edition, [etc.]

Newcastle : Printed by and for S. Hodgson ; For
G. & J. Robinson, Paternoster-Row, and J. Mawman,
Poultry, London.　1802.

12mo. Pp. viii, 208. With a facsimile of the signature of "A. Fisher" at the end of the Introduction, said to be by Thomas Bewick. I have the original Block.

Good copy, in old calf.

(4135.) 105. The Fashionable Songster.
Newcastle: 1802.

18mo. With frontispiece by Thomas Bewick.
Imperfect copy.

(4136.) 106. The Prettiest Book For Children: Being The History Of the Enchanted Castle, Situated in one of the Fortunate Isles, And governed by the Giant Instruction. Written for the Entertainment of the Little Masters and Misses of Great Britain. By Don Stephano Bunyano, Under-Secretary to the Giant Instruction.
York: Printed by T. Wilson and R. Spence, High-Ousegate. 1802. (Price Sixpence.)

18mo. Pp. 81. With a frontispiece and thirteen cuts, of which I believe hardly one, if one, to be by Bewick.
Good copy, in its original boards.

(4137.) 107. The Holy Bible Abridged; Containing the History Of The Old Testament. No. (3784.).

Another copy, in its original boards.

(4138.) 108. Anecdotes Of The Clairville Family; To which is added, The History of Emily Wilmont. By Mrs. C. Mathews.
York: Printed by and for T. Wilson and R. Spence, High-Ousegate, 1802. (Price One Shilling.)

18mo. Pp. 107. With four cuts. The book was reprinted in 1809.

Good copy, in its original boards.

(4139.) 109. An History of Birds, With A Familiar Description of each In Verse and Prose. By Tommy Trip. With Cuts by Bewick.

York: Printed by T. Wilson and R. Spence, High-Ousegate. 1802. Price Sixpence.

Square 18mo. Pp. 81.

Good copy, in its original Dutch paper boards.

(4140.) 110. The Wonderful Life And Surprising Adventures Of Robinson Crusoe; Who lived 28 Years On An Uninhabited Island. With Cuts by Bewick.

York: Printed by and for T. Wilson and R. Spence, High-Ousegate. 1802. (Price Sixpence.)

18mo. Pp. 82. With a frontispiece and six full-page cuts.

Good copy, in its original boards.

(4141.) 111. (No. I.) Of the Newcastle Songster; Or, Tyne Minstrel. Containing a Selection of Modern and Original Songs. Second Edition.

Newcastle upon Tyne: Printed and Sold by David Bass, Foot of Pilgrim Street. 1803. (Price Six-pence.)

12mo. Pp. 68. With cut, on the title, of the top of the Newcastle Old Exchange and the crow's nest, by Thomas Bewick, of which the original Block is in my possession.

No. II., which is bound in the same volume, pp. 72, bears the date of 1805; and No. III., pp. 60, of 1806. Each of them has the same cut on its title.

Good copy, half-bound in calf.

(4142.) 112. 1. Thomas Lovechild's Only Method To Make Reading Easy, Or, Little Masters' & Misses' Best Instructor: [etc.] The whole adorned with pretty Emblematic Cuts by Thomas Bewick, of Newcastle.

York: T. Wilson and R. Spence, High Ousegate. Newcastle, Emerson Charnley, Bigg Market. 1803.

18mo. Pp. vi, 108. Hastie's Reading Easy, printed by "J. Rewcastle, Printer," Newcastle, with a different title.

Good copy, in its original boards.

(4143.) 112. 2. Another copy.

(4144.) 113. The Holy Bible Abridged; Containing the History Of The New Testament. Adorned with Cuts. For the Use of Children.

York: Printed by T. Wilson and R. Spence, High-Ousegate. 1803. (Price Sixpence.)

18mo. Pp. 84. With thirty-one cuts.

Good copy, in its original boards.

(4145.) 114. The Pleasing Moralist: [etc.] No. (190.).

Another copy, in its original boards.

(4146.) 115. 1. The History Of Little Goody Two-Shoes; Otherwise called Mrs. Margery Two-Shoes. With The Means by which she acquired her Learning and Wisdom, and, in Consequence thereof, her Estate. [etc.]

York: Printed by T. Wilson and R. Spence, High Ousegate. 1803.

18mo. Pp. 84. With a frontispiece and thirty-one cuts.

Good copy, in its original boards.

(4147.) 115. 2. Another copy, imperfect.

(4148.) 116. The Holiday Present; Containing

Anecdotes Of Mr. and Mrs. Jennet, And Their Little Family, viz. Master George, Master Charles, Master Thomas, Miss Maria, Miss Charlotte, and Miss Harriot. Interspersed with instructive and amusing Stories and Observations.

York: Printed by T. Wilson and R. Spence, High-Ousegate. 1803. (Price Sixpence.)

18mo. Pp. 82. With a frontispiece and twenty-four cuts. Good copy, in its original boards.

(4149.) 117. The History Of the Goodville Family; Or, The Rewards of Virtue and Filial Duty.

York: Printed for T. Wilson and R. Spence, High-Ousegate. (Price Sixpence.) [n. d.]

18mo. Pp. 80. With a frontispiece and seventeen cuts. Good copy, in its original boards.

(4150.) 118. 1. Memoirs Of A Peg-Top. By The Author of Adventures of a Pincushion. [etc.]

York: Printed by and for T. Wilson and R. Spence, High-Ousegate. (Price Sixpence.) [n. d.]

18mo. Pp. vi, 84. With a frontispiece and twenty-seven cuts. Good copy, in its original boards.

(4151.) 118. 2. Another copy, in its original boards.

(4152.) 119. The History of England, From the Invasion of Julius Cæsar To the Abdication of James the Second. By David Hume, Esq. With the Author's Last Corrections. In Eight Volumes. Embellished with Portraits.

Edinburgh: Printed by Oliver and Co. For T.

Brown, Bookseller, North Bridge, and T. Oliver, Netherbow. 1803.

> 8 vols. 12mo. With a few tailpieces in the 1st, 3rd, 4th, 5th, and 8th volumes, some of which I believe to be by Thomas Bewick.
> Good copy, in old calf.

(4153.) 120. The Grave. A Poem. By Robert Blair. With Gray's Celebrated Elegy In a Country Church Yard.

. Newcastle : Printed by K. Anderson, in the Side. 1804.

> 12mo. Pp. 36. With cut on the title, thought to be by Thomas Bewick.
> Good copy, half-bound.

(4154.) 121. Mrs. Pleasant's Story Book : Composed for The Amusement Of Her Little Family. To which are added Instructions For the Proper Application of them. Adorned with Cuts by Bewick.

York : Printed by T. Wilson and R. Spence, High-Ousegate. 1804. (Price Sixpence.)

> 18mo. Pp. 84. With a frontispiece and sixteen cuts.
> Good copy, in its original boards.

(4155.) 122. The Sugar-Plum ; Or, Sweet Amusement For Leisure Hours. Being an Instructive and Entertaining Collection of Stories. To which is added, The History of Mr. Ashfield. Embellished with Elegant Cuts.

York : Printed by T. Wilson and R. Spence. 1804. (Price Sixpence.)

18mo.   Pp. 84.   With a frontispiece and ten cuts.
Good copy, in its original boards.

(4156.) 123. The Renowned History Of Primrose Prettyface, Who, By her Sweetness of Temper and Love of Learning, Was raised from being the Daughter of a Poor Cottager, To Great Riches; And To the Dignity of the Lady of the Manor. [etc.]   Adorned with Cuts by Bewick.

York: Printed by T. Wilson and R. Spence, 1804. (Price Sixpence.)

18mo.   Pp. 84.   With a frontispiece and thirty-six cuts.
Good copy, in its original boards.

(4157.) 124. The Sleeping Beauty In the Wood; With other Instructive and Entertaining Stories.   Designed to promote Good Humour and Proper Conduct.

York: Printed by T. Wilson and R. Spence, High-Ousegate.   1804.   (Price Sixpence.)

18mo.   Pp. 81.   With seven cuts.
Good copy, in its original boards.

(4158.) 125. The Picture Room: No. (194.).

Another copy, in its original boards.

(4159.) 126. Fables Of Æsop, &c.   Translated into English.   With Instructive Applications.   By Samuel Croxall, D.D. Late Archdeacon of Hereford.   With Cuts.   A New Edition, Improved.

London: Published and sold by all the Booksellers, and by T. Wilson and R. Spence, Printers, High-Ousegate, York.   1804.

12mo. Pp. xxxvi, 336. With upwards of fifty cuts by Thomas
Bewick, with others older than his time.
Good copy, in old calf.

(4160.) 127. Poems By Goldsmith And Parnell.
London: Printed by W. Bulmer and Co. Shak-
speare Printing-Office, Cleveland-Row. 1804.
4to. Pp. xxvii, 68. A reprint of No. (78.).
Fine copy, half-bound in morocco.

(4161.) 128. The Gentle Shepherd; A Scots Pastoral. By Allan Ramsay. With the Original Music.
Embellished with beautiful Engravings.
Edinburgh; Printed by Oliver & Co. Netherbow.
1804.

18mo. Pp. 95. With cuts used by the publishers in other books.
Good copy, in its original boards.

(4162.) 129. A Father's Legacy To his Daughters.
By the late Dr. Gregory, of Edinburgh.
London: Published by Vernor and Hood, Poultry;
And Champante and Whitrow, Jewry-Street. 1805.
[Printed by G. Miller, Dunbar.]

Small 18mo. Pp. 72. With a frontispiece and four cuts. The
former is used on the title of Relph's Poems, 8vo, Carlisle,
1798, No. (124.).
Good copy, in its original half-binding.

(4163.) 130. The Newcastle Chronicle Newspaper,
for 1805, 1806, and 1807.

Large folio. Containing many engravings by Thomas Bewick,
of which I possess other impressions cut from similar papers,
enumerated and described in the Divisions, "Cuts for Various

Societies and Companies," "Tradesmen's Newspaper Cuts," and " Newspaper Cuts."
Good copies, half-bound in calf.

(4164.) 131. The Man Of Feeling. A New Edition. Newcastle on Tyne: Printed and Sold by J. Mitchell, Dean-Street. 1805.

12mo. Pp. vi, 128. With a copperplate frontispiece and four woodcuts, the latter of which are by Thomas Bewick, and had been used in other works.
Poor copy, half-bound in calf.
This, although with a similar title to No. (202.), is printed in different type, and with fewer cuts.

(4165.) 132. Charms Of Literature: Consisting of An Elegant Assemblage Of Curious, Scarce, and Interesting Pieces, In Prose and Poetry; [etc.] Embellished with Engravings on Wood, By Bewick, &c. Third Edition.

Newcastle upon Tyne: Printed and Sold by J. Mitchell, 1805.

18mo. Pp. vi, 434. A reprint of No. (154.). See Note to No. (4130.).
Good copy, in old calf.

(4166.) 133. 1. The Fairing; Or, Golden Toy. York: Printed by T. Wilson and R. Spence, High-Ousegate. 1805. (Price Sixpence.)

18mo. Pp. 84. With a frontispiece, representing Tommy Trip in his chariot, and thirty cuts.
Good copy, in its original boards.

(4167.) 133. 2. Another copy, in its original boards.

(4168.) 134. Three Instructive Tales For Little

Folk.   Simple and Careless.   Industry and Sloth.
And The Cousins.   By C. P——.

London : Printed for J. Harris, (Successor to E.
Newbery), Corner of St. Paul's Church-Yard.   (Price
Three-pence.)   [n. d.]

> 24mo.   Pp. 83.   With eight cuts, thought to be by John Bewick.
> I have the original Block of that at p. 44, of which the follow-
> ing is an impression.

Good copy, in its original cover.

(4169.) 135. Elmina ; Or, The Flower that never
Fades.   A Tale for Young People.

London : Printed for J. Harris, (Successor to E.
Newbery) corner of St. Paul's Church-Yard.   By
J. Crowder, Warwick-square.   (Price Two-Pence.)
[n. d.]

> 24mo.   Pp. 60.   With a frontispiece and eight full-page cuts.
> A reprint of No. (4108.), under which a specimen of the illus-
> trations has been given.
> Good copy, in its original cover.

(4170.) 136. The Village Tatlers ; Or, Anecdotes Of the Rural Assembly.　Embellished with Cuts.

London : Printed by J. D. Dewick, Aldersgate-street, For J. Harris, Successor to E. Newbery, Corner of St. Paul's Church-Yard.　Price Two-pence. [n. d.]

24mo.　Pp. 64.　With a frontispiece and twelve cuts.　Of those at pp. 14 and 54 I possess the original Blocks.　An impression follows of the former.　It is probably attributable to Jackson.

Good copy, in its original cover.

(4171.) 137. 1. The Wonderful Life And Adventures Of Robinson Crusoe.

York : Printed by T. Wilson and R. Spence, High-Ousegate.　[n. d.]

24mo.　Pp. 29.　With a frontispiece and thirteen cuts, some of which, with two on the cover, are by Thomas Bewick.

Good copy, in its original cover.

(4172.) 137. 2. Another copy, imperfect.

(4173.) 138. Prayers To be said Before and after

Mass, And in the Afternoon, On all Sundays and Festivals, In the Catholic Chapels Of Preston and Blackburn. To which is added The Ordinary of the Mass. Printed at the Request of Messrs. Dunn and Morgan, Preston, and Dr. Dunn, Blackburn, by whom the present Edition has been corrected and considerably enlarged.

Manchester, Printed by Haydock and Wardle, Market-street-lane. 1805.

> 12mo. Pp. 128. With cut, perhaps by Thomas Bewick, on the title. It occurs also in Nos. (4095.) and (4115.).
>
> I have great doubt of the propriety of my attribution of the cut to Thomas Bewick, but there are lines to recommend it to favourable consideration.
>
> Good copy, in its original boards.

(4174.) 139. Measure for Measure, A Comedy, By William Shakspere.

Manchester, Printed and Sold by R. & W. Dean, 9, Spring-gardens. Sold also by Sael & Co., 192, Strand, and T. Knott, Lombard-street, London; and all other Booksellers. 1800.

> 18mo. Pp. 78. With cut on the title, "W. M. Craig, del. T. Bewick, sculp."
>
> Good copy, in its original cover.

(4175.) 140. An Abridgment Of the History Of England, [etc.] By Dr. Goldsmith. The Twelfth Edition. With Heads by Bewick.

London: Printed by T. Maiden, Sherbourn-Lane, Lombard-Street, For Clarke and Co. and Thomson and Son, Manchester; Deighton, Cambridge; Upham,

Exeter; W. Jones, Liverpool; Hazard, Bath; Tod, York; and Rodford, Hull. 1806.

> 12mo. Pp. 384. With the usual cuts.
> Fine copy, in shagreen calf.

(4176.) 141. Steel's Naval Chronologist Of The Late War, [etc.] The Fourth Edition, Corrected and greatly enlarged.

London: Printed for P. Steel, at the Navigation-Warehouse, Little Tower-Hill; and to be had of every Bookseller in the United Kingdom. 1806. (Price Five Shillings.)

> Small 4to. Pp. 12, civ, 123. With the frontispiece of the pre-
> vious editions. See No. (169.).
> Good copy, in its original half-calf binding.

(4177.) 142. The Young Reader. No. (212.).

> Another copy, in old calf.

(4178.) 143. Charms For Children. [etc.] With Cuts by Bewick.

York: Printed by T. Wilson and R. Spence, High-Ousegate. 1806. (Price Fourpence.)

> 24mo. Pp. 93.
> Good copy, in its original Dutch paper cover.

(4179.) 144. The House That Jack Built. To which is added, Some Account of Jack Jingle; Showing by what Means he acquired his Learning, and in consequence thereof got rich, and built himself a House. Adorned with Cuts; [etc.]

York: Printed by T. Wilson and R. Spence, High-Ousegate. 1806. (Price One Penny.)

24mo. Pp. 29. With twelve cuts, one of which is by Thomas
Bewick.
Good copy, in its original cover.

(4180.) 145. The History Of Little King Skilful.
Wherein is shown The Reward of Goodness And The
Punishment of Vice. Adorned with Cuts.

York: Printed by T. Wilson and R. Spence, High-
Ousegate. 1806. (Price Twopence.)

24mo. Pp. 63. With a frontispiece and twelve cuts.
Good copy, in its original boards.

(4181.) 146. The History Of Master Charles And
Miss Kitty.

York: Printed by T. Wilson and R. Spence, High-
Ousegate. 1806. (Price Twopence.)

24mo. Imperfect.

(4182.) 147. The Little Moralists; Or, The History Of Amintor and Florella, The Pretty Little Shepherd and Shepherdess Of the Vale of Evesham. Embellished with Cuts.

London: Printed for J. Harris, Successor to E.
Newbery, the Corner of St. Paul's Church-yard. 1806.
By J. Crowder, Warwick-Square. (Price Three-
Pence.)

24mo. Pp. 95. With a frontispiece and twelve cuts, some of
which bear the name of Jackson, and others are probably by
Lee. I possess the original Blocks of those at pp. 49 and 75.
The following is an impression of the former.

Good copy, in its original cover.

(4183.) 148. The Mountain Piper; Or, The History Of Edgar and Matilda. To which is added, A Journey to London. A Moral Tale. Embellished with Cuts.

London: Printed by Rider and Weed, Little Britain. For J. Harris (Successor to E. Newbery), Corner of St. Paul's Church-yard.   [n. d.]

24mo.   Pp. 96.   With a frontispiece and twelve cuts.
Good copy, in its original cover.

(4184.) 149. Observations On the Utility, Form and Management Of Water Meadows, And the Draining and Irrigating Of Peat Bogs, [etc.]   By William Smith, Engineer and Mineralogist.

Norwich: Printed by R. M. Bacon, Cockey-Lane; and sold By Longman, Hurst, Rees, and Orme, Paternoster-Row, London; and all other Booksellers. 1806.

8vo.   Pp. xviii, 121.   With several vignettes which may be attributed to Thomas Bewick.
Fine copy, in its original boards.

(4185.) 150. The History Of Ripon: With Descriptions of Studley-Royal, Fountains' Abbey, Newby, Hackfall, &c. &c. [etc.] Second Edition.—With Engravings.

Ripon: Printed and Sold by W. Farrer: Sold also by Longman & Co., Pater-Noster-Row, London: And by Wilson and Spence, York. 1806.

12mo. Pp. 314. With cut of a man fishing at p. 43, and repeated at pp. 167, 221, and 262, probably by Thomas Bewick. Fine copy, half-bound in calf.

(4186.) 151. A Walk Through Leeds, Or, Stranger's Guide To Every Thing worth Notice in that Ancient and Populous Town; With an Account of the Woollen Manufacture Of the West-Riding of Yorkshire. With Plates. Pannus mihi Panis.

Leeds: Printed by J. H. Leach, And sold by John Heaton, (Successor to the late Mr. Binns) J. Spence, W. Fawdington, J. H. Leach, M. Robinson, and J. Ryley. 1806. Price One Shilling and Sixpence.

12mo. Pp. iv, 55. With the Arms of Leeds, and three insignificant cuts, thought to be by Thomas Bewick. Good copy, in its original cover.

(4187.) 152. A Spring-Day: Or, Contemplations On Several Occurrences Which naturally strike the Eye in that Delightful Season. By James Fisher. The Second Edition, Carefully Corrected and Improved.

Edinburgh: Printed for the Author, By John Moir, Royal Bank Close; Sold by Ogle and Aikman, Edinburgh; William Smith, Stationers Court; and Ogle,

Great Turn-Style, London; And many of the Principal Booksellers In Great Britain. 1806.

> 8vo. Pp. viii, 338. With four very beautiful cuts by Thomas Bewick.
>
> Fine copy, in its original boards.

(4188.) 153. The Fables Of Mr. John Gay. Complete in Two Parts. With Cuts by T. Bewick, of Newcastle.

York: Printed by and for T. Wilson and R. Spence, High-Ousegate. 1806.

> 12mo. Pp. 252. Very similar to the edition published by the same firm in the same year, No. (215.), but with a few verbal differences.
>
> Fine copy, in its original boards.

(4189.) 154. The British Primer, Or, First Book; Adapted to the Capacities of Children. Embellished with a Beautiful Frontispiece, And several Engravings of Birds and Beasts, By T. Bewick. Fifth Edition.

Newcastle upon Tyne: Printed by and for J. Mitchell, and sold by every respectable Bookseller in Great Britain. [n. d.]

> 18mo. Pp. 42. With a frontispiece, and cuts of the Cat, Dog, Goat, Ass, Horse, Bull, Eagle and Serpent, Owl, and Robin Redbreast.
>
> Good copy, in its original paper cover.

(4190.) 155. Memoirs Of Two Veteran Soldiers: Or, The Military Hospital. [etc.]

Newcastle on Tyne, Printed and sold by J. Mitchell, Dean-Street. 1807.

> 12mo. Pp. 40. With a frontispiece by Thomas Bewick.
>
> Good copy, in its original cover.

(4191.) 156. Interesting Anecdote Of the late Princess of Wales, Mother of His present Majesty. [etc.] Embellished with an elegant Engraving.
Newcastle on Tyne, Printed by J. Mitchell. [n. d.]

12mo. Pp. 36. With a frontispiece by Thomas Bewick, "The Female Exile," No. (1712.), used in various other works.
Good copy, in its original cover.

(4192.) 157. The Interesting Story Of Wolkmar and his Dog. By Drake. Embellished with an elegant Engraving. [etc.]
Newcastle on Tyne, Printed and Sold by J. Mitchell. [n. d.].

12mo. Pp. 36. With a frontispiece by Thomas Bewick.
Good copy, in its original cover.

(4193.) 158. The Absent Man ; Or, Life & Singular Eccentricities Of George Harvest, [etc.]
Newcastle on Tyne : Printed by J. Mitchell, Dean-Street. [n. d.]

12mo. Pp. 36. With a frontispiece by Thomas Bewick.
Good copy, in its original cover.

(4194.) 159. The Life Of Daniel Dancer, Esq. The Celebrated Miser. Embellished with an elegant Engraving. [etc.]
Newcastle upon Tyne : Printed by J. Mitchell. [n. d.]

12mo. Pp. 36. With a frontispiece by Thomas Bewick.
Good copy, in its original cover.

(4195.) 160. Ducks And Pease ; Or, The Newcastle Rider. A Dramatic Piece. Embellished with an accurate Portrait, by T. Bewick.

Newcastle on Tyne, Printed by J. Mitchell, Dean-Street.   Price Sixpence.   [n. d.]

12mo.   Pp. 24.   With a frontispiece by Thomas Bewick.
Good copy, in its original cover.

(4196.) 161. Sporting Anecdotes ; [etc.]
Albion Press Printed, For J. Cundee, Ivy-Lane, Paternoster-Row; And J. Harris, St. Paul's Church-yard.   [n. d. but about 1807.]

12mo.   Pp. xv, 579.   With cut on the title used in the ' British
   Field Sports,' the original Block of which is in my possession.
Good copy, in its original cover.

(4197.) 162. The Easter Gift : [etc.]   Published for the Amusement of all the Little Gentry in Christendom.   Embellished with Cuts.
York : Printed by T. Wilson and R. Spence, High-Ousegate.   1807.   (Price Two-pence.)

24mo.   Pp. 63.   With a frontispiece and twenty-four cuts, one
   of which is by Thomas Bewick.
Good copy, in its original cover, which has two cuts.

(4198.) 163. Works Of the late celebrated Robert Burns; With a Sketch of his Life.
Edinburgh : Printed by John Johnstone, High Street.   1807.

24mo.   Pp. xii, 252.   With a frontispiece, " View of the Cottage
   where Burns was born."
Good copy, in old calf.

(4199.) 164. The Cotter's Saturday Night.   By Robert Burns.
Newcastle : 1807.

12mo. With frontispiece by Thomas Bewick.
Imperfect copy.

(4200.) 165. The Scottish Minstrel; A Selection Of The Most Favourite Songs of Caledonia; Adapted for the Voice, German Flute, and Violin.

Edinburgh: Printed by Oliver & Co. Netherbow. 1807.

12mo. Pp. vii, 216. A reprint of No. (143.).
Good copy, in its original cover, and uncut.

(4201.) 166. Oliver's Choice Selection Of Comic Songs. Second Edition.

Edinburgh; Printed by Oliver & Co. Netherbow. For Champante & Whitrow, Jewry-Street, Aldgate; Lane, Newman, & Co. Leadenhall-Street; and T. & R. Hughes, Ludgate-Street, London. 1807.

18mo. Pp. 216. With a frontispiece and several vignettes, about which I feel considerable doubt.
Good copy, in its original boards.

(4202.) 167. A History Of England, In a Series of Letters From a Nobleman to his Son. The Continuation to April, 1808, By J. Bigland, [etc.]

London: Printed for J. Brambles, A. Meggitt, and J. Waters, By H. Mozley, Gainsborough. 1808.

12mo. In two vols. Vol. I. pp. iii, 317. Vol. II. pp. 347.
With the large series of the Portraits of the Sovereigns, similar to that in No. (3797.), issued by the same printer at Gainsborough in the previous year.
Very fine copy, in old calf.

(4203.) 168. A Spring-Day: Or, Contemplations

On Several Occurrences Which naturally strike the eye in that Delightful Season. By James Fisher. The Third Edition, Carefully Corrected and Improved.

Edinburgh: Printed for the Author, By John Moir, Royal Bank Close; And sold by Ogle & Aikman, Edinburgh; Williams & Smith, Stationers Court; and Ogle, Great Turnstyle, London; and many of the Principal Booksellers In Great Britain.   1808.

8vo. Pp. x, 338. With the four admirable cuts.
Fine copy, in its original boards.

(4204.) 169. The Repository Of Select Literature. No. (232.).

Another good copy, in its original boards.

(4205.) 170. The British Miscellany, A Selection Of Humorous, Sentimental, and Moral Poems, From the most approved Authors. By Duncan Donaldson, Esq.

Pontefract: Printed by and for B. Boothroyd: Sold by Longman, Hurst and Co. Paternoster-Row; T. Williams, Stationers'-Court, London; and may be had of all other Booksellers.   1808.

12mo. Pp. viii, 196. With two vignettes, among others, which may be by Thomas Bewick.
Good copy, in its original half-calf.

(4206.) 171. The Grave, A Poem. By Robert Blair. To which is added Gray's Elegy In a Country Church Yard. With Notes Moral, and Explanatory.

Alnwick: Printed by Catnach and Davison. Sold by the Booksellers in England, Scotland, And Ireland. 1808.

12mo. Pp. xiv, 72. With a frontispiece and other cuts by Thomas Bewick, of which the original Blocks are in my possession.   An impression of the former is here given.

Fine copy, in its original cover.

(4207.) 172. The Caledonian Tea-Table Miscellany. Choice Songs.

Edinburgh: Printed by Oliver & Boyd, Netherbow. 1808.

18mo. Pp. xii, 219. With cut on the title, thought to be by Thomas Bewick.

Good copy, in its original boards.

(4208.) 173. A History Of British Birds. The Figures Engraved on Wood by T. Bewick.

Newcastle : Printed by Edward Walker, for T.
Bewick : Sold by him, And Longman and Co. London.   1809.

> 8vo.   Part I. pp. xlii, 328.   Part II. pp. xviii, 360.
> Beautiful copy, in old calf.

(4209.) 174. A Natural History Of British Quadrupeds, Foreign Quadrupeds, British Birds, Water Birds,
Foreign Birds, Fishes, Reptiles, Serpents, & Insects.
Embellished with 247 Engravings on Wood, By Thomas Bewick, of Newcastle.

Alnwick : Printed at the Apollo Press, By and for
W. Davison.   1809.

> 18mo.   Each of the divisions consists of 36 pages.   The whole
> comprises Nos. (284.) to (297.), but issued at an earlier date
> than I was formerly led to suppose.
> Beautiful copy, in calf gilt.

(4210.) 175. The History Of the Castle, Town, and
Forest, Of Knaresborough, With Harrogate, And it's
Medicinal Springs : [etc.]   By E. Hargrove.   Sixth
Edition ; With considerable Additions.

Knaresborough : Printed by Hargrove and Sons ;
[etc.]   1809.

> 12mo.   Pp. 423.   With a number of cuts, and among them the
> beautiful engraving of the Cornwall Arms at page 100.
> Good copy, in its original boards.

(4211.) 176. Every Man His Own Farrier ; Or,
The Whole Art of Farriery Laid Open : [etc.]   By
Francis Clater.   The Eighteenth Edition.

London : Printed, by Assignment of A. Tomlinson,

Newark, For B. Crosby and Co., Stationers' Court, Paternoster-Row, Which is the only Wholesale House. Sold also by S. and J. Ridge, Newark; [etc.] 1809.

> 8vo. Pp. xi, 179. With a frontispiece, a cut at p. 179, and two cuts on the cover.
> Good copy, in its original boards.

(4212.) 177. Furnass's Practical Surveyor. No. (236.).

> Another very beautiful copy, half-bound in green morocco.

(4213.) 178. Rural Felicity; Or the History Of Tommy and Sally. Embellished with Cuts.
London: Printed for J. Harris, successor to E. Newbery, the Corner of St. Paul's Church-Yard. 1809. By J. Crowder, Warwick-Square.

> 24mo. Pp. 31. With a frontispiece and seven cuts. I possess the original Block of that at p. 18, of which an impression is given at page 491.
> Good copy, in its original cover.

(4214.) 179. The Visits Of Tommy Lovebook To his neighbouring Little Misses and Masters. Embellished with Cuts.
London: Printed for J. Harris, (Successor to E. Newbery) Corner of St. Paul's Church-Yard, 1809. By J. Crowder, Warwick-Square. (Price Two Pence.)

> 24mo. Pp. 64. With a frontispiece and twelve cuts. I possess the original Blocks of those at pp. 14, 24, 33, 53, and 62. Impressions of those at pp. 14 and 53 are here given, and one of that at p. 33 is to be found under No. (3619.).

Good copy, in its original cover.

(4215.) 180. The History Of Tommy Careless, Or, The Misfortunes Of A Week.   Embellished with Cuts.

London : Printed for J. Harris, successor to E. New-bery, the Corner of St. Paul's Church-Yard.   1809. By J. Crowder, Warwick Square.   (Price One Penny.)

24mo.   Pp. 31.   With a frontispiece and seven cuts.   Of that at p. 22 I possess the original Block.

Good copy, in its original cover.

(4216.) 181. The Foundling; Or, the History Of Lucius Stanhope. Embellished with Cuts.

London: Printed for J. Harris, Successor to E. Newbery, at the Corner of St. Paul's Church-Yard; by J. Crowder, Warwick-square. 1809. (Price One Penny.)

24mo. Pp. 31. With a frontispiece and seven cuts, of the authenticity of which I have great doubt.

Good copy, in its original cover.

(4217.) 182. The Lay of the Reedwater Minstrel. No. (243.).

Another very fine copy, in its original boards.

(4218.) 183. The Gentle Shepherd; A Scots Pastoral. By Allan Ramsay.

Edinburgh: Printed by and for Oliver and Boyd, Netherbow. [n. d. The cover bears date 1809.]

18mo. Pp. 71. The frontispiece is certainly not by Thomas Bewick, but a vignette on the wrapper is possibly his work. It also occurs at p. 157 of the 'Scottish Minstrel,' published by the same house, No. (143.), etc.

Good copy, in its original paper wrapper.

(4219.) 184. The Antiquities Of The Anglo-Saxon Church. The Second Edition. By The Rev. John Lingard.

Newcastle: Printed by Edward Walker. Sold by J. Booker, and Keating and Co. London. 1810.

8vo. Similar to No. (249.), with the exception of the imprint.

The following is an impression from the original Block in my possession, representing the Preaching of S. Augustine.

Fine copy, half-bound.

(4220.) 185. The Historie of Frier Rvsh : how he came to a houfe of Religion to feeke feruice, and being entertained by the Priour, was firft made vnder Cooke. Being full of pleafant mirth and delight for young people. Imprinted at London by Edw. All-de, dwelling neere Chrift-Church. 1620.

London : Reprinted by Harding and Wright, St. John's-Square ; For Robert Triphook, 37, St. James's-Street. 1810.

4to. Pp. 38. With a fac-simile of an old woodcut on the title, said to be by Thomas Bewick.

Fine copy, half bound in calf. It formerly belonged to " John Caley., Greys Inn. F.A.S. 1810." who has written on the fly-leaf some particulars of this curious production.

(4221.) 186. The New English Tutor, Or, Modern Preceptor. [etc.] The Thirteenth Edition: With the Author's Last Corrections. [etc.] By A. Fisher, Author of the English Grammar, with Exercises of Bad English.

Newcastle: Printed by S. Hodgson. And Sold by the Booksellers in General. 1810.

12mo. Pp. vii, 121. With the cuts of the previous Editions. Good copy, in old calf.

(4222.) 187. The New Museum Of Natural History. With Engravings on Wood by Bewick.

Edinburgh: Published by Oliver & Boyd, Nether-bow. 1810.

12mo. Pp. 100. With cuts which, though positively stated to be by him, certainly do not add to Bewick's fame. Good copy, in its original boards.

(4223.) 188. A Treatise On the Choice, Buying, and General Management Of Live Stock; [etc.] Second Edition, Revised, Corrected, and Enlarged. Embellished with beautiful Wood Engravings of some of the most profitable Breeds. By the Author of The Complete Grazier.

London: Printed for B. Crosby and Co. Stationers'-Court, Paternoster-Row; And sold by Ridges, Newark; Poole, Taunton; Wood, Wakefield; [etc.] 1810. (J. G. Barnard, Printer, Skinner-Street.)

8vo. Pp. viii, 232. With many cuts of stock, some of which are by Thomas Bewick, and very beautiful. Good copy, in its original boards.

(4224.) 189. Fables Of Æsop, And Others: Translated into English. With Instructive Applications; And a Print before each Fable. By Samuel Croxall, D.D. Late Archdeacon of Hereford. The Twentieth Edition, Carefully Revised and Improved.

London: Published and Sold by all the Booksellers, and by Thomas Wilson and Son, Printers, High-Ousegate, York. 1810.

> Sm. 8vo. Pp. xxiv, 336. With many cuts previously used in the Select Fables of 1784, No. (24.), among many which are older than Bewick.
>
> Beautiful copy, in tree-calf.

(4225.) 190. Yorick's Budget; Or, Repository Of Wit, Humour, and Sentiment. [etc.]

London: Published by Vernor, Hood, and Sharpe; R. Scholey; And T. Tegg.

Newcastle on Tyne, Printed and Sold by J. Mitchell. 1810.

> 12mo. Pp. iv, 260. With an admirable cut on the title by Thomas Bewick.
>
> Good copy, in its original boards.

(4226.) 191. The Indian Cottage, Or A Search after Truth. By M. Saint Pierre, [etc.]

Newcastle on Tyne, Printed and Published by J. Mitchell, And sold by all the Booksellers in the United Kingdom. 1810.

> 12mo. Pp. 72. With a beautiful frontispiece, a cut on the title, and another at p. 17, by Thomas Bewick.
>
> Very fine copy, in its original boards.

(4227.) 192. The Fables Of Mr. John Gay. Complete in Two Parts. [etc.] With Cuts by T. Bewick, of Newcastle.

York: Printed by and for T. Wilson and Son. High-Ousegate. 1810.

12mo. Pp. 252. A reprint of the edition of 1806.
Fine copy, in old calf.

(4228.) 193. The Poetical Fabulator. No. (257.)

Another copy, in its original cover.

(4229.) 194. Original Miscellaneous Poetry, On different Incidents. By Veterinary, Doctor Marshall, South-Street, Durham. [etc.]

Barnard-Castle; Printed by John Soulby, And sold by Crosby and Co. Stationer's-Court, London; Mundell and Stevenson, Edinburgh; Fauer, Dublin; and by all the Booksellers, in the United Kingdom. 1810.

12mo. Pp. 36. With a few insignificant cuts, some at least of which are believed to be by Thomas Bewick.
Good copy, in its original cover.

(4230.) 195. Reading Exercises For the Use of Schools, [etc.] By The Rev. David Blair. The Sixth Edition, Corrected.

London: Printed for Richard Phillips, Bridge Street, Blackfriars. [etc.] 1811. W. Flint, Printer, Old Bailey, London.

8vo. Pp. iv, 212. With a number of cuts, a few of which, representations of animals, have certainly much to recommend them as the work, in part at least, of Thomas Bewick.
Good copy, in old calf.

(4231.) 196. Robin Hood; Or, A Complete His-

tory Of all the Notable Exploits Performed by Him
and his Merry Men. [etc.]

York: Printed by and for Thomas Wilson and Son,
High-Ousegate.   1811.   (Price One Shilling.)

> 18mo. Pp. iv, 106. With cuts, one or two of which may be
> the early productions of Thomas Bewick, though the accuracy
> of this attribution is questionable.
> Fine copy, in its original boards.

(4232.) 197. The Northumbrian Minstrel. No.
(267.).

> Another very fine and clean copy of the three parts, in their ori-
> ginal paper covers.

(4233.) 198. The Grave, A Poem. By Robert
Blair. To which is added Gray's Elegy In a Country
Churchyard.

Alnwick: Printed by and for W. Davison, and Sold
by A. K. Newman, & Co. London, J. and J. Robertson, & Oliver & Boyd, Edinburgh.   1811.

> 18mo. Pp. xii, 46. With a frontispiece and two cuts, of which
> I possess the original Blocks. An impression of the first has
> already been given under No. (4206.), of which this edition is
> a reprint.
> Good copy, in its original cover.

(4234.) 199. A Garland Of New Songs, Containing, 1. Be Quick, for I'm in Haste. [etc.]

W. Appleton, Printer, Darlington.   1811.

> 12mo. Pp. 8. With cut of a Swan, thought to be by Thomas
> Bewick, on the title.
> Good copy, uncut.

(4235.) 200. 1. A Spelling-Book, Wherein the Pro-

nunciation and Spelling Of the English Tongue Are
reduced to a very few Principles, or General Heads.
For the Use of English Schools. By John Warden,
Teacher of English in Edinburgh. A New Edition,
With considerable Additions and Improvements.
Newcastle: Printed at the Shakespeare Printing-
Office, By E. Humble and Son, Mosley-Street. 1812.

 12mo. Pp. viii, 180. With admirable cuts of the Horse, Cow,
  Deer, Cat, Dog, Lion, and Bear, by Thomas Bewick, at pp.
  148-154. That of the Deer was afterwards, if not before,
  used for the head of a Bar Bill, and occurs in this Collection,
  Nos. (2623.)-(2625.). The original Blocks are in my possession. Impressions of "The Horse" and "The Cow" are here
  given, and one of "The Deer" will be found in the Department "Bar Bills."

Beautiful copy, in half-russia.

(4236.) 200. 2. Another copy, in old calf.

(4237.) 201. The New Testament Of Our Lord and Saviour Jesus Christ, Translated out of the Latin Vulgat: Diligently compared with the Original Greek: And first published by The English College of Rhemes, Anno 1582. [etc.]
Newcastle Upon Tyne: Printed by Preston & Heaton. 1812.

> 12mo. Pp. vi, 412. With a very beautiful cut of Our Lord on the Cross, on the title, by Thomas Bewick.
> Fine copy, in old calf.

(4238.) 202. The Hive Of Ancient & Modern Literature: [etc.] The Fourth Edition, Illustrated with a Number of Engravings on Wood, by T. Bewick and L. Clennell, both of Newcastle.
Newcastle: Printed by and for S. Hodgson, and the Booksellers in general. 1812.

> 12mo. Pp. vii, 338. With the cuts of the previous editions, of which I possess the original Blocks. That on the title has already been given at page 371.
> Good copy, in old calf.

(4239.) 203. Choice Emblems, Natural, Historical, Fabulous, Moral, and Divine. [etc.] Written for the Amusement of a Young Nobleman. The Eleventh Edition.
London: Printed for J. Harris, Corner of St. Paul's Church-Yard; Longman and Co. Pater-Noster Row; Scatcherd and Co. Ave-Maria Lane; and Rivingtons, St. Paul's Church-Yard. 1812.

18mo. Pp. xxi, 226. The cuts added in the third edition are, perhaps, the work of John Bewick. A reprint of No. (13.), etc. See the note to that Number.

Good copy, in half-calf.

(4240.) 204. A Description Of more than Three Hundred Animals, Including Quadrupeds, Birds, Fishes, Serpents, and Insects, [etc.] A New Edition, Carefully Revised, Corrected, and considerably Augmented. By A. D. M[cQuin]. H.F.S.A.

London: Printed for B. and R. Crosby, and Co. Stationers'-Court, Ludgate-Street, And Sold by all the Booksellers in the United Kingdom. 1812.

8vo. Pp. xx, 364. With numerous woodcuts, of some of which I possess the original Blocks, and imagine them to be by Thomas Bewick. Most of them are certainly not by him, and perhaps none are.

Good copy, in its original boards.

(4241.) 205. The Parents' Best Gift.
York: Printed by Thomas Wilson and Son, High-Ousegate. 1812. (Price One Penny.)

24mo. Pp. 62. With a frontispiece and thirteen cuts.
Imperfect copy.

(4242.) 206. The Sister's Gift; Or, the Naughty Boy Reformed. Published for The Advantage of the rising Generation.
York: Printed by Thomas Wilson and Son, High-Ousegate. 1812. (Price One Penny.)

24mo. Pp. 30. With a frontispiece and seven cuts.
Good copy, in its original cover, on which are two cuts.

(4243.) 207. 1. Entertaining Fables For The In-

struction of Children.   Embellished with Cuts.   To
which is added, The Trial of an Ox for killing a
Man.   Also A Moment's Advice to Children, and Young
People.

York: Printed by Thomas Wilson and Son, High-
Ousegate.   1812.   Price One Penny.

24mo.   Pp. 31.   With a frontispiece and seventeen cuts.
Good copy, in its original cover, on which are two cuts.

(4244.)   207.   2.   Another copy, in its original cover.

(4245.)   207.   3.   Another copy.

(4246.)   208.   History Of Sir Richard Whittington
And His Cat.   Adorned with Cuts.

York : Printed by Thomas Wilson and Son, High-
Ousegate.   1812.   (Price One Penny.)

24mo.   Pp. 30.   With a frontispiece and twelve cuts.
Good copy, in its original cover, which has two cuts.

(4247.)   209.   The London Cries, For the Amusement Of all the Good Children Throughout the World.
Taken from Life.

York : Printed by Thomas Wilson and Son, High-
Ousegate.   1812.   (Price One Penny.)

24mo.   Pp. 31.   With a frontispiece and twenty-seven cuts.
Good copy, in its original cover.   The two cuts which embellish
   the latter are, in my opinion, the only specimens of Bewick's
   work which the little volume contains.

(4248.)   210.   The History Of Little Tommy Two-
Shoes, Own Brother to Mrs. Margery Two-Shoes.
Adorned with Cuts.

York: Printed by Thomas Wilson and Son, 1812. (Price One Penny.)

> 24mo. Pp. 28. With a frontispiece and nine cuts, the authenticity of which, as well as of the two on the cover, is, in my judgment, very doubtful.
> Good copy, in its original cover.

(4249.) 211. The Affecting History Of the Babes in the Wood. Embellished with Cuts.

York: Printed by Thomas Wilson and Son, High-Ousegate. 1812. (Price One Penny.)

> 24mo. Pp. 31. With a frontispiece and eight cuts.
> Good copy, in its original cover, on which are two cuts.

(4250.) 212. 1. Cinderella; Or, the History Of the Little Glass Slipper.

York: Printed by Thomas Wilson and Son, High-Ousegate. 1812. (Price One Penny.)

> 24mo. Pp. 30. With a frontispiece and eight cuts, two of which, together with two that ornament the cover, are to be attributed to Thomas Bewick.
> Good copy, in its original cover.

(4251.) 212. 2. Another copy, in its original cover.

(4252.) 213. The History Of Little Francis: Intended for the Instruction of Boys and Girls not Six Feet High. To which is added, Learned, Religious, and Moral Lessons for all the Little Gentry in the Kingdom. With Cuts by Bewick.

York: Printed by Thomas Wilson and Son, High-Ousegate. 1812. (Price One Penny.)

> 24mo. Pp. 30. With a frontispiece and eight cuts.
> Good copy, in its original cover, on which are two cuts.

(4253.) 214. Rhymes Of Northern Bards; [etc.] No. (302.).

Another copy, in its original boards, and lettered at the back in the handwriting of Mr. W. Garret. It formerly belonged to Mr. Thomas Bell, and has his bookplate.

(4254.) 215. Elegant Poems: Containing, Pope's Essay on Man, Blair's Grave, Gray's Elegy, Goldsmith's Traveller, And Goldsmith's Deserted Village.

Gainsborough: Printed by and for Henry Mozley. 1812.

18mo. Pp. 119. With a frontispiece.
Good copy, in its original boards.

(4255.) 216. The History Of Alnwick, The County Town Of Northumberland.

Alnwick: Printed by and for W. Davison. 1813.

12mo. Pp. 142. With a view of Alnwick Castle for the frontispiece, of which I possess the original Block.
Fine copy, in its original boards.

(4256.) 217. The Honey-Jug; Containing A Variety of Pleasant Stories, For Youthful Amusement. With cuts by Bewick.

York: Printed by Thomas Wilson and Sons, High-Ousegate. 1813. (Price Twopence.)

24mo. Pp. 31. With a frontispiece and twelve cuts.
Good copy, in its original cover, on which are two cuts.

(4257.) 218. The House That Jack Built; To which is prefixed the History of Jack Jingle; [etc.]

Edinburgh: Printed and Published by G. Ross. 1813. Price One Penny.

24mo. Pp. 19. With a frontispiece and eleven cuts. In my opinion, although I give them the benefit of a doubt, they are copies, more or less clever, of those by Thomas Bewick, but are not by the Artist himself.

Good copy, in its original paper cover.

I possess a number of Ross's Children's Books, including

> Cock Robin.
> Master Jackey And Miss Harriot.
> Tom Thumb's Play-Book.
> Jacky Dandy's Delight.
> The Royal Fabulist.
> Nursery Songs.
> The Golden Present.
>
> etc. etc. etc.

But I consider even the most clever of their illustrations to be copies, and nothing more.

(4258.) 219. Ballads, In the Cumberland Dialect, By Robert Anderson. [etc.]
Alnwick: Printed by W. Davison, Bondgate Street. Sold by all Booksellers. [n. d.]

18mo. Pp. xvi, 224. With a few cuts, used in other publications, and of which I have the original Blocks.

Good copy, in its original cloth boards.

(4259.) 220. Newcastle Reprints. A volume containing the following :—

1. Biographical Memoirs of William Ged. No. (365.).
2. Santander's Origin of Printing. No. (367.).
3. Willett's Origin of Printing. No. (369.).
4. Hodgson's Origin of Stereotype Printing. No. (370.).

All are on large paper, with the autograph attestation to each by

the printer of the number of copies printed. Of the three
first-named pieces, thirty copies were printed on this large
paper, and of the fourth thirty-six copies.

A very beautiful royal 8vo volume, handsomely half-bound in calf.

(4260.) 221. Newcastle Reprints. A volume containing the following :—

1. Cheviot. No. (351.).
2. The Marriage Of the Coquet and the Alwine.
   No. (352.).
3. An Account Of The Great Floods. No. (359.).
4. An Exact Narration Of the Life and Death Of
   the Reverend and Learned Prelate, and Painfull
   Divine, Launcelot Andrewes, Late Bishop of
   Winchester.
5. A Short View Of the Long Life and Raigne Of
   Henry the Third, King of England. No.
   (355.).
6. A Memoir On The Origin of Printing. By
   Ralph Willett. [etc.] No. (369.).
7. Observations On the Origin of Printing, In
   a letter to Owen Salisbury Brereton, Esq.
   By Ralph Willett, Esq. F.R. and A.SS. Newcastle: Printed by S. Hodgson, Union-Street.
   MDCCCXIX. With autograph presentation "To
   Thomas Davidson, Esqr. from J. Murray. Newcastle, September 27th, 1819.", and autograph
   note inserted.

Very fine copies. The volume, which is half-bound in calf, belonged to Thomas Davidson, Esq., Clerk of the Peace for the
county of Northumberland, whose book-plate is inserted, and
to whom these original copies were presented.

"It contains the most rare and valuable of all the Newcastle Typographic Publications. The Ordinary Selling Price of the Life of Bishop Andrewes is One Guinea, Cheviot 10*s*. 6*d*., but seldom or ever to be had even at these Prices for Love or Money."—Mr. R. Robinson, 1866.

(4261.) 222. The First Report Of a Society for Preventing Accidents In Coal Mines, [etc.] Illustrated by Plans and Sections, By John Buddle.

Newcastle: Printed by Edward Walker, Pilgrim-Street. 1814.

8vo. Pp. iv, 28. Figure VII., on page 11, is attributed to Thomas Bewick.

Good copy, in paper wrapper.

(4262.) 223. Davison's Halfpenny Books. No. (310.).

The following should be added as of special merit :—

1. The English Alphabet.
2. The Picture Alphabet.
3. The House That Jack built.
4. The Book of Wild Beasts.
5. The British Picture Book of Birds.
6. The History of Monkeys.
7. Juvenile Song Book.
8. The Guess Book, A Collection of Ingenious Puzzles.

Good copies, in their original state.

(4263.) 224. Natural History of British Quadrupeds—British Birds—Water Birds—Fishes—Reptiles,

Serpents, and Insects—Foreign Quadrupeds—Foreign Birds.   Nos. (284.)–(297.).

Another copy of each, very fine and clean, in their original covers.

(4264.) 225. A New Family Herbal: [etc.]   By Robert John Thornton, M.D. [etc.]
London: 1814.

8vo.   A reprint of the edition of 1810, No. (253.).
Good copy, in its original boards.

(4265.) 226. Mother Bunch's Fairy Tales.   Published for the Amusement Of all those Little Masters and Misses, Who, By Duty to their Parents, and Obedience To their Superiors, Aim at becoming Great Lords and Ladies.   Embellished with Engravings.
Glasgow: Published by J. Lumsden and Son. (Price Sixpence.)   [n. d. but about 1814.]

Square 24mo.   Pp. 71.   With a frontispiece.
Fine copy, in half-morocco.
I am in great doubt of the correctness of the attribution to Thomas Bewick of the cuts in Lumsden's publications, but not sufficiently assured of the want of genuineness of some to refuse them a place in this Catalogue.

(4266.) 227. A Selection of Stories; Containing the History Of the Two Sisters, The Fisherman, The King and Fairy Ring, And Honesty Rewarded.   Embellished with Copperplates.
Glasgow, Published and Sold by J. Lumsden & Son. Price Sixpence.   [n. d. but about 1814.]

Square 24mo.   Pp. 60.   With five cuts.
Fine copy, in half-morocco.

(4267.) 228. Christmas Tales For the Instruction Of Good Boys and Girls, By M^r. Solomon Sobersides. Embellished with Engravings.

Glasgow: Published by J. Lumsden & Son. & Sold By Stoddart & Craggs, Hull. Price Sixpence. [n. d. 1814?]

Square 24mo. Pp. 61. With cut at p. 61.
Fine copy, in half-morocco.

(4268.) 229. 1. Gammer Gurton's Garland, [etc.] No. (315.)

Another copy, in its original cover.

(4269.) 229. 2. Another copy, in its original cover.

(4270.) 230. Beauty And The Beast. A Tale. For the Entertainment of Juvenile Readers. Ornamented with Elegant Engravings.

Glasgow: Published by J. Lumsden & Son. Price Sixpence.

18mo. Pp. 48. With cut, thought to be by Thomas Bewick, at page 48.
Good copy, in its original cover.

(4271.) 231. An Elegy On the Death and Burial Of Cock-Robin.

Glasgow: Published and Sold, Wholesale, By Lumsden and Son. (Price One Penny.) [n. d.]

24mo. Pp. 14. With thirteen cuts.
Good copy, in its original cover.

(4272.) 232. The Waggon Load Of Amusement.

Glasgow: Published and Sold, Wholesale, By Lumsden and Son. (Price One Penny.) [n. d.]

24mo.   Pp. 14.   With twenty-one charming cuts.
Good copy, in its original cover.

(4273.) 233. The History of Selima and Azor.
Derby : Printed by and for Henry Mozley, Brook-
Street.   [n. d.]

24mo.   Pp. 47.   With a frontispiece and five cuts, three of
which appear to be the work of Thomas Bewick.
Good copy, in its original cover.

(4274.) 234. Divine Songs, In Easy Language, For
the Use of Children.   By I. Watts, D.D.
Edinburgh : Printed and Sold by G. Ross.   Price
Two-Pence.   [n. d. but about 1814.]

24mo.   Pp. 31.   With a frontispiece and eight cuts.
Good copy, in half-calf.

(4275.) 235. The Poems Of Allan Ramsay. A New
Edition, Greatly Enlarged.   To which is prefixed, A
Life of the Author.   In Two Volumes.
Leith : Printed by and for A. Allardice, And to be
had of all Booksellers.   1814.

18mo.   With a few vignettes.
Good copy, in its original boards.

(4276.) 236. The Recreation Of Leisure Hours;
Being Original Songs and Verses, Chiefly in the Scot-
tish Dialect.   By P. Buchan, Jun. Peterhead. [etc.]
Edinburgh : Printed for and Sold by the Author,
A. Clark, and W. Mortimer, Peterhead, and all the
principal Booksellers in Scotland.   Oliver & Boyd,
Printers.   Price Two Shillings.   [n. d. but about
1814.]

12mo. Pp. 138. With a frontispiece and numerous cuts, some
of which I am willing to believe to be by Thomas Bewick.
Good copy, in its original boards.

(4277.) 237. An Introduction To Spelling and
Reading : [etc.] By the Rev. Francis Fox, M.A.
Rector of St. Mary, Reading. The Twentieth Edition. Corrected and Improved.
London : Printed for F. C. and J. Rivington, Booksellers to the Society for Promoting Christian Knowledge, No. 62, St. Paul's Church-Yard. 1815.

12mo. Pp. v., 108. With the cuts mentioned under No. (4049.),
of which it is a reprint.
Good copy, in old calf.

(4278.) 238. A Tour through Sweden, Swedish-
Lapland, Finland, and Denmark. In a Series of Letters. By Matthew Consett, Esq. Second Edition.
Stockton : Printed by Christopher and Jennett.
1815.

8vo. Pp. viii., 148. With a frontispiece of "The Lapland
Sledge," on wood, by Thomas Bewick. It faced page 86,
and was the only woodcut, in the previous edition.
Good copy, in its original boards.

(4279.) 239. Fabliaux or Tales, Abridged from
French Manuscripts Of the XIIth and XIIIth Cen-
turies By M. Le Grand, Selected and Translated into
English Verse, By the late G. L. Way, Esq. With A
Preface, Notes, and Appendix, By the late G. Ellis,
Esq. A New Edition, Corrected. In Three Volumes.
London : Printed for J. Rodwell, (Successor to Mr.

Faulder,) New Bond Street, By S. Hamilton, Wey-
bridge, Surrey.　1815.

> Sm. 8vo.　A reprint of the edition of 1796–1800, No. (95.),
> with the same cuts.
> Fine copy, in red morocco.

(4280.)　240. A Copy of A Letter, Written by Our
Blessed Lord & Saviour, Jesus Christ. [etc.]

[Marshall, Printer.]

> 12mo.　Pp. 8.　With the cut of an Evangelist, already men-
> tioned, No. (3282.), as illustrating a Christmas Carol, issued
> by the same Printer.
> Good copy, uncut.

(4281.)　241. Divine Songs, Attempted in Easy
Language, For the Use of Children.　By I. Watts,
D.D. [etc.]

Louth : Printed and Published by B. Fotherby,
Mercer-Row, And sold by all Booksellers.　Price
Sixpence.　[n. d. but about 1815.]

> 18mo.　Pp. 46.　With a frontispiece of doubtful authenticity.
> Good copy, in its original cover.

(4282.)　242. A Garland Of New Songs.　Containing Blow high, blow low. [etc.]

M. Angus & Son, Printers, Newcastle.　[n. d.]

> 12mo.　Pp. 8.　With an early cut, by Thomas Bewick, on the
> title, of which the following is an impression from the original
> Block, obtained, as those which follow, from Angus's Office,
> the whole of the Bewick cuts of which have passed, through
> the hands of Mr. Emerson Charnley and Mr. Dodd, into my

possession. This cut is also used on the title of No. (15) Poor Jack. [etc.], presently mentioned.

In many numbers, of eight pages each, sometimes bearing the imprint, " Newcastle : Printed by M. Angus & Son, Side." Among others, those containing (1.) Thomas Clutterbuck and Polly Higginbottom. [etc.], (2.) Tho' Fortune shuns my Lowly Cot. [etc.], (3.) The Blue Bell of Scotland. [etc.], (4.) Ewie wi' the crooked horn. [etc.], (5.) The Flowing Can. [etc.], (6.) God save the King. [etc.], (7). The Bay of Biscay, O. [etc.], (8.) Meg of Wapping. [etc.], (9.) My Nannie, O. [etc.], (10.) The New Ploughboy. [etc.], (11.) Old Towler. [etc.], (12.) When o'er the Midnight Billow. [etc.], (13.) The Old Ram of Derby. [etc.], (14.) On the green Sedgy Banks. [etc.], (15.) Poor Jack. [etc.], (16.) Of a' the Airts. [etc.] (17.) Jamie Reilly's Courtship. [etc.], (18.) Kitty o' the Clyde, [etc.], (19.) Lash'd to the Helm. [etc.], (20.) Sequel to Sweet Poll of Plymouth. [etc.], (21.) The Soldier's Adieu. [etc.], (22.) The Tempest. [etc.], (23.) William at Eve. [etc.], (24.) The Banks of the Dee. [etc.], (25.) The Blaeberries. [etc.], (26.) Duke William's Ramble. [etc.], (27.) The Greenwich Pensioner, [etc.], (28,) The Golden Days of Good Queen Bess. [etc.], (29.) A song in the Opera of Inkle and

Yarico. [etc.], and (30.) The Whip-Club. [etc.], have cuts on their titles done by Thomas Bewick in his early days, most of the original Blocks of which are in my possession.

The following is the cut on the titles of Nos. (1.) Thomas Clutterbuck and Polly Higginbottom. [etc.], and (18.) Kitty o' the Clyde. [etc.] :—

The next occurs on Nos. (2.) Tho' Fortune shuns my Lowly Cot. [etc.], (14.) On the green Sedgy Banks. [etc.], (16.) Of a' the Airts. [etc.], and (17.) Jamie Reilly's Courtship. [etc.] :—

The following is on Nos. (3.) The Blue Bell of Scotland. [etc.], and (25.) The Blaeberries. [etc.] :—

The next is on Nos. (4.) Ewie wi' the crooked horn. [etc.], and (13.) The Old Ram of Derby. [etc.] :—

The following occurs on Nos. (5.) The Flowing Can. [etc.], and (9.) My Nannie, O. [etc.] :—

This cut also occurs in Bell's Right Merry Garland of Northumberland Heroes, No. (303.), page 13.

The following is on Nos. (6.) God save the King. [etc.], and (28.) The Golden Days of Good Queen Bess. [etc.] :—

The next occurs on Nos. (7.) The Bay of Biscay, O. [etc.],
(12.) When o'er the Midnight Billow. [etc.], (19.) Lash'd
to the Helm. [etc.], (22.) The Tempest. [etc.], (26.) Duke
William's Ramble. [etc.], and (27.) The Greenwich Pensioner. [etc.] :—

The following is on No. (8.) Meg of Wapping. [etc.] :—

The next is on Nos. (10.) The New Ploughboy. [etc.], and (29.) A song in the Opera of Inkle and Yarico. [etc.] :—

The following is on No. (11., Old Towler. [etc.] :—

The following occurs on Nos. (20.) Sequel to Sweet Poll of Plymouth. [etc.], and (23.) William at Eve. [etc.] :—

The next is on No. (21.) The Soldier's Adieu. [etc.] :—

And the following is on No. (30.) The Whip-Club. [etc.] :—

Good copies, uncut.

(4283.) 243. A Collection Of New Songs. Containing 1. The Bleaberries. [etc.]
George Angus, Printer, Side, Newcastle.   [n. d.]

12mo.   Pp. 8.   With cut of the Scotch Piper, already given.
In many numbers, some with the above imprint, and others with
"M. Angus & Son, Printers, Newcastle."   Another, containing 1. Happy Harry. [etc.], has the following cut on the title,
by Thomas Bewick.

Most of the rest commence with the same songs, and are illustrated with the same cuts as those mentioned and given above
among the Garlands, which were printed at the same house,
and from which they differ only in the designation on their
titles.

Good copies, uncut.

(4284.) 244. The Jovial Sailor's Garland.

Licensed and entered according to Order. [no place
nor date.]

12mo. Pp. 8. With the following cut, used also on the title of
Bell's Right Merry Garland of Northumberland Heroes,
No. (303.).

Good copy, uncut.

(4285.) 245. The True Lover's Garland.

Licensed and Entered according to Order. [no place
nor date.

12mo.　Pp. 8.　With the following cut, used also on the title of Bell's Garland of Bells, No. (335.).

Good copy, uncut.

(4286.) 246. The Jovial Gamester's Garland.
Licensed and Entered according to Order. [no place nor date.]

12mo.　Pp. 8.　With cut used in No. (335.), given above.
Good copy, uncut.

(4287.) 247. The Fortunate Miller's Garland.
Licensed and Entered according to Order. [no place nor date.]

12mo.　Pp. 8.　With cut used on the title of the Contented Couckould, No. (336.), and also in the Garlands (4.) and (13.) mentioned above, of which an impression has been given.
Good copy, uncut.

(4288.) 248. The Cuckold's Cap Garland.　1. The Buxom Dame of Reading. [etc.]

Licensed and entered according to Order. [no place nor date.]

12mo. Pp. 8. With cut used in No. (336.), etc. as stated above. Good copy, uncut.

(4289.) 249. The London Rake's Garland. Beautified with several choice New Songs.

Licensed and entered according to Order. [no place nor date.]

12mo. Pp. 8. With cut on the title, which occurs also on the title of 'Figures in Rhymes,' No. (304.). The following is an impression from the original Block in my possession.

Good copy, in paper cover.

(4290.) 250. The Ewie wi' the crooked Horn Garland. [etc.]

Licensed and Entered according to Order.

12mo. Pp. 8. With the cut used in No. (336.), etc., of which an impression has been given. Good copy, uncut.

(4291.) 251. Poor Jack's Garland, [etc.]

Newcastle: Printed in this present year. [n. d.]

12mo, Pp. 8. With the cut of Sailor and Lass, already given.
Good copy, uncut.

(4292.) 252. Meg of Wapping's Garland, [etc.]
Newcastle : Printed in this present year.   [n. d.]

12mo. Pp. 8. With the cut used in Garland No. (8.), already
given,
Good copy, uncut.

(4293.) 253. Nelson's Garland Of New Songs.
[No place nor date.]

12mo. Pp. 8. With the cut of a Ship, used in Garlands Nos.
(7.), (12.), etc. given above.
Good copy, uncut.

(4294.) 254.   The Midford Garland.
[No place nor date.]

12mo. Pp. 8. With cut of a Galloway, used also in the Rhymes
of Northern Bards, No. (302.), of which I have the original
Block.
Good copy, uncut.

(4295.) 255. The Comical and witty Jokes Of
John Falkirk. [etc.]
Printed in this present year.

12mo. Pp. 8. With the cut already given under No. (4284.).
Good copy, uncut.

(4296.) 256. A Garland Of New Songs.
Newcastle upon Tyne : Printed by J. Marshall, in
the Old Flesh-Market.   No. (138).

12mo. To those already mentioned should be added, as containing cuts of special merit, the numbers beginning The Blackbird, The Bonny Scotch Lad and his Bonnet so Blue, and The

Woodpecker, with a figure of a Blackbird; The Post Captain, The Tempest, The Bay of Biscay, O, and Oh! Lady fair, with a figure of a Ship; and The Roving Bachelor, and Muirland Willie, with that of a Gentleman walking.

Good copies, uncut.

(4297.) 257. A Garland Of Newcastle Songs.
Newcastle upon Tyne: Printed by J. Marshall, in the Old Flesh Market.

12mo. Pp. 8. With cut of a Gentleman walking.
Good copy, uncut.

(4298.) 258. A Garland Of New Songs, Containing The Hungry Fox. [etc.]
Newcastle: Printed by David Bass, Foot of Pilgrim Street. [n. d.]

12mo. Pp. 8. With cut of the Fable of the Fox and the Grapes.
Another number, containing The Lammy, [etc.], has a figure of Fortune.
Good copies, uncut.

(4299.) 259. Excellent New Songs.
Alnwick: Printed and Sold by W. Davison. [n. d.]

12mo. Pp. 8. With a cut on the title of each number, used by Davison in others of his publications.
Good copies, in their original covers.

(4300.) 260. An Introduction To Reading and Spelling. Written on a New Plan, For the Use of Schools, In Two Parts. [etc.] By the Rev. John Hewlett, B.D. Author of Sermons in Two Volumes; Vindication of the Parian Chronicle, &c. A New Edition.
London: Printed for Baldwin, Cradock, and Joy,

47, Paternoster Row, And. R. Hunter, 72, St. Paul's Church-Yard. 1816.

> 12mo. Pp. viii, 172. With Fable cuts at pp. 8, 11, 22, 23, 25, 30, 33, 41, 45, 47, 50, and 51, most of which are by Thomas Bewick. Those at pp. 22, 33, 50, and 51, are signed with his initials.
>
> Very fine copy, in its original boards, and uncut.

(4301.) 261. The Youth's Historical Companion, Containing A Variety Of Anecdotes. Embellished with Cuts.

Derby: Printed and Sold by Henry Mozley, Brook-Street. 1816.

> 18mo. Pp. 72. With a frontispiece, and cut at p. 5, the authenticity of each of which is doubtful.
>
> Good copy, in its original boards.

(4302.) 262. Dr. Goldsmith's Abridgment Of his History of England, From the Invasion of Julius Cæsar, To The Death of George II. To which is added, A very Extensive and Faithful Continuation From that Period to March, 1816. By an Eminent Historian. Ornamented with a Frontispiece, and with Heads by Bewick.

Derby: Printed by and for Henry Mozley, Brook-Street, 1816.

> 12mo. Pp. 428. With the larger Heads of Sovereigns, as in Nos. (299.), (3797.), etc.
>
> Good copy, in old calf.

(4303.) 263. 1. A History Of Hartlepool. By Sir Cuthbert Sharp, Knight, F.S.A. No. (343.)

> Another, a presentation, copy, "To the Ettrick Shepherd, a tes-

timony of affectionate regard and esteem, from the Author. Hartlepool. July 9. 1816."
Good copy, in its original boards.

(4304.) 263. 2. Another copy, presented by the Author to Mr. Sykes, the publisher, "With Sir C. Sharp's best respects to Mr. Sykes."

Very fine copy, in its original boards.

(4305.) 264. An Account Of the Great Flood. [etc.] No. (345.).

Another copy, one of the twenty-four printed on writing demy paper, ruled with red lines, with the extra leaf and MS. signature, and half-bound in calf. It belonged to J. T. Brockett, Esq., and has his book-plate.

(4306.) 265. The Custom House Garland. [etc.] No. (347.).

Another of the fifty copies printed. It is on azure-blue paper, and curiously bound in blue calf gilt, bearing the initials I. S. It belonged to John Straker, Esq., and has also his autograph signature, "Jno. Straker, 1816," and his book-plate. I had it from an old gentleman of Newcastle, who believed it to be unique.

(4307.) 266. The Budget; Or Newcastle Songster. For 1816, [etc.]
Newcastle: Printed for the Union Lodge of Odd Fellows, By J. Marshall, Old Flesh-Market. 1816.

12mo. Pp. 24. With the Arms of Newcastle on the title.
Good copy, uncut.

(4308.) 267. An Account Of The Interment Of Her Royal Highness the Princess Charlotte, In St.

George's Chapel, Windsor, On Wednesday, Nov. 19, 1817.

Newcastle: Printed for J. S.   MDCCCXVII.

8vo. With Bewick's cut of a Female Figure leaning on a Tomb, used by J. Mitchell in No. (281.), etc.

Good copy, in its original paper cover.

(4309.) 268. A Select Collection Of Anecdotes, Tales, Poems, &c.   Compiled By G. Thompson.

Newcastle upon Tyne, Printed by Preston & Heaton, Side.   1817.

12mo.   Pp. 24.   With cut on the title, said to be by Thomas Bewick, of which I have the original Block.

Good copy, half-bound.

(4310.) 269. The Little Teacher, Or Child's First Spelling Book.   By a Parent.   A New Edition.

London: Printed for Darton, Harvey, and Darton, No. 55, Gracechurch-Street.   1818.

12mo.   Pp. 96.   A reprint of No. (256.).   The early period at which the Alphabet cuts were executed, and their great similarity to others of Bewick's works at the same time, induce me to concede to this little volume a place in the present Catalogue.

Good copy, in its original boards.

(4311.) 270. Wilkinson's Treatise On two of the most Important Diseases Which attack The Horse. No. (409.).

Another very fine copy, in its original boards, and uncut.

(4312.) 271. The Highland Girl; Or, The Advantages of Early Piety Exemplified, In The Life and Death Of Jane M'Gregor.

Newcastle : Printed by Edward Walker, Pilgrim-Street, For the Newcastle Religious Tract Society. 1818.

12mo. Pp. 15. With a cut on the title, No. (3461.).
Good copy, half-bound.

(4313.) 272. A Historical and Descriptive View Of the Parishes of Monkwearmouth and Bishopwearmouth, And the Port and Borough of Sunderland. Compiled from Publications of Undoubted Authority, Original Communications, and Personal Research. By George Garbutt.

Sunderland : Printed by and for the Editor ; And sold by Longman, Hurst, Rees, Orme, and Brown, Paternoster-Row ; Nichols and Son, Red-Lion Passage, Fleet-Street, London ; and the Booksellers in the Counties of Durham and Northumberland. 1819.

8vo. Pp. vii, 422, 72, 18. With a " South-west View of the Custom-House, with Part of Fitter's Row," at page 420, said to be by Thomas Bewick, of which I possess the original Block.
Good copy, half-bound in calf.

(4314.) 273. Chronicon Mirabile Seu Excerpta Memorabilia E Registris Parochialibus Com. Pal. Dunelm. Pondere non Numero.

[Book I.] G. Garbutt, Sunderland. MDCCCXIX.

8vo. Pp. vi, 26.

[Book II.] Bishopweremouth : George Garbutt, Typographer. MDCCCXXV.

8vo. Pp. 23. With cut, at p. 3, of the " Friarage, Hartlepool, used in the History of that Town, No. (343.).

[Book III.]   [no place or date.]

8vo.   Pp. iv, 27.   With the cut at p. i, used in the ' Bishoprick
    Garland,' No. (490.), etc.
Fine copy, half-bound in morocco.

(4315.) 274. A Collection Of Classical Songs. [etc.]
Part I.
Newcastle upon Tyne : Printed and Sold by J. Marshall, In the Old Flesh-Market.   1819.   Price Two-
pence.

18mo.   Pp. 16.   With cut of music and instruments on the title.
Fine copy, in its original paper cover.

(4316.) 275. A Collection Of Popular Newcastle
Songs, [etc.]
Newcastle upon Tyne : Printed and Sold by J.
Marshall, In the Old Flesh-Market.   1819.   Price
Twopence.

12mo.   Pp. 16.   With the Arms of Newcastle on the title.
Good copy, uncut.

(4317.) 276. A Collection Of Original Newcastle
Songs, [etc.]
Newcastle upon Tyne : Printed and Sold by J.
Marshall, In the Old Flesh-Market.   1819.   Price
Twopence.

12mo.   Pp. 16.   With the Arms of Newcastle on the title.
Good copy, uncut.

(4318.) 277. Emerson Charnley's Catalogue For
1820.

8vo.   Pp. 163.   With the View of Newcastle Castle, on the
    title ; cut of the Elephant, at p. 24 ; two Fable cuts at p. 25 ;

the Hon. Horace Walpole's Book-plate, given under No. (2112.), and of which I possess the original Block, at p. 76; the Goose, at p. 85; fishing scene, at p. 86 (query if by Bewick); and Mr. Adamson's book-plate, given under No. (1929.) of the 'Bewick Collector,' at p. 158.

Good copy, in its original paper cover.

(4319.) 278. Scraps For The Curious; Being a Miscellaneous Collection Of Interesting Events, &c. &c. Selected from Authentic Sources.

Newcastle upon Tyne: Printed by William Hall, New Wheat-Market, For the Publishers. 1820. (Price One Shilling & Sixpence.)

12mo. Pp. 34. With cut on the title, which may be by Thomas Bewick.

Good copy, half-bound.

(4320.) 279. A Collection Of Original Newcastle Songs, [etc.]

Newcastle upon Tyne: Printed and Sold by J. Marshall, In the Old Flesh-Market. 1820. Price Twopence.

12mo. Pp. 16. With the Arms of Newcastle on the title.

Good copy, uncut.

(4321.) 280. The Gododin, And The Odes of the Months, Translated from the Welsh. [etc.] [By William Probert.]

London: Sold by E. Williams, 11, Strand, Bookseller to the Prince Regent and to the Duke and Dutchess of York; W. Davison, Alnwick; E. Charnley. Newcastle upon Tyne; and P. Blair, Morpeth.

Alnwick: Printed by W. Davison.   [n. d. but published in 1820.]

12mo.   Pp. v, 120.   With cut of the Bard on the title.
Good copy, in its original boards.

(4322.) 281. A Selection Of Engravings on Wood By Thomas Bewick. [etc.]
Newcastle: Printed at the Mercury Press.   1821.

4to.   Consisting of a title and nineteen leaves, printed on one side only, and containing fifty-one cuts, among which are those of Tynemouth Priory, No. (65.), and the Knight, No. (3798.).
Fine copy, in its original grey paper cover.

(4323.) 282. Mynshul's Essayes And Characters Of a Prison, and Prisoners.   No. (436.).

Another copy, in its original boards.

(4324.) 283. Catalogue Of James Oviston's Circulating Library, In Collingwood-Street, Newcastle upon Tyne; [etc.]
Newcastle: Printed by Preston & Heaton.   1821. Price Sixpence.

12mo.   With cut on the title, similar to that of No. (4309.).
Good copy, in its original cover.

(4325.) 284. The Hermit Of Warkworth: [etc.] With Engravings on Wood by Bewick.
Alnwick: Printed and Sold by W. Davison.   1821.

12mo.   Pp. vii, 50.   With a frontispiece, "South View of the Hermitage," given at p. 449, and three other cuts.
Good copy, half-bound in calf.

(4326.) 285. Specimen Of Printing Types, &c. In the Newcastle Printing Office, Newgate Street.
J. Clark, Printer.—1822.

8vo. With " J. C.," encircled with palm, oak, etc., on the title; a view of Clark's Shop, No. (2429.); Profile of Clark; Arms of Newcastle, No. (3007.); Arms of Newcastle, of which an impression is given at page 291; view of the Newcastle Theatre, No. (2187.); view of Sunderland Bridge; etc. etc., by Thomas Bewick, the original Blocks of some of which are in my possession.

This volume is another specimen of a class of books in which the present Supplement is so happily rich, consisting of impressions of the Blocks in the possession of various publishers. All of them are of extreme rarity. Of the one before us I have never seen or heard of another copy.

Good copy, half-bound.

(4327.) 286. Collections For A History Of The Ancient Family Of Carlisle.   No. (438.).

Another copy. A presentation copy, in its original boards, and uncut, from the author to Mr. Charles Devon, with the following autograph note inserted:—" Somerset Place, 29th Jan'. 1823. Mr. Nich'. Carlisle presents his Compliments to Mr. Devon, & begs his acceptance of a copy of His Family History." It is endorsed, " Mr. Charles Devon. by favour of Mr. Caley."

One hundred copies only were printed, as presents, and not published.

(4328.) 287. 1. An Address Delivered in the Loyal Northumbrian Social Society: By W. G. Thompson. No. (3813.).

Another fine copy, in its original cover.

(4329.) 287. 2. Another Copy.

The impression was limited to one hundred copies.

(4330.) 288. The Little Child's Tutor, Or First Book, For Children, The Twenty-ninth Edition.

Derby: Printed by and for Henry Mozley. Price Sixpence. 1823.

> 18mo. Pp. 72. With two cuts on the frontispiece and one on the title, of doubtful authenticity.
> Good copy, in its original cover.

(4331.) 289. The Fables of Æsop, And Others. With Designs on Wood, by Thomas Bewick. The Second Edition.

Newcastle: Printed by E. Walker, For T. Bewick and Son. Sold by them, Longman and Co. London, And All Booksellers. 1823.

> 8vo. Pp. xxiv, 376. A reprint of No. (408.).
> Fine copy, in calf gilt.

(4332.) 290. New General County Rate Schedules, Ordered by the Court of Quarter Sessions at Durham, on the 2nd of August, 1823, to be Printed and Distributed.

Durham: Printed by Francis Humble and Co. [1823.]

> 4to. Pp. 18. With cut of the Seal of the Clerk of the Peace, Durham, by Thomas Bewick.
> Good copy, in its original cover.

(4333.) 291. The Sorrows of Yamba, Or the Negro Woman's Lamentation, By Hannah More. [etc.]

Newcastle: Printed by Edward Walker, Pilgrim-Street, For the Newcastle Religious Tract Society. 1823.

8vo. Pp. 12. With Bewick's cut of the Kneeling Negro, No. (3446.).
Good copy, half-bound.

(4334.) 292. Negro Sale At Demerara.
Newcastle: [etc.] [n. d.]

8vo. Pp. 12. With the same cut.
Good copy, with the former.

(4335.) 293. A Bibliographical And Descriptive Tour From Scarborough To the Library of a Philobiblist, In it's Neighbourhood. By John Cole, Bookseller, Scarborough.

Scarborough: Printed and Published by John Cole and by Longman, Hurst, Rees, Orme, Brown and Green, W. Baynes and Son, and Richard Baynes, Paternoster-row, J. Taylor, Great Surrey Street; Isaac Wilson, Hull; J. and G. Todd, York; and Birdsall and Son, Northampton. 1824.

8vo. Pp. iv, 92. With a view of Hunmanby Church, by Thomas Bewick, on the title.
Good copy, in its original boards.
The impression consisted of fifty copies, whereof twenty-four were on large paper, of which the present is one.

(4336.) 294. A Descriptive Catalogue Of a Select Portion Of the Stock Of John Cole, Bookseller, Scarborough. [etc.]
Scarborough: Printed by John Cole, 1825.

2 copies on Drawing Paper.
6   ,,   Tinted Paper.
25   ..   Medium Writing.

8vo. Pp. 66. With Bewick's view of Hunmanby Church at
page 29.
Good copy, on medium writing-paper, in its original boards.

(4337.) 295. History Of the Earl of Derwentwater.
Sold by T. Huntley, 11, High Street, Sunderland;
And 13, Dean Street, Newcastle.   [n. d.]

12mo. Pp. 24. With cut of " The Female Exile," No. (1712.),
on the cover.
Good copy, in its original cover.

(4338.) 296. The History Of Fortunatus. [etc.]
Edinburgh : Printed for the Booksellers in Town
and Country.   [n. d.]

12mo. Pp. 24. With cut on the title, which appears to be by
Thomas Bewick.
Good copy, uncut.

(4339.) 297. New Penny Histories.
Morpeth : Published by J. Mackay, Bridge Street.
[n. d.]

12mo.   Pp. 24.   In various numbers, of which,
No. 4. The Three Meetings ;
No. 7. The Falcon Inn ;
No. 9. The Rival Cousins ;
No. 11. Helen Bertram ;
and No. 16. The Fatal Stroke,
contain cuts which have much of the style of Thomas Bewick.
Good copies, uncut.

(4340.) 298. Storys of The Three Beggars, [etc.]
Glasgow : Printed for the Booksellers.   No. 31.
[n. d.]

12mo.   Pp. 24. With several cuts, which appear to be taken
from stereotypes, obtained, no doubt, from Davison, of Alnwick.

Other numbers of the same series are similarly illustrated.
Good copy, uncut.

(4341.) 299. The Tyne Side Minstrel. No. (459.).

Another copy. Of the frontispiece I have considerable doubt; but, as the original Block is in my possession, I give an impression of it. It is probably by Isaac Nicholson.

(4342.) 300. Poems, By James Stirling.

Newcastle: Printed for the Author By Preston & Heaton. [1824.]

12mo. Pp. 24. With cut on the title, used in No. (4309.), etc. Good copy, in its original paper cover.

(4343.) 301. Hymns, In Prose. For Children: Calculated to impress The Infant Mind with Early Devotion. By Mrs. Barbauld.

Alnwick: Printed by William Davison, Bondgate Street. [n. d.] [1824?]

18mo. Pp. 35. With a number of cuts, among which are several by Thomas Bewick, used by Davison in others of his publications.
Good copy, in its original boards.

(4344.) 302. An Account Of the Charitable Dona-
tions To the Poor Of the Parish of Gateshead, With
Extracts from the Wills of several of the Benefactors:
To which is added An Account of the Plate belonging
to St. Mary's Church, And St. Edmund's Chapel,
Gateshead.

Newcastle: Printed by J. & R. Akenhead. 1825.

4to. Pp. 7. With Bewick's cut of Tynemouth Priory on page 7.
"To the Rev. W. Hawks with James Charlton's Respects."
Good copy, in its original wrapper.

(4345.) 303. The Hermit Of Warkworth: [etc.]
With Engravings on Wood by Bewick.

Alnwick: Printed and Sold by W. Davison. 1825.

18mo. Pp. viii, 50. With a frontispiece, "South View of the
Hermitage," given at page 449, and three other cuts. A re-
print of No. (4325.)
Good copy, in its original cover.

(4346.) 304. The Battle of Chevy Chase. By
Richard Shele. [etc.]

Alnwick: Printed and Sold by W. Davison, Bondgate Street, [n. d.]

12mo. Pp. 24. With several vignettes used elsewhere.
Good copy, uncut.

(4347.) 305. The Hermit of Warkworth, [etc.]
Alnwick: Printed and Sold by W. Davison, Bondgate Street. [n. d.]

12mo. Pp. 24. With view of the Hermitage on the title, and vignette at page 22.

Good copy, uncut.

(4348.) 306. The Yorkshire Garland, Containing the Celebrated old Songs of " Yorke Yorke, for me Monie," And the Pattern of True Love ; Or, Bowes Tragedy. [etc.]

Northallerton : Printed and Sold by E. Langdale ; Sold also by T. Langdale, Ripon ; W. Langdale, Knaresbro', and the principal Booksellers in the County. 1825.

12mo. Pp. 34. With a frontispiece by Thomas Bewick.

Good copy, in its original cover.

(4349.) 307. The Diverting History Of John Gilpin, [etc.]

York : Printed and Sold Wholesale and Retail, by C. Croshaw, Pavement. Price One Penny.

24mo. Pp. 15. With a frontispiece, in the manner at least of Thomas Bewick.

Good copy, in its original cover.

(4350.) 308. The Universal Battledore.

Printed and Sold by C. Croshaw, Pavement, York. Price One Penny. [n. d.]

12mo. With twelve cuts, of which I possess the Blocks. They are a portion of those which illustrate the rare " Picture Book" printed at Stockton. See No. (4101.).

Good copy, in its original state.

(4351.) 309. The Yorkshire Battledore.

Printed and Sold by C. Croshaw, Pavement, York. Price One Penny. [n. d.]

12mo. With nineteen cuts, fifteen of which illustrate the " Picture Book," just mentioned, and of which I possess most of the original Blocks.

Good copy, in its original state.

(4352.) 310. The Pretty Battledore. To Instruct and Amuse.

Printed and Sold by C. Croshaw, Pavement, York. Price One Penny.

12mo. With seven cuts, used in the previous articles.

Good copy, in its original state.

(4353.) 311. 1. A Battledore, To Instruct and Amuse.

Printed and Sold by C. Croshaw, Pavement, York. Price One Penny.

12mo. With seven of the cuts used above.

Good copy, in its original state.

(4354.) 311. 2. Another good copy.

(4355.) 312. The Royal Battledore.

Printed by C. Croshaw, Pavement, York. Price One Penny.

12mo. With eleven cuts, most of them already mentioned.

Good copy, in its original state.

(4356.) 313. Weightman's New Battledore.

York: Printed by T. Weightman, 44, Goodram-gate. Price One Penny.

12mo. With twenty cuts, nine of which are the same as those in No. (4060.).

Good copy, in its original state.

I have other Battledores, published by R. & J. Richardson, High-Ousegate, and T. Weightman, Goodramgate, York; Thomas Richardson, Derby; R. Harrild, Great East Cheap; S Bennett,

Market Place, Nottingham ; J. Rosewarne, Belper ; and others ;
but, though not without an interest of their own, they have no
claim to a place in the present Catalogue.

(4357.) 314. 1. The Infant's Alphabet. Neatly
embellished with Cuts.
York: Printed & Sold by C. Croshaw, Pavement.
Price One Penny.

32mo. With twenty-eight cuts, most of them used in the foregoing articles.

(4358.) 314. 2. Another copy.

Several of the same cuts are used to adorn the covers of various
toy-books of the same publisher, as The History of Goody
Two-Shoes, The History of Jack the Giant Killer, The Interesting History of Charlotte & Francis, The History of Whittington And His Cat, etc. etc.

(4359.) 315. 1. The Juvenile Scrap-Book.
Printed & Sold by J. Bishop, Taunton. (Price Sixpence.) [n. d. but about 1825.]

Square 12mo. With one hundred and ninety-seven cuts, including nine on the outside of the cover.
Fine copy, in its original cover.

(4360.) 315. 2. Another fine copy.

An eminent London bibliopolist describes this little book as fol-
lows :—
"EXTREMELY RARE, £2 12s 6d
"This beautiful BEWICK gem is of the HIGHEST RARITY, the
cuts being full of life and character. Amongst the AMUSING
CONTENTS may be mentioned, Jack, Mermaid, Giant, Murder,
Bed, Horse, Shepherd, Boat, Rabbit, Woodman, Robber, Ship,
Gardeners, Goat with Dog Riding on his back, Ghastly Skele-
tons (treated in the most curious manner), Smoking Dog, the
Bull Finch, a large Cut, and Finis.
"The publisher believes this very rare volume to be almost price-

less to the BEWICK COLLECTOR, being PERFECTLY CLEAN THROUGHOUT."

I am sorry that I cannot endorse this enthusiastic description. In deference to my friend's authority, I allow the volume a place in this Supplement, but I do not believe that Thomas Bewick cut a single line in one of the cuts which illustrate—I can hardly say, embellish—it.

(4361.) 316. A List Of the Knights and Burgesses, Who have represented the County and City of Durham, In Parliament. Fifty Copies Printed.

Durham : Printed by Francis Humble. 1826.

4to. Pp. vi, 41. The work was by Sir Cuthbert Sharp, and is illustrated with a cut, by Thomas Bewick, at the head of the Preface, which he had previously used in his ' Bishoprick Garland,' No. (490.), and elsewhere. Possibly that also at page 28 is by him, but I am in great doubt of its being genuine. The original Block is in my possession, and an impression follows. I believe it to be by Isaac Nicholson.

Good copy, in its original cover.

(4362.) 317. Narrative Of the Adventures Of A Greenwich Pensioner. [etc.]

Newcastle: Printed by R. T. Edgar, Pilgrim Street. 1826.

12mo. With cut by Thomas Bewick.

Good copy, in its original paper cover.

(4363.) 318. The English Portion Of The Library Of the Ven. Francis Wrangham, M.A. F.R.S., Archdeacon of Cleveland.

Malton: Printed by R. Smithson, Jun. Bookseller and Stationer, in Yorkersgate. 1826. (Only Seventy Copies.) Unpublished.

8vo. Pp. x, 645. With cuts at pp. 128 and 181, said to be by Thomas Bewick.

Good copy, in its original boards.

(4364.) 319. The Antiquarian Trio, [etc.] To which is added A Finale, Called The Poet's Favourite Tree, By the Rev. Archdeacon Wrangham; with A brief Description of Hunmanby.

Scarborough: Printed and published by John Cole, Library, Newborough Street, 1826.

8vo. Pp. ii, 27. With Bewick's View of Hunmanby Church, at page 24.

Good copy, in its original boards.

(4365.) 320. Splinters, [etc.]   No. (477.).

Another fine copy, in half-morocco.

(4366.) 321. The History And Antiquities Of Filey, In the County Of York. By John Cole. [etc.]

Scarborough, Printed and Published by J. Cole 1828.

8vo.   Pp. vi, 160.   With Bewick's View of Hunmanby Church,
at p. 150.
Very fine copy, on large paper, in its original cloth boards.

(4367.) 322. Sykes's Tracts: Verses on Alnwick
Castle, Hermitage of Warkworth, Quakers' Burial
Ground at Cullercoats.
Printed for John Sykes, Bookseller, At Johnson's
Head, 179, Pilgrim Street, Newcastle.   MDCCCXXIX.
8vo.
Good copy, in its original cover.

(4368.) 323. The Gentle Shepherd, A Scots Pastoral, In Five Acts.   By Allan Ramsay.
Alnwick : Printed and Sold by W. Davison.   1830.
18mo.   Pp. 60.   With a frontispiece and cut on the title, used
in other publications, of which I have the original Blocks.
Good copy, in its original boards.

(4369.) 324. Transactions Of the Natural History
Society, Of Northumberland, Durham, And Newcastle
upon Tyne.
Newcastle : Printed by T. & J. Hodgson, Union
Street, For Emerson Charnley, And Longman & Co.,
London.   1831.
4to.   With the Seal of the Society, by Thomas Bewick, on the
title.   An impression is given under No. (2189.).   The second
volume was published in 1838, with a similar title.
Good copy, half-bound in calf.

(4370.) 325. A List Of the Knights and Burgesses
Who have represented the County and City of Durham In Parliament.   Second Edition.

Sunderland : Printed by Marwood and Co. Herald Office. 1831.

4to. Pp. xi, 55, 8. With the cuts of the former edition, No. (4361.).

Good copy, in blue cloth boards.

(4371.) 326. Robin Hood : A Collection Of all the ancient Poems, Songs, and Ballads, Now extant Relative to that celebrated English Outlaw. To which are prefixed Historical Anecdotes of his Life. By Joseph Ritson, Esq. [etc.] Second Edition.

London : William Pickering : J. and G. Todd, York. 1832.

2 vols. Small 8vo. Vol. I. pp. cxxxv, 148. Vol. II. pp. vi, 261. With the cuts of the first edition, No. (86.), of which this is a very beautiful reprint.

Good copy, in its original boards, and uncut.

(4372.) 327. Service's Metrical Legends Of Northumberland. No. (489.).

Another copy, in its original boards.

(4373.) 328. Markham's Spelling Book. No. (495.).

Another copy, in cloth boards.

(4374.) 329. The Hermit of Warkworth, A Northumberland Tale. In Three Parts. By Dr. Thomas Percy, Bishop of Dromore.

Alnwick : Stereotyped and Printed by W. Davison, 22, Bondgate Street. And Sold by all Booksellers. [n. d.]

12mo. Pp. vi, 44. With the cuts previously used, the original Blocks of which are in my possession. Davison was in the habit of protecting his blocks by the use of stereotypes, for which care I have much reason to thank him. See note to No. (298.).

(4375.) 330. The Jolly Huntsman's Garland. Printed by W. A. Mitchell, Newcastle. [n. d.]

Sm. 8vo. Pp. 14. With three cuts attributed to Thomas Bewick. Fine copy, in its original cover.

(4376.) 331. A Treatise On Wood Engraving, Historical and Practical. With upwards of Three Hundred Illustrations, Engraved on Wood, By John Jackson.

London: Charles Knight and Co. Ludgate Street, 1839.

Imp. 8vo. Pp. xvi, 749. With a large number of cuts, most of which, as stated on the title, are by Jackson. Among the rest, engraved by Charlton Nesbit, Luke Clennell, John Thompson, Robert Branston, and William Harvey, is a solitary one, at page 634, stated to be " by Thomas Bewick." Of this I have the pleasure of possessing the original Block, and the following is an impression from it.

Fine copy, in half morocco.

(4377.) 332. 1. Obituary Of Charles Newby Wawn, Esq.   No. (396.).

Another fine copy, on large 4to paper, in its original paper cover.
A presentation to " Thomas Bell, Esq. from John Fenwick."

(4378.) 332. 2. Another fine copy, on large 4to paper, in its original paper cover.

(4379.) 333. 1. Obituary Of Charles Newby Wawn, Esq.

Newcastle : From the Newcastle Chronicle of 30th May, 1840.

4to.   Pp. 10.   With Mr. Fenwick's cut on the title.
Fine copy, on large 4to paper, in its original paper cover.

(4380.) 333. 2. Another fine copy, on large 4to paper, in its original paper cover.

(4381.) 334. The Hermit of Warkworth, A Northumberland Tale, [etc.]   Illustrated with Engravings by Bewick, From Designs by Craig.

Alnwick : Printed by W. Davison, Bondgate Street. MDCCCXLI.

Sm. 8vo.   Pp. xii, 88.   With cuts used by Davison in the former editions of this Poem, and others of his publications. The frontispiece is the View of Warkworth Hermitage, given at p. 449 of the ' Bewick Collector,' from the original Block in my possession.   The present copy is printed on thick and large paper, and is one of the best specimens of Davison's press.
Good copy, in its original cloth boards.

(4382.) 335. Obituary=Resolutions [etc.]   No. (397.).

Another fine copy, on large 4to paper, in its original paper cover.

(4383.) **336.** Fables, By John Gay. With upwards
of One Hundred Embellishments.

Alnwick : Printed by W. Davison, Bondgate Street.
1842.

> Large 12mo. Pp. xii, 216. With many of the vignettes which
> illustrate Davison's other publications. The cuts to the
> Fables are free versions rather than copies of those which
> ornament the editions of Saint, and Wilson and Spence, and
> are not by Bewick.
> Good copy, in its original cloth boards.

(4384.) **337.** Biographical Sketch Of the late John
Trotter Brockett, Esq., F.S.A. [etc.]

Newcastle : Printed by T. & J. Hodgson, For Emerson Charnley. M.DCCC.XLIII.

> 4to. Pp. vi, 16. With Mr. Fenwick's cut on the title, and Mr.
> Brockett's arms and cut at pp. 7 and 13.
> Fine copy, on large 4to paper, in its original paper cover.

(4385.) **338.** The Gathering Ode Of The Fenwyke.
No. (401.).

> Fine copy, on large 4to paper, in its original paper cover.

(4386.) **339.** Biographical Sketches Of Joshua
Marshman, D.D. Of Serampore.

Newcastle Upon Tyne : Emerson Charnley.
MDCCCXLIII.

> 4to. Pp. xiv, 25. With Mr. Fenwick's cut on the title.
> Fine copy, on large 4to paper, in its original paper cover.

(4387.) **340.** Biographical Notice Of The Rev. William Carey, D.D. Of Serampore, By The Hon. & Rev.
William Herbert. [etc.]

Newcastle. T. & J. Hodgson, Union Street.
MDCCCXLIII.

4to. Pp. 8. With Mr. Fenwick's cut on the title.
Fine copy, on large 4to paper, in its original paper cover.

(4388.) 341. Memorial To the Senate of Hamburgh, And Letter To the King of Denmark.
Newcastle: MDCCCXLIII.

4to. Pp. ix, 20. With Mr. Fenwick's cut on the title.
Fine copy, on large 4to paper, in its original paper cover.

(4389.) 342. Memoir of Farrer. No. (403.).

Another copy, on large 4to paper, in its original boards, and uncut.

(4390.) 343. Obituary Notice Of the late Mr. William Anthony Hails. [etc.]
Newcastle: T. & J. Hodgson, Union Street.
MDCCCXLV.

4to. Pp. 8. With Mr. Fenwick's cut on the title.
Fine copy, on large 4to paper, in its original paper cover.

(4391.) 344. Memoir Of the late John Trotter Brockett, Esq. F.S.A.
Newcastle Upon Tyne: Printed by T. & J. Hodgson, Union Street. MDCCCXLVI.

4to. Pp. 15. With Mr. Fenwick's cut on the title.
Fine copy, on large 4to paper, in its original paper cover.

(4392.) 345. Obituary Notice Of the Life and Ministry Of the late Reverend John Mack Of Serampore.
Newcastle T. & J. Hodgson, Union Street.
MDCCCXLVI.

4to. Pp. 16. With Mr. Fenwick's cut on the title.
Fine copy, on large 4to paper, in its original paper cover.

(4393.) 346. A Brief Summary Of the Contents of a Manuscript, Formerly belonging to the Lord William Howard, Of Naworth.

Imprinted by M. A. Richardson, In Grey Street, Newcastle. MDCCCXLVIII.

    8vo. Pp. 36. With the cut, at page 5, which the editor, Sir Cuthbert Sharp, had previously used in his ' Bishoprick Garland,' No. (490.).

    Fine copy, in half-morocco.

(4394.) 347. Catalogue Of Rare and Curious Books, Copperplates and Wood Cuts, And Valuable Literary Copyrights, To be Sold By Public Auction, By order of the Executors of the late Sir Cuthbert Sharp, F.S.A., Knt., &c., At the Residence, No. 65, Northumberland Street, Newcastle-Upon-Tyne, On Monday and Tuesday, October 29th and 30th, 1849. Mr. George Hardcastle, Auctioneer. [etc.]

H. J. Dixon, Printer, Bishopwearmouth. [1849.]

    8vo. Pp. 28. With various specimens of the woodcuts which illustrate Sir Cuthbert's History of Hartlepool, No. (343.), etc., and other works.

    Good copy, in its original cover, on which are five cuts.

(4395.) 348. Letters Between Ellis and Scott. No. (510.).

    Another copy, on large 4to paper, in its original paper cover.

(4396.) 349. A Genealogy Of the Family of Radclyffe, [etc.] No. (511.).

    Another fine copy, on large 4to paper, in its original paper cover.

(4397.) 350. Dialogue Between the North and South Tyne Rivers, In Northumberland.

Newcastle-Upon-Tyne : Printed by George Bouchier Richardson, 38, Clayton-Street-West. MDCCCL.

4to. Pp. 14. With Mr. Fenwick's cut on the title.
Fine copy, on large 4to paper, in its original paper cover.

(4398.) 351. The Foundation Stone : A Hymn. By the Right Hon. Stephen Lushington, D.C.L. Judge of the High Court of Admiralty.

Newcastle-Upon-Tyne : Printed by George Bouchier Richardson, 38, Clayton-Street-West. MDCCCL.

4to. Pp. 8. With Mr. Fenwick's cut on the title.
Fine copy, on large 4to paper, in its original paper cover.

(4399.) 352. History of Hartlepool, By the late Sir Cuthbert Sharp, Knight, F.S.A. [etc.]

Hartlepool : Printed and Published by John Procter ; [etc.] 1851.

8vo. A reprint of the edition of 1816, No. (343.).
Good copy, in its original boards.

(4400.) 353. A Description Of Alnwick Castle. For the Use of Visitors.

Alnwick : Published by W. Davison, Bondgate Street. 1851.

12mo. Pp. 40. With a vignette by Thomas Bewick at page 24, and the beautiful cut of the Percy Arms at page 40. The latter has been given at page 400.
Good copy, in its original cover.

(4401.) 354. Treasure Trove In Northumberland.
Imprinted by George Bouchier Richardson, at the Sign of the River-God Tyne, Clayton-Street-West ; Printer to the Society of Antiquaries, and to the Typo-

graphical Society, both of Newcastle-upon-Tyne.
1851.

Large 4to, Pp. x, 68. With Mr. Fenwick's cut on the title.
Fine copy, on large 4to. paper, in its original paper cover.

(4402.) 355. The New Reading Made Easy; Consisting of a Variety of Useful Lessons.
Alnwick: Published by W. Davison. Price Twopence. [n. d.]

18mo. Pp. 33. With a cut by Thomas Bewick on the title.
Good copy, in its original cover.

(4403.) 356. Inscription On A Tablet In the Abbey Church of Hexham.
Newcastle-Upon-Tyne: Imprinted by George Bouchier Richardson, At the Sign of the River-God Tyne, 38, Clayton-Street-West. 1852.

4to. Pp. 12. With Mr. Fenwick's cut on the title.
Fine copy, on large 4to. paper, in its original paper cover.

(4404.) 357. Rustic Sketches; Being Rhymes on Angling. [etc.] By G. P. R. Pulman.
London: John Gray Bell, Bedford St. Covent Garden. MDCCCLIII.

12mo. Pp. ix, 78. With a vignette, said to be by Thomas Bewick, at p. 48.
Good copy, in its original cover.

(4405.) 358. The Protest Of Certain Lords against the Bill of Attainder Of Sir John Fenwick, Bart.
Newcastle-upon-Tyne: Imprinted by G. Bouchier Richardson, at the Sign of the River-god-Tyne, Clayton-street-west: Printer to the Society of Antiquaries,

and to the Typographical Society, both of Newcastle-upon-Tyne. M.DCCC.LIV.

> Large 4to. Pp. 17. With Mr. Fenwick's cut on the title.
> Fine copy, on large 4to. paper, in its original paper cover.

(4406.) 359. Specimens Of Early Wood Engraving: Being Impressions of Wood-cuts From the Collection of Mr. Charnley, Newcastle.

Newcastle-Upon-Tyne : Privately Printed for Emerson Charnley, Bigg Market. 1858.

> 4to. A title and ninety leaves, with a large number of cuts printed on one side only. Since the publication of this work, of which there were " Only 20 Copies printed," many of the original Blocks, including all which were either known or believed to be by Thomas Bewick, have passed into my possession.
> Fine copy, half-bound in morocco, gilt, with gilt top.

(4407.) 360. " The Thomas Bell Library." The Catalogue Of 15,000 Volumes Of Scarce & Curious Printed Books, and Unique Manuscripts, Comprised in the unrivalled Library collected by The late Thomas Bell, Esq. F.S.A., Which will be Sold by Auction, [etc.] on Monday, 15. October, 1860, and following Days, [etc.]

Imprinted by J. G. Forster, at the Sign of the River God Tyne, in Clayton Street, Newcastle upon Tyne. 1860.

> Folio. Pp. vi, 276. With an impression of Mr. Thomas Bell's book-plate, and several other cuts, by Thomas Bewick.
> Fine copy, on the largest paper, in its original cover.

(4408.) 361. 1. Impressions From Wood Blocks,

Engraved by Thomas Bewick and Others, Formerly in
the Possession of Messrs. T. and J. Hodgson.
Newcastle-upon-Tyne: MDCCCLXV.

> 4to.   A title and forty-two leaves, with impressions of three hun-
> dred and ninety-one cuts, printed on one side of the leaves only.
> One of twelve copies taken off for Mr. Hodgson, before he
> disposed of the Blocks to me.
> Fine copy, in half morocco.

(4409.) 361. 2. Another copy.

(4410.) 361. 3. Another copy.

(4411.) 362. Newcastle in the Olden Time: Being
155 Views Of Ancient Churches, Chapels, and Monas-
teries; [etc.] Reprinted from Richardson's Table
Book.

Newcastle-upon-Tyne: William Dodd, 5, Bigg
Market, Printed by J. G. Forster, at the Sign of the
River-God Tyne, 81, Clayton Street.   1865.   20
Copies Printed.

> Folio. With four cuts believed to be by Thomas Bewick.
> Good copy, in its original cover.

(4412.) 363. A Pretty Book Of Pictures For Little
Masters and Misses, [etc.] The Fifteenth Edition.

London: Printed for, and Published by, Edwin
Pearson, Bewick Repository, 64, St. Martin's Lane,
Trafalgar Square. W.C. MDCCCLXVII.

> Sm. 4to. Pp. xvi. 124. A reprint of the famous 'Tommy
> Trip,' with cuts from the original Blocks, which—although
> they have been retouched, especially those used by Charnley in

the ' Select Fables ' of 1820—still retain very much of the beauty of their original state.

Good copy, in half-morocco.

" For this elegant Reprint of an exceedingly rare and interesting little tome, right precious and dear to the heart of the genuine Bewick Collector, we are indebted in the first place to the liberality of our talented townsman, Robert White, Esq. The worthy living depository of so much of the traditionary lôre of the ' North Countrie,' Mr. White, who is in possession of a copy of the original work, kindly placed the same in the hands of Mr. Edwin Pearson, the bookseller, who has evinced much good taste in the getting up of this very limited edition."— *Newcastle Courant Newspaper*, 25 *Oct.*, 1867.

ADDITIONS

TO

PROOFS, ETC., OF THE CUTS

IN

THE 'HISTORY OF QUADRUPEDS.'

(4413.) 1. A Series of eight Quadrupeds, similar to those described under Nos. (534.), (535.), and (536.).

They consist of the Bull, Giraffe, Elk, Wild Boar, Weasel, Bull Dog, Mastiff, and Water Rat, as they appear in the first edition. It is, doubtless, to these impressions that Bewick refers in his Letter in the 'Monthly Magazine' of November, 1805, where he says, "As the cuts [of the Quadrupeds] were engraved, we employed the late Mr. Thomas Angus, of this town, printer, to take off a certain number of impressions of each, many of which are still in my possession."

(4414.) 2. A Series of the Quadrupeds, and Vignettes belonging to that Work, taken off without the letter-press, one on a page.

8vo. In old calf.   It formerly belonged to Mr. Thomas Bell, of Newcastle, and has his bookplate.   It cost a subsequent possessor ten guineas.

I have been told that these brilliant impressions were taken off for Mr. John Bell during the printing of the fifth edition of the book in 1807.   Almost all have above and below them the marks of the letter-press without ink, similar to what I have already described in my notices of those curious and most beautiful proofs of the Birds, Nos. (663.) to (668.).

(4415.) 3. A Series of fifty-three of the Quadrupeds, with marks of the type, etc., of a similar character to those of the last article.

8vo.   In shagreen calf.   Bound together with the Proofs of the Birds noticed under No. (4419.).

It formerly belonged to Mr. J. T. Brockett.

(4416.) 4. 1. The Improved Cart Horse.   (No. 546.)   Another impression.   *Proof on paper.*

(4417.) 4. 2. Another.   A cutting from Charnley's Book Catalogue, 1817.

(4418.) 5. The Common Bull.   No. (557.).   Another impression.   *On a card.*

ADDITIONS

TO

PROOFS, ETC., OF THE CUTS

IN

THE 'HISTORY OF BRITISH BIRDS.'

———◆———

(4419.) 1. A Series of twenty-eight of the Birds, and of thirteen Vignettes, most of which are of a character similar to those described under Nos. (663.) to (668.).

> Among them are splendid impressions of the Hen-harrier, Domestic Cock, Pheasant, Turkey, Peacock, Pintado, Partridge, Quail, Water Hen, and Tame Duck—the loveliest gems of the ' British Birds.'
>
> 8vo. In shagreen calf. Bound together with the Proofs of the Quadrupeds noticed under No. (4415.).

(4420.) 2. The Office Proofs of the First Volume of the Birds. " Price 1l. 1s. in Boards. 1797."

> Imp. 8vo., with occasional leaves in royal 8vo. The last leaf

has the advertisement of the third edition of the Quadrupeds. The volume is roughly printed on coarse paper, and is still in its original uncut state. It was given by Bewick to Mr. R. Wingate, whose name, as also that of Thomas Wingate, is written in several places, with various sketches of animals and birds, inside the cover, and who has coloured several of the figures with his usual ability. The Jay and the Mountain Finch are specially excellent, and the entire volume is a most interesting relic of the earliest days of the celebrated work whose history it illustrates.

BRITISH LAND BIRDS.   No. (117.).

(4421.) 3. Title.   *Proof on paper.*   From Mr. W. Garret.

BRITISH WATER BIRDS.   No. (117.).

(4422.) 4. Title.   *Proof on paper.*   From Mr. W. Garret.

ADDITIONS

TO

PROOFS, ETC., OF THE CUTS

IN

'ÆSOP'S FABLES.'

(4423.) 1. Vignette. "There will be sleeping enough in the Grave." No. (1603.). Another impression. *Proof on paper.*

(4424.) 2. The Fowler and the Lark. On a cancelled leaf. No. (1610.). Another.

ADDITIONS

TO

PROOFS OF THE CUTS, ETC.,

IN

MISCELLANEOUS BOOKS & PAMPHLETS.

———◆———

Hutton's Mensuration. No. (1.).

(4425.) 1. The entire Series of the Cuts, cuttings from the book, mounted on crayon paper.

Fisher's New English Tutor. No. (4029.).

(4426.) 2. The entire Series of Cuts. *On white India paper.* From the original Blocks in my possession.

Impressions have been given under No. (4029.).

Grey's Epitome of the Annals of Great Britain. No. (4033.).

(4427.) 3. The twenty-four Figures of the Sovereigns. *On white India paper.* From the original Blocks in my possession.

Impressions will be found under No. (4033.).

(4428.) 4. The entire Series of the Cuts.   *On white India paper.*   From the original Blocks in my possession.

The following are specimens.

(4429.) 5. The twenty-four Alphabet Cuts.   *Proofs on drawing paper.*

(4430.) 6. The Old Hound.   *Fine old proof on 8vo. paper.*

(4431.) 7. The Foolish Stag.   *Fine old proof on 8vo. paper.*

An impression has been given under No. (1619.).

NEW YEAR'S GIFT.   No. (4034.).

(4432.) 8. Six Cuts, illustrating the Story of Little Red Riding Hood.   *On white India paper.*   From the original Blocks in my possession.

Specimens will be found under No. (4034.).

"DEED FOR THE INSURANCE OF SHIPS IN THE LOYAL CLUB. NORTH-SHIELDS: PRINTED BY MATTHEW BROWN. M.DCC.LXXXII."

(4433.) 9. Proof of Title.

CURIOUS HIEROGLYPHIC BIBLE.   No. (4045.).

(4434.) 10. Cut " representing a Gentleman seated in an arm-chair, with four boys beside (before) him. The border of this cut is of the same kind as that of the large cut of the Chillingham Bull."   Chatto, in ' Jackson's Hist. of Wood-Engraving,' p. 566.   *An impression on vellum.*

FOX'S SPELLING BOOK.   No. (4049.)

(4435.) 11. The Series of Cuts.   *Proofs on paper.*

THE CHILDREN'S MISCELLANY.   Nos. (30.), (193.).

(4436.) 12. Nineteen Cuts, mounted on crayon paper.

HARGROVE'S KNARESBOROUGH.   No. (38.)

(4437.) 13. The Bewick Cuts, including the Arms of the Priory of Knaresborough, the Cornwall Arms, at page 61.   *On white India paper.*   From the original Blocks in my possession.

LOOKING GLASS FOR THE MIND.   No. (66.), ETC.

(4438.) 14. A Series of nineteen Cuts. *On white India paper.* From the original Blocks in my possession.

> They consist of the cut on the title; the large cuts at pp. 38, 75, 122, 132, 187, 202, 257, and 263; and the vignettes at pp. iv, 37, 53, 117, 174, 201, 223, 241, 256, and 262. See note respecting them in the Department "Wood Blocks."

> The following are impressions of the cut on the title, and of that at p. 202.

SPORTING MAGAZINE.   No. (71.).

(4439.) 15. Horse Racing. Large Cut on the cover. *On white India paper.* From the original Block in my possession.

> An impression will be found in the Department "Wood Blocks."

(4440.) 16. 1. The Cuts mentioned under No. (71.) of "The Bewick Collector." Early cuttings.

(4441.) 16. 2. Another Series.   Early cuttings.

Tales for Youth.   No. (72.), etc.

(4442.) 17. The entire Series of thirty Cuts.   *On white India paper.*   From the original Blocks in my possession.

Of these celebrated cuts, the finest examples of the work of John Bewick for juvenile publications, I am happy to offer the two following specimens, which occur at pages 40 and 55.   See note respecting them in the Department "Wood Blocks."

KINGS OF ENGLAND.   No. (4078.)

(4443.) 18. Cut on the title, and Portrait of King George III. *On white India paper.* From the original Blocks in my possession.

HISTORY OF ENGLAND.   No. (83.).

(4444.) 19. The Series of Illustrations.   Fine impressions.

THE OECONOMIST.   No. (127.).

(4445.) 20. The Series of Cuts.   *On white India paper.*   From   the   original   Blocks   in   my   possession.

The cut on the title has been given under No. (1966.).

THE HIVE.   Nos. (128.), (209.), ETC.

(4446.) 21. The Series of Cuts.   *Old proofs, on 8vo paper.*

The original Blocks are in my possession.   The cut on the title will be found at page 371, and the following illustrate 'The Story of Fidelia,' and 'The Beggar's Petition.'

THE PICTURE BOOK. NO. (4101.).

(4447.) 22. A Series of thirty-eight Cuts. *On white India paper.* From the original Blocks in my possession.

Specimens will be found under No. (4101.), etc.

THE NEW SONGSTER. NO. (139.).

(4448.) 23. The two Cuts on the frontispiece, " Blekell Murry-Neet " and " Worton Weddin." *On white India paper.* From the original Blocks in my possession.

THE VOCAL MISCELLANY. NO. (141.).

(4449.) 24. Cut on the title. *On white India paper.* From the original Block in my possession.

THE PLEASING INSTRUCTOR. NO. (4103.).

(4450.) 25. Cut on the title. *On white India paper.* From the original Block in my possession.

Elmina.   No. (4108.).

(4451.) 26. The Frontispiece.   *On white India paper.*   From the original Block in my possession.

The Forsaken Infant.   No. (4111.).

(4452.) 27. The Series of nine large oval Cuts.   *On white India paper.*   From the original Blocks in my possession.   The following is a specimen:

Reay's Sportsman's Friend.   No. (163.).

(4453.) 28. The Bay Pony.   *On white India paper.*   From the original Block in my possession. An impression is given on the next page.

Fisher's Grammar Improved.   No. (4134.).

(4454.) 29. Facsimile of Signature.   *On white India paper.*   From the original Block in my possession.

OSTERWALD'S BIBLE.   No. (207.).

(4455.) 30. A Series of thirteen copper-plate Engravings, as follow, each " Engraved by Beilby & Bewick."

> Lot's Hospitality.
> The Meeting of Jacob & Rachel.
> Moses in the Ark of Bulrushes.
> Moses' Rod turned into a Serpent.
> The Israelites departing out of Egypt.
> Aaron.
> The Two Spies.
> Jephthah's rash Vow.
> Sampson with the Gates of Gaza.
> The Judgment of Solomon.
> The Adoration of the Shepherds.
> Peter Delivered.
> S! Paul.

THE HERMIT OF WARKWORTH.   Nos. (217.), (221.), ETC.

(4456.) 31. Large Cut facing page 83. On the back of a card with the Multiplication Table. " Davison, Printer, Alnwick."

(4457.) 32. Cut at p. 69. On a proof title of an intended work descriptive of the works of Thomas and John Bewick.

Specimens will be found at pp. 400 and 449.

THE PICTURE OF NEWCASTLE UPON TYNE.   No. (218.).

(4458.) 33. Cut on the title. *On white India paper.* From the original Block in my possession. I add an impression.

POEMS OF BURNS.   Nos. (230.), (480.), (1685.), ETC.

(4459.) 34. The whole Series of Cuts.   *Fine old Proofs on 8vo paper.*

(4460.) 35. A Series of eight Cuts.   *Old Proofs on 12mo paper.*

Specimens will be found at pp. 429, 473, and 487 of 'The Bewick Collector,' and at p. 125 of the present Supplement.

(4461.) 36. Tam o'Shanter.   On a proof title of the intended work before referred to.

An impression has been given under No. (3599.).

MEMOIR OF FARRER.   No. (262.).

(4462.) 37. Portrait.   No. (1702.).   *Proof on large 4to paper.*

WARDEN'S SPELLING BOOK.   No. (4235.).

(4463.) 38. The entire Series of Cuts.   *On white India paper.*   From the original Blocks in my possession.

Specimens have been given under No. (4235.).

Rhymes of Northern Bards. No. (302.).

(4464.) 39. The Cuts at pages 149, 174. *On white India paper*. From the original Blocks in my possession.

Garland of Northumberland Heroes. No. (303.).

(4465.) 40. Cut on title, the only Cut. *On white India paper*. From the original Block in my possession.

An impression will be found under No. (4284.).

Figures in Rhymes. No. (304.).

(4466.) 41. Cuts on title and pages xiv, xvi, the only Cuts. *On white India paper*. From the original Blocks in my possession.

An impression of the first is given under No. (4289.).

Garland of Bells. No. (335.).

(4467.) 42. Cut on title, the only Cut. *On white India paper*. From the original Block in my possession.

For an impression see under No. (4285.).

The Contented Couckould. No. (336.).

(4468.) 43. Cut on title, the only Cut. *On white India paper*. From the original Block in my possession.

An impression is given under No. (4282.).

Garland of New Songs. No. (4282.).

(4469.) 44. A Series of thirteen Cuts. *On white India paper*. From the original Blocks in my possession.

Impressions will be found under No. (4282.).

COLLECTION OF NEW SONGS. No. (4283.)

(4470.) 45. Cut on title. *On white India paper.* From the original Block in my possession.

An impression will be found under No. (4283.).

ACCOUNT OF THE GREAT FLOOD. No. (345.).

(4471.) 46. Arms of Newcastle on title. *On white India paper.* From the original Block in my possession.

An impression will be found under No. (2169.).

MEMOIRS OF BLACKETT. No. (364.).

(4472.) 47. Cut on title. No. (1737.). *On white India paper.*

BATTLE OF FLODDON FIELD. No. (377.).

(4473.) 48. 1. Vignette. No. (1746.). *On white satin.*

(4474.) 48. 2. Another impression. *On white India paper.* From the original Block in my possession.

An impression has been given under No. (1746.).

MITCHELL ON THE PLEASURE AND UTILITY OF ANGLING. No. (384.).

(4475.) 49. Cut on the title. *On white India paper.* From the original Block in my possession.

An impression will be found in the Department "Cuts for various Societies, etc."

CHICKEN'S COLLIER'S WEDDING. No. (391.)

(4476.) 50. Vignette on page 1. *Proof on large 4to paper.*

Carlisle's Collections. Nos. (438.), (4327.).

(4477.) 51. 1. Cut on title. *On an 8vo leaf of white India paper.* From Mr. W. Garret.

(4478.) 51. 2. Another impression. *On a similar leaf.* From Mr J. G. Bell.

Tom Thumb's Play Book. No. (456.).

(4479) 52. The entire Series of Cuts. *On white India paper.* From the original Blocks in my possession.

The Tyne Side Minstrel. No. (459.).

(4480.) 53. The frontispiece. *On white India paper.* From the original Block in my possession.

An impression has been given under No. (4341.).

Stanzas on Intended New Road. No. (466.).

(4481.) 54. Arms of Gateshead on the title. *On white India paper.* From the original Block in my possession.

List of Knights and Burgesses of Durham. No. (4361.).

(4482.) 55. Panel in Sir J. Duck's house in Silver Street, Durham, page 28. *On white India paper.* From the original Block in my possession.

An impression will be found under No. (4361.).

The Bishoprick Garland. No. (490.).

(4483.) 56. The Hilton Crest, page 84. *On white India paper.* From the original Block in my possession. An impression follows.

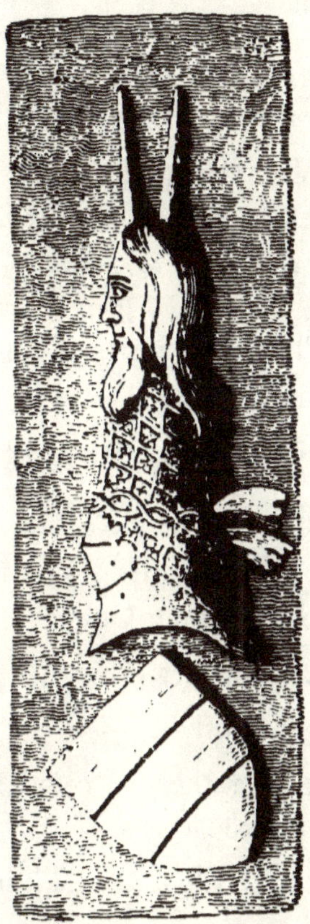

(4484.) 57. Vignette at page 634. *On white India paper.* From the original Block in my possession.

An impression has been given under No. (4376.).

IMPRESSIONS OF CHARNLEY'S WOOD BLOCKS. No. (4406.).

(4485.) 58. A Series of twenty Cuts, besides those elsewhere enumerated, amounting to one hundred and thirty-five. *On white India paper.* From the original Blocks in my possession.

MEMOIR OF THOMAS BEWICK. No. (528.).

(4486.) 59. Prospectus of the Work. 8vo. With specimen of the illustrations.

(4487.) 60. Vignette, page 207. The Ass and the Bees. No. (1905.). *Proof on paper.*

WOOD BLOCKS FORMERLY BELONGING TO MR. HODGSON.
No. (4408.).

(4488.) 61. The entire Series of Cuts. *On white India paper.* From the original Blocks in my possession.

Specimens are given under Nos. (3594.), (3742.), (3743.), (3744.), etc.

TOMMY TRIP. No. (4412.).

(4489.) 62. 1. Prospectus of the work. 4to. With a portrait and six specimen Cuts.

(4490.) 62. 2. Another copy.

(4491.) 62. 3. Another.

(4492.) 62. 4. Another, *on vellum.*

" Only six copies printed on vellum."

(4493.) 63. Three Illustrative Photographs of Title, MSS. notes. etc.

" Rev. Thomas Hugo, with Edwin Pearson's Respectful Compliments."

ARISTOTLE'S MASTERPIECE. (An unknown Edition).

(4494.) 64. Four Cuts of Monsters. *On white India paper.* From the original Blocks in my possession.

HISTORY OF ENGLAND.

(4495.) 65. The Series of twenty-seven large Portraits of the Sovereigns. *On white India paper.* From the original Blocks in my possession.

Specimens will be found amongst the " Wood Blocks."

(4496.) 66. A Series of Alphabet Cuts, having a great resemblance to those in 'Hastie's Reading Easy,' No. (11.), etc., but executed, as it appears to me, a little later.

Taken off on coarse blue paper, and mounted in an imp. 8vo volume, which, after lying about the office for a considerable time, Bewick gave as a scrapbook to Mr. G. Watson, sen., of Gateshead, when a child. It afterwards passed into the possession of S. Longstaffe, Esq., of Gateshead, and from him became my property.

(4497.) 67. Another Series of Alphabet Cuts, larger than the foregoing, but also bearing a general resemblance to those in ' Hastie's Reading Easy.'

On coarse white paper. Mounted in the same volume.

(4498.) 68. A Set of Alphabet Cuts on two Blocks. *On white India paper.* From the original Blocks in my possession.

Of these clever little cuts impressions are annexed.

(4499.) 69. A Set of Alphabet Cuts on one Block. *On white India paper.* From the original Block in my possession.

(4500.) 70. A Set of twenty-four Alphabet Cuts. *On white India paper.* From the original Blocks in my possession.

(4501.) 71. Part of an Alphabet, sixteen letters. *On white India paper.* From the original Blocks in my possession.

(4502.) 72. "M" for Merchant. Alphabet Cut. *On white India paper.* From the original Block in my possession.

(4503.) 73. Boys gathering Apples. *On white India paper.* From the original Block in my possession.

(4504.) 74. Boys gathering Apples. *On white*

India paper. From the original Block in my possession.

Both of these, I presume, were done for Spelling Books.

(4505.) 75. A Series of fifty-seven Cuts in rectangular borders, for book illustrations. *On white India paper.* From the original Blocks in my possession.

Specimens will be found among the "Wood Blocks."

(4506.) 76. A Series of sixty-two Vignettes, for book illustrations. *On white India paper.* From the original Blocks in my possession.

Specimens will be found among the "Wood Blocks."

(4507.) 77. Eleven book-illustrations, in square borders, similar in style of execution to those which occur in Saint's publications.

Among them are cuts for the 'History of a Fly,' 'Cock Robin,' etc.

On coarse paper, of various colours. Mounted in the volume previously noticed.

(4508.) 78. "T B" formed by the bodies of two posture-makers.

On coarse white paper. Mounted in the same volume.

(4509.) 79. Six London Cries, in scroll borders.

On coarse white paper. Mounted in the same volume.

(4510) 80. A pair of large Fable Cuts of the Fox and the Stork, $4\frac{1}{10}$ inc. by $2\frac{9}{10}$ inc., each occupying an oval in a square, the corners filled with beautiful flowers on a black ground.

On white paper. Mounted in the same volume.

(4511.) 81. " Gardening." A Large Cut for the covers of copy books.

(4512.) 82. John Gilpin. With extract from Cowper's poem. For the cover of a copy book.

(4513.) 83. A Series of fourteen Vignettes, printed two on each leaf of an 8vo pamphlet.

> The two first represent a man driving a pig from market, and a dog rescuing a drowning child. Among the rest are a man shooting a hare, a post chaise stopping at a gate with post boy paying toll, jockeys weighing, sportsman loading his gun, etc. They were apparently intended for the illustrations of some book, and printed about the year 1820.
>
> Though they are not wanting in ability, the attribution of these cuts to Bewick is very far from certain.

(4514.) 84. Two Fable Cuts, The Shepherd's Boy, and Old Man and Death. In octangular borders. *On white India paper.* From the original Blocks in my possession.

(4515.) 85. Robinson Crusoe, bringing off boxes, casks, etc., from the wreck. *On white India paper.* From the original Block in my possession.

(4516.) 86. Portrait of Robert Burns. In an oval border. *Proof on paper.*

(4517.) 87. A Plough and a Pitchfork. *On white India paper.* From the original Block in my possession.

> Done for some agricultural work.

(4518.) 88. A line of Music. *On white India paper.* From the original Block in my possession.

(4519.) 89. Two pages of different kinds of hand-writing, used in various Spelling Books. *On white India paper.* From the original Blocks in my possession.

(4520.) 90. A Mariner's Compass. *On white India paper.* From the original Block in my possession.

(4521.) 91. A Series of thirteen Plans of Coal Mines, etc., to illustrate the working of the same. *On white India paper.* From the original Blocks in my possession.

(4522.) 92. A Series of fifty Geometrical Diagrams. *On white India paper.* From the original Blocks in my possession.

ADDITIONS

TO

BOOK PLATES.

—◆—

It is proper to state that the majority of the Articles in this and the eight following Divisions, except of course the impressions on India paper from Blocks since obtained, should have been included in the previous volume, from which they were unintentionally omitted.

Mr. Adamson's Cut.   No. (1928.).

(4523.) 1. Another impression. *On yellow China paper.*

An impression is given under No. (1929.).

Affleck's Book Plate.   No. (1936.).

(4524.) 2. Another impression. *On white India paper.* From the original Copperplate in my possession.

(4525.) 3. " Matt^w Anderson   St Petersburg "
Tyne-side scene, with distant view of Newcastle.   *On
white India paper.*   From the original Block in my
possession.   An impression follows.

" Wm. Armstrong."   No. (1950.).

(4526.) 4. Another impression.   *Proof on paper.*

(4527.) 5. " George Atkinson."   Arms alone.   *Proof
on paper.*

(4528.) 6. " John Bell, Gateshead."   An angel
blowing a trumpet, and holding in the left hand a
palm.   The name is introduced among the clouds on
which the figure reposes.

(4529.) 7. Mr. Brockett's Cut.   A copy executed,
as I believe, by Bewick himself.   *On white India paper.*
From the original Block in my possession.

(4530.) 8. W. S. Burn, M.D.   Arms alone.   Copperplate.

(4531.) 9. " J. Cockerill."   Rock and trees, with Tynemouth in the distance.

To this are also to be referred Nos. (2050.), (2051.).

(4532.) 10. Viscount Galway.   Arms alone.   *On white India paper.*   From the original Block in my possession.

" J. Green."   No. (2021.).

(4533.) 11. Another impression.   *Proof on white India paper.*

M. Hewitson.   No. (2030.).

(4534.) 12. Another and most beautiful impression, for which I am indebted to the kindness of the Rev. C. J. Newmarch, rector of Leverton, Boston.

(4535.) 13. "W^m. Nicholson."   River scene, a mill in the distance.   A most beautiful copy of Mr. Archbold's cut, No. (1945.).   *On white India paper.*

Query, if not by Luke Clennell.

(4536.) 14. " William Robson." Arms alone. *Proof on paper.*

J. W. Sanders.   No. (2080.).

(4537.) 15. 1. Another impression.   *On white India paper.*   From the original Block in my possession.

(4538.) 15. 2. Another.   *On white satin.*

An impression is given under No. (2080.).

(4539.) 16. " Britiffe Skottowe."   Arms and crest, with flowers and foliage.

Query, if by Bewick, although positively state so to be.

Straker. No. (2095.).

(4540.) 17. 1. Another impression. *On white India paper.*

(4541.) 17. 2. Another. *On white India paper.*

(4542.) 18. Initial Letter T, with books. *On white India paper.* From the original Block in my possession.

"William Thomas." No. (2102.).

(4543.) 19. Another impression. With the name cut out, and the figure of a Fisherman inserted. *Proof on paper.* It thus appears in the 'Fisher's Garland' for 1842.

(4544.) 20. A blank oval, in a border of oak, palm, etc., apparently intended for a book-plate. *On white India paper.* From the original Block in my possession.

(4545.) 21. Tyne-side scene, with rock in the foreground, from which a name has apparently been removed. *On white India paper.* From the original Block in my possession.

Afterwards used for the heads of ballads, etc.

(4546.) 22. A blank Shield among foliage. *On white India paper.* From the original Block in my possession.

(4547.) 23. Four Shields of Arms. *On white India paper.* From the original Blocks in my possession.

Query, if by Bewick.

ADDITIONS

TO

CUTS FOR VARIOUS SOCIETIES, COMPANIES, ETC.

———◆———

1. ALBION FIRE AND LIFE INSURANCE COMPANY.

(4548.) 1. Figure of St. George and the Dragon. Very similar to but not the same as No. (2124.). Newspaper cut.

2. BERWICK BANK.

(4549.) 2. Their note for One Guinea, No. 13090. Copperplate.   Dated March 8th, 1799.

Believed to be by Thomas Bewick.

3. CARLISLE BANK.

(4550.) 3. Their note for One Pound. With the arms of Carlisle in a festoon of flowers. Copperplate.

4. CHRISTIANSSUND BILL OF LADING.

(4551.) 4. A blank form. " C & M " in floreated capitals.

5. Cowpen Colliery.

(4552.) 5. Bill. Prince of Wales' plume. Copperplate.

6. Clerk of the Peace, Durham.

(4553.) 6. Circular seal, containing a Shield with the arms of Durham. *On white India paper.* From the original Block in my possession.

7. Forresters' Lodge.

(4554.) 7. Forrester's Arms. *On white India paper.* From the original Block in my possession.

8. Freemasons' Lodge.

(4555.) 8. Freemason's cut. *On white India paper* From the original Block in my possession.

9. Parish of Gateshead.

(4556.) 9. Gateshead Parish Boundary Token, 1824. *On white India paper.* From the original Block in my possession.

(4557.) 10. "Merit," on a medal with ribbon. *On white India paper.* From the original Block in my possession.

10. Kirby Stephen Bank.

(4558.) 11. Their note for One Guinea, No. $\frac{11}{87}$. Dated 12th August, 1807. With view of the Bank. Copperplate.

Said to be by Thomas Bewick.

11.—Lambton's Bank, Newcastle.

(4559.) 12. 1. Cheque. "R I L & Co" in floreated capitals.

(4560.) 12. 2. Another.

(4561.) 12. 3. Another.

12. "Lottery Office."

(4562.) 13. Figure of Mercury, with cornucopiæ. All but identical with the Cut at page 484. *On white India paper.* From the original Block in my possession.

13. Morpeth Hunt.

(4563.) 14. 1. Vignette. Coursing. For the head of their notices. *Proof on paper.*

(4564.) 14. 2. Another impression. *Proof on paper.* Query, if by Bewick.

14. Newcastle Bank.

(4565.) 15. Order, No. 2177., for payment of £45. 18. 11, Dated Oct. 22. 1806. Arms of Newcastle, in a scroll border. Copperplate.

(4566.) 16. Acknowledgment of Receipt of Money. Arms of Newcastle. Copperplate.

" The notes of Ridley and Co.'s Bank were for many years engraved and printed under the superintendence of Bewick, who, after Mr. Beilby's retirement, still continued the business of copper-plate engraving and printing, and for this purpose always kept presses of his own." Chatto, in Jackson's ' History of Wood Engraving,' p. 598.

15. Newcastle Royal Exchange Assurance Office.

View of the Royal Exchange. No. (2140.).

(4567.) 17. Another impression. *On white India paper.* From the original Block in my possession.

View of the same.   No. (2146.).

(4568.) 18. 1. Another impression.   Dated March 14, 1816.

(4569.) 18. 2. Another.   Dated Dec. 12, 1816.

View of the same.   No. (2147.).

(4570.) 19. Another impression.   Dated March 18, 1814.

(4571.) 20. 1. View of the same.   Very small.   Dated September 24, 1819.   Newspaper cut.

(4572.) 20. 2. Another impression.   Dated December 23, 1819.

16. NEWCASTLE-UPON-TYNE FIRE OFFICE.

Figure of Neptune, etc., No. (2148.).

(4573.) 21. 1. Another impression.   At the head of " Proposals," etc.

(4574.) 21. 2. Another.   At the head of " Pro posals," etc.

(4575.) 21. 3. Another.   Cutting from a Policy.
An impression has been given under No. (2150.).

(4576.) 22. 1. Figure of Neptune.   Copperplate.

(4577.) 22. 2. Another impression.

(4578.) 22. 3. Another.
From the head of a Policy.   It was this of which Bewick's celebrated engraving on wood, the last article, was a copy.   The
  copperplate, so far as I am aware, is not his work.

Figure of a Fire Engine.   No. (2157.).

(4579.) 23. Another impression.   *On white India paper*.   From the original Block in my possession.

17. " Newcastle Broad & Crown Glass Comp^y."

(4580.) 24. Bill, No. 5856, for *£*27. 17*s*. 2*d*. dated Newcastle upon Tyne, Decr. 22^d, 1779. With the Arms of Newcastle, above " N B & C G C " in ornamental capitals, both enclosed in a scroll border. Copperplate.

18. Newcastle Waltonian Club.

(4581.) 25. River scene, with anglers supporting a shield of arms. No. (2239.). *On white India paper.* From the original Block in my possession. An impression follows.

19. Northumberland Life Boat.

(4582.) 26. 1. The Northumberland Life Boat, with Tynemouth in the distance. *Old proof on paper.*

(4583.) 26. 2. Another impression. *On white India paper.* From the original Block in my possession, of which the following is an impression.

The Northumberland Life Boat.   No. (3482.).

(4584.) 27. 1. Another impression. *Proof on paper.*

(4585.) 27. 2. Another.   *Proof on paper.*

(4586.) 27. 3. Another.   *On white India paper.*

20. PHŒNIX FIRE OFFICE.

Phœnix.   No. (2194.).

(4587.) 28. Another impression.   *On white India paper.*   From the original Block in my possession.

Phœnix.   In a black oval.   No. (2203.).

(4588.) 29. Another impression.

(4589.) 30. Phœnix. *On white India paper.* From the original Block in my possession.

(4590.) 31. Phœnix. *On white India paper.* From the original Block in my possession.

21. SOUTH SHIELDS ——— ?

(4591.) 32. "South Shields, No.   I owe the Bearer Five Shillings." With the Royal Arms, under an Oak. Very fine. The original Block has lately come into my possession.

22. SUN FIRE OFFICE.

The Sun.　No. (2212.).

(4592.) 33. Another impression.

23. WEAR BANK, SUNDERLAND.

(4593.) 34. Their note for One Pound.　No. 10511.
With view of Sunderland Bridge.　Dated 15th Feb-
ruary, 1815.　Copperplate.

Said to be by Thomas Bewick.

[I have notes, among others, of Barnard Castle Bank, Stockton
and Cleveland Bank, Tees Bank, and Sunderland and Wear-
mouth Bank, etc.; but the attribution of these to Bewick is
very problematical.]

24. UNION LODGE.

Four Hands.　No. (2231.).

(4594.) 35. Another impression.　*Proof on paper.*

25. WOOLCOMBERS' COMPANY.

(4595.) 36. Their Arms.　*On white India paper.*
From the original Block in my possession.

(4596.) 37. Female Figure.　"Britannia" on the
exergue.　In a circular border.　*On white India paper.*
From the original Block in my possession.

(4597.) 38. Figure of Fortune, standing on a wheel
and holding a cornucopiæ.　An ancient tower in the
distance.　*On white India paper.*　From the original
Block in my possession.

(4598.) 39. Figure of Hope, done, I presume, for

some Society or Company. *On white India paper.*
From the original Block in my possession. Not unlike
that given at page 337, but reversed, and of better
execution.

(1599.) 40. Figure of Hope. Very similar to the
last. *On white India paper.* From the original Block
in my possession.

ADDITIONS

TO

CUTS FOR EXHIBITIONS, ETC.

———◆———

(4600.) 1. "Coronation Balloon." "Edgar, Printer, Pilgrim Street, Newcastle." A bill of Mr. Green's 30th Ascent, from the Nun's Field, Newcastle.

With a Figure of the Balloon.

(4601.) 2. Balloon among Clouds, inscribed "Coronation." *On white India paper.* From the original Block in my possession.

(4602.) 3. The Cockpit. *On white India paper.* From the original Block in my possession.

(4603.) 4. A Series of eleven Cuts of Fighting Cocks. *On white India paper.* From the original Blocks in my possession.

[See also under "Newspaper Cuts."]

(4604.) 5. "Ingleby, Sen." In white letters on

black ground. For advertisements of his Conjuring Performances. Newspaper cut.

(4605.) 6. "Ingleby." In white letters on black ground. For similar advertisements. At the head of a programme of performances at the Town Hall, Morpeth, on the 11th and 13th of May, 1818.

(4606.) 7. Mr. Sadler, the Aeronaut. View of his descent in the Irish Channel. For a notice of one of his exploits. *Proof on paper.*

Said to have been engraved for Mr. Sadler, on the occasion of one of his ascents, from Newcastle, 1 Sept., 1815.

(4607.) 8. Mr. Sadler. Another view of his descent. Very similar to the last. *On white India paper.* From the original Block in my possession.

(4608.) 9. Mr. Sadler. View of his balloon among clouds. *On white India paper.* From the original Block in my possession.

(4609.) 10. A Bill of Performances on the tight rope and of learned dogs at North Shields. With four cuts by Thomas Bewick. Dated 1st August, 1786.

(4610.) 11. "Theatre, North Shields." A label for the head of the play bills. *On white India paper.* From the original Block in my possession.

(4611.) 12. "Theatre-Royal. For the Benefit of Miss Jervis. Gal." Good woodcut square border.

(4612.) 13. "Tradesmen's Subscription Assembly. Stranger's Ticket. No.   ."   Good woodcut oval border.

(4613.) 14. "George Wilson." "Preston & Heaton, Printers, Newcastle. Price Sixpence."

A portrait of Wilson, the pedestrian, at the head of an Account of his various Performances.

ADDITIONS

TO

RACING CUTS.

———◆———

For the greater number of the articles in the present Division I have to thank an old and well-known Sportsman in the North of England, who, during fifty years past, had collected these memorials, not for their artistic excellence, but as records of other, and to him more interesting, triumphs.

———◆———

(4614.) 1. Racing Cut. Small. Three Horses, to the left. Probably older than Bewick.

Racing Cut. No. (2271.), etc.

(4615.) 2. 1. Another impression. " Newcastle Races, 1816." " G. Angus, Printer, Side, Newcastle." At the head of a List of the Horses and Prizes.

(4616.) 2. 2. Another impression. " Newcastle

Races, 1819." "G. Angus, Printer, Newcastle." At the head of a similar List.

(4617.) 2. 3. Another impression. "Newcastle Races, 1821." "G. Angus, Printer, Newcastle." At the head of a similar List.

(4618.) 2. 4. Another impression. "Chester-le-Street Easter Races." "Atkinson, Printer, Chester-le-Street." At the head of a List of Prizes to be run for on the 19th and 20th of April, 1824.

Racing Cut. No. (2284.), etc.

(4619.) 3. 1. Another impression. "Newcastle Races, 1816." "G. Angus, Printer, Side, Newcastle." At the head of a List of the Horses and Prizes.

(4620.) 3. 2. Another impression. "Newcastle Races, 1822." "G. Angus, Printer, Newcastle." At the head of a similar List.

(4621.) 3. 3. Another impression. "Newcastle Races, 1824." At the head of a similar List.

An impression is given under No. (2286.).

Racing Cut. No. (2287.), etc.

(4622.) 4. 1. Another impression. At the head of a "List of Horses, &c., Entered to run on the Town Moor, Newcastle Upon Tyne, in June, 1804." "M. Angus and Son, Printers, Newcastle upon Tyne."

(4623.) 4. 2. Another impression. "Willington Races." "Printed by E. Humble, Mosley-Street, Newcastle." At the head of a List of Prizes " to be Run for, at Willington, on Whitsun Tuesday, May 27th, 1817."

(4624.) 4. 3. Another impression. "Newcastle Races, 1822." "G. Angus, Printer, Newcastle." At the head of a List of Horses and Prizes.

(4625.) 4. 4. Another impression. "Newcastle Races, 1823." "G. Angus, Printer, Newcastle." At the head of a similar List.

An impression is given under No. (2292.).

Racing Cut. No. (2293.), etc.

(4626.) 5. Another impression. At the head of "A Humoursome and Interesting Dialogue between a Lady and Gentleman." "Catnach, Printer, 2, Monmouth Court, 7 Dials."

The impression shows that the block is cracked in four or more pieces. No portion, after a long and minute search through all the stock of Catnach's office, has been recovered. It has not been seen for a number of years, and has doubtless perished.

Racing Cut. No. (2295.), etc.

(4627.) 6. 1. Another impression. "Newcastle Races, 1815." "Marshall, Printer, Old Flesh Market, Newcastle." At the head of a similar List.

(4628.) 6. 2. Another impression. "Newcastle Races, 1825." "J. Marshall, Printer, Newcastle." At the head of a similar List.

Racing Cut. No. (2310.), etc.

(4629.) 7. 1. Another impression. Date and place cut off.

(4630.) 7. 2. Another. "Lambton Park Meeting, 1825." "Newcastle : Printed by W. Boag, Foot of Dean Street." At the head of a similar List.

(4631.) 7. 3. Another similar.

Racing Cut. No. (2313.), etc.

(4632.) 8. Another impression. "Newcastle Races, 1815." "Marshall, Printer, Old Flesh Market, Newcastle." At the head of a similar List.

Racing Cut. No. (2317.), etc.

(3633.) 9. Another impression. "Newcastle. King's Meadow's Races & Regatta, 1830." "W. Boag, Printer, Newcastle." At the head of a List of various Amusements on the 19th, 20th, and 21st of May, in that year.

Racing Cut. No. (2320.), etc.

(4634.) 10. Another impression. *On white India paper.* From the original Block in my possession.

(4635.) 11. 1. Racing Cut. "Car-Hamilton Races." "K. Anderson, Printer, Side, Newcastle." Three Horses, to the left. At the head of a List of Prizes "To be Run for, over Car-Hamilton, on Monday the 6th of June, 1803."

(4636.) 11. 2. Another impression. "Stanhope Races, 1812." "K. Anderson, Printer, Newcastle." At the head of a List of Prizes "To be Run for, at Stanhope in the County of Durham, on Thursday the 21st of May."

(4637.) 12. Racing Cut. "Newcastle Races, 1826." "W. Boag, Printer, Newcastle." Three Horses, to the right. At the head of a List of Horses and Prizes.

(4638.) 13. Racing Cut. Three Horses, to the left. Place and date cut off.

I fear that this may be later than any work of Thomas Bewick, but it is so like his as to deserve the benefit of the doubt.

(4639.) 14. Racing Cut. Two Horses, to the left. Probably older than Bewick. *On white India paper. From the original Block in my possession.*

(4640.) 15. Racing Cut. Small. Two Horses, to the right. *On white India paper.* From the original Block in my possession. I give an impression.

(4641). 16. Racing Cut. Small. Two Horses, to the right. Very similar to the last. *On white India paper. From the original Block in my possession.*

(4642.) 17. Racing Cut. Small. Two Horses, to the left. *On white India paper.* From the original Block in my possession.

(4643.) 18. Racing Cut. Small. Three Horses, to the right. *On white India paper.* From the original Block in my possession.

(4644.) 19. Racing Cut. Small. Three Horses, to the right. *On white India paper.* From the original Block in my possession.

(4645.) 20. Racing Cut. Three Horses, to the left. In a border. *On white India paper.* From the original Block in my possession.

The gentleman whom I have to thank for this addition informed

me that it had been in his family for a great number of years,
and that it was believed to be the first effort of Thomas Bewick
in the line in which he was afterwards so unrivalled.

(4646.) 21. Racing Cut. Three Horses, to the left.
On white India paper. From the original Block in my
possession.

(4647.) 22. Racing Cut. Three horses, to the left.
On white India paper. From the original Block in my
possession. An impression follows.

(4648.) 23. Racing Cut. Three Horses, to the left.
Very similar to the last. *On white India paper.* From
the original Block in my possession.

(4649.) 24. Racing Cut. Three Horses, to the left.
On white India paper. From the original Block in my
possession. An impression is given on the opposite page.

(4650.) 25. Racing Cut. Three Horses, to the left.
On white India paper. From the original Block in my
possession. An impression is given on the opposite page.

(4651.) 26. Racing Cut. Four horses, to the left.
On white India paper. From the original Block in my
possession.

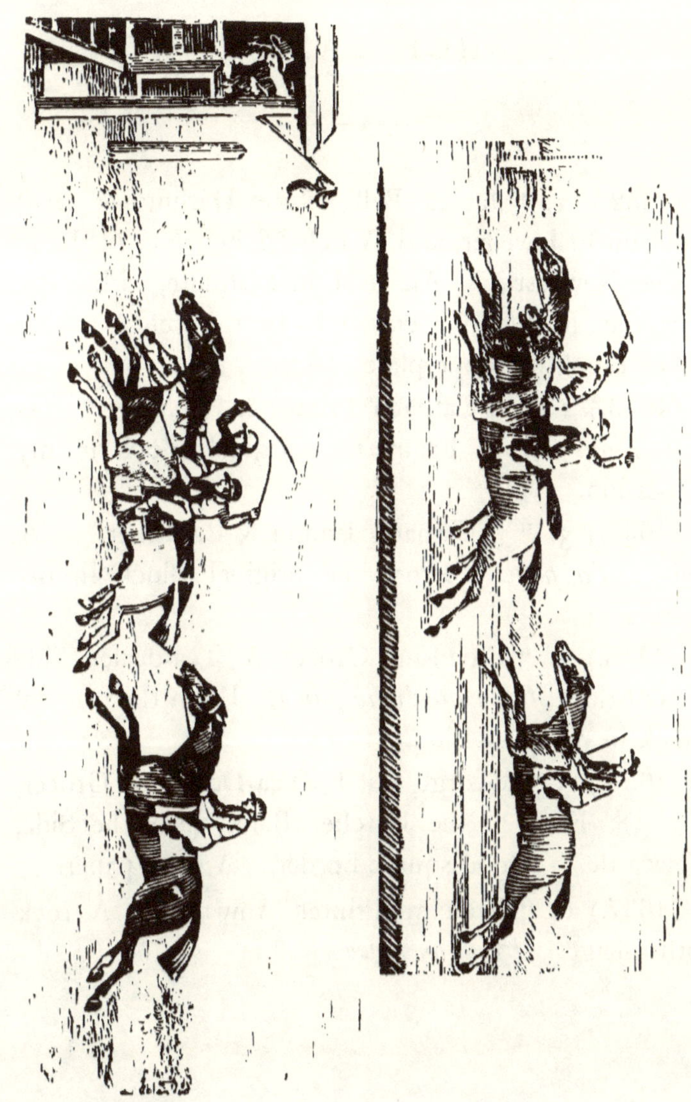

ADDITIONS

TO

SHOP CARDS.

———◆———

(4652.) 1. " James Bell, (Late Darling & Bell) Goldsmith, Jeweller, and Watch Maker, No. 19, Dean Street, Newcastle." An oval in a square, with cups, urns, etc., in the four corners. In the centre " The Silver Lion." Copperplate.

(4653.) 2. " J. Catnach Printer & Publisher." *On white India paper.* From the original Block in my possession.

(4654.) 3. " J. Catnach Printer & Publisher." *On white India paper.* From the original Block in my possession.

(4655.) 4. " Davidson Grocer & Tea-dealer Side Newcastle." *On white India paper.* From the original Block in my possession.

(4656.) 5. " George Estell, Tea-Dealer & Grocer, No. 38, Foot of the Butcher Bank, near the Side, Newcastle." Good square border. A shop paper.

(4657.) 6. " Graham Printer Alnwick." A rock with foliage. *Proof on paper.*

John Harrop.   No. (2359.).

(4658.) 7. Another impression.

(4659.) 8. " S. H."   Solomon Hodgson.   An oval, with the letters in white on a black ground, palm branches on either side, festoons of flowers, etc.

(4660.) 9. " D. Laidler, Taylor," etc. " Westgate-Street, (near the end of Denton Chare) Newcastle." The Royal Arms.   Copperplate.

(4661.) 10. " Mitchell, Merchants Auctioneer."   A scroll, with books, plans, table with pen and ink, etc. Copperplate.

(4662.) 11. " J. Neil, Northumberland-Street, Day or Evening Drawing School."   Clever oval border.

(4663.) 12. " All sorts of Sportsmens Instrum[ts] Guns Pistols &c"   Done for Mr. W. D. Noad, Gun-maker, of Morpeth, about the year 1810.   *On white India paper.*   From the original Block in my possession, of which the following is an impression.

(4664.) 13. 1. " S. Stephenson Letter Founder, London."   Weapons of the chace, bow, arrows, quiver, shield, etc., with a leopard's skin thrown across a club.   *On vellum.*

(4665.) 13. 2. Another impression. *On white satin.* Very similar in style of execution to the emblematical cuts at the beginning of each of the Books of "Somervile's Chace."

(4666.) 14. "Turnbull, Tyne Bridge End Newcastle." A cartouche bearing a Hat, supported by a beaver and a ram. Copperplate.

(4667.) 15. "J. Weir, Boot and Ladies' Shoe Maker, No. 4, Collingwood-Street, Newcastle." Woodcut scroll border, dated in M.S. "June 26, 1812."

(4668.) 16. "B. Wilson, (Late Master of the Alexander,) Dealer in Marine Stores, North Shore, Newcastle upon Tyne." Oval border. Similar to J. Neil, No. (4662.).

(4669.) 17. An oval border, for a shop-card. *On white India paper.* From the original Block in my possession.

(4670.) 18. Border for a shop-card. *On white India paper.* From the original Block in my possession. An impression follows.

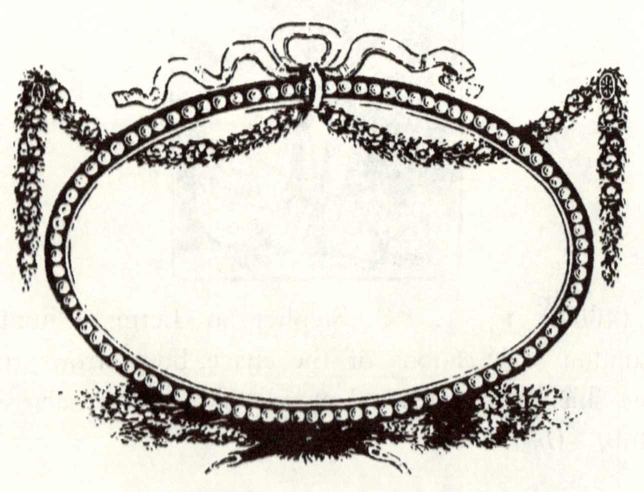

———◆———

IT is not improbable that a few of these were used as Newspaper Advertisement Cuts.

(4671.) 1. 1. "Thomas Appleby Stationer Printer and Bookseller. North Shields." A scroll hanging over a heap of books, with " Pilots Charts, Books of Navigation and Commerce, Genuine Medicines," etc. Copperplate. Dated in M.S. Aug^{st.} 20, 1810.

(4672.) 1. 2. Another impression.

Probably by Lambert.

" J. Blackwell and Co." No. (2423.).

(4673.) 2. 1. Another impression. On a leaf on which three other impressions are pasted. From Mr. John Bell.

(4674.) 2. 2. Another impression. *On white India*

paper. From the original Block in my possession, for which beautiful work of art I have to thank Mr. Blackwell. An impression follows.

(4675.) 3. Bookseller's and Stationer's Cut. A curtain, in front of which is an open volume. *On white India paper.* From the original Block in my possession.

(4676.) 4. Bookseller's and Stationer's Cut. Very similar to the last, but with the addition of two palm branches and flowers below the volume. *On white India paper.* From the original Block in my possession.

(4677.) 5. "Bray Chymist." In an oval, above which is a pestle and mortar. *On white India paper.* From the original Block in my possession.

(4678.) 6. Breeches' Maker's Cut. A pair of breeches and a glove. *On white India paper.* From the original Block in my possession.

(4679.) 7. "J. C." White letters on a black

ground. An oval, with border of palm and oak. Done for John Clark, Printer, Newcastle.

(4680.) 8. Chemist's Cut. A curtain surmounting an oval in which is a bust of "Glauber." *On white India paper.* From the original Block in my possession.

(4681.) 9. Chemist's Cut. A pestle and mortar. *On white India paper.* From the original Block in my possession.

(4682.) 10. Currier's Cut. A currier at work. *On lwhite ndia paper.* From the original Block in my possession.

(4683.) 11. Cutler's Cut. A knife grinder at work. *On white India paper.* From the original Block in my possession.

(4684.) 12. "Original Daffy's Elixir." A bottle, with "True Daffy's Elixir," in a circular border with the above inscription. *On white India paper.* From the original Block in my possession.

(4685.) 13. Grocer's Cut. A Turk drinking Coffee. Barrells with "Coffee," "Tobacco," etc. A Ship in the distance. *On white India paper.* From the original Block in my possession.

(4686.) 14. "Harris." "Juvenile Library." Square view of his shop, corner of St. Paul's Churchyard, with part of the front of the Cathedral. *On white India paper.* From the original Block in my possession.

(4687.) 15. "Harris." "Juvenile Library." Square view of his shop, corner of St. Paul's Churchyard, with the whole front of the Cathedral. *On white India paper. From the original Block in my possession.*

(4688.) 16. "Harris's Cabinet of Amusement & Instruction." Circular view of his shop, with the whole front of the Cathedral, in a border of oak and bay. *On white India paper.* From the original Block in my possession.

(4689.) 17. "I Harris" On a rock with foliage. *On white India paper.* From the original Block in my possession. An impression follows.

(4690.) 18. "I Harris" On part of a frame supporting a bee-hive, with flowers, etc. *On white India paper.* From the original Block in my possession.

These old relics of the celebrated House, from which emanated so many and well-known publications, have a special interest apart from the artistic ability which they display.

(4691.) 19. Ironmonger's Cut. Figure of Justice, with anchor and key. Very similar to No. (2449.).

On white India paper. From the original Block in my possession. I give an impression.

(4692.) 20. Ironmonger's Cut. Figure of Hope. *On white India paper.* From the original Block in my possession.

David Laidler. No. (2448.).

(4693.) 21. Another impression. Dated Mar. 14, 1805.

(4694.) 22. Lockwood & Cockburn, Engine Bridge Factory, Huddersfield. View of the works. Copperplate. Dated in MS. 4 May, 1819.

Query, if by Bewick.

(4695.) 23. View of a mill; two horses carrying sacks of corn in the foreground, a farm house and yard in the rear. On a miller's bill, as I presume, but the scrip has unfortunately been cut off. Copperplate.

(4696.) 24. Printer's Cut. A printing press, with sheets hanging to dry. *On white India paper.* From the original Block in my possession.

(4697.) 25. Printer's Cut. Printers at work. *On white India paper.* From the original Block in my possession.

(4698). 26. Shipbuilder's Cut. A ship on the stocks. *On white India paper.* From the original Block in my possession.

(4699.) 27. Silversmith's Cut. An urn, etc. *On white India paper.* From the original Block in my possession.

(4700.) 28. Tea Dealer's Cut. A Chinaman, with tea chest, etc. *On white India paper.* From the original Block in my possession.

(4701.) 29. Tea Dealer's Cut. A Chinaman, with tea chest: a pagoda in the distance. *On white India paper.* From the original Block in my possession.

(4702.) 30. Tea Dealer's Cut. A Chinaman, with tea chest inscribed " Fine Tea," etc. *On white India paper.* From the original Block in my possession.

(4703.) 31. Tea Dealer's Cut. A canister inscribed " Fine Tea." *On white India paper.* From the original Block in my possession.

(4704.) 32. Tea Dealer's Cut. A canister inscribed " The Chinese Tea Warehouse." *On white India paper.* From the original Block in my possession.
Very similar to No. (2498.)

(4705.) 33. Tea Dealer's Cut. A canister inscribed " The Chinese Tea Warehouse." *On white India paper.* From the original Block in my possession.

(4706.) 34. Tea Dealer's Cut. Large Chinese landscape, with figures of an Englishman and a Chinaman and tea chests, and a ship and pagoda in the distance. *On white India paper.* From the original Block in my possession.

(4707.) 35. Tea Dealer's Cut. Chinese landscape, with Chinamen, tea chests, etc. *On white India paper.* From the original Block in my possession.

(4708.) 36. Tea Dealer's Cut. A Chinese lady and child drinking tea. *On white India paper.* From the original Block in my possession.

(4709.) 37. Tea Dealer's Cut. Chinese, etc. *On white India paper.* From the original Block in my possession.

(4710.) 38. Tea Dealer's Cut. A Grasshopper. *On white India paper.* From the original Block in my possession.

(4711.) 39. Tobacco Cut. An Indian holding tobacco leaves; by his side are four hogsheads, the nearest inscribed "Virginia." *On white India paper.* From the original Block in my possession.

(4712.) 40. Tobacco Cut. Two Indians leaning on a hogshead. *On white India paper.* From the original Block in my possession.

(4713.) 41. Tobacco Cut. A man smoking, leaning against a hogshead inscribed "Best Virginia." *On white India paper.* From the original Block in my possession.

(4714.) 42. Tobacco Cut. Tobacco plant, with chest and hogshead. *On white India paper.* From the original Block in my possession.

(4715.) 43. Tobacco Cut. A hogshead inscribed "W S W" "Long Strip", with tobacco plant in the rear. Palms and a ship in the distance. *On white India paper.* From the original Block in my possession.

(4716.) 44. Tobacco Cut. A Scotchman leaning on a hogshead. *On white India paper.* From the original Block in my possession.

(4717.) 45. Tobacco Cut. A West Indian planter smoking, leaning on a hogshead. *On white India paper.* From the original Block in my possession.

(4718.) 46. Tobacco Cut. "Fein Toback." An Indian smoking, with tobacco plant, hogsheads, etc. *On white India paper.* From the original Block in my possession.

(4719.) 47. Upholsterer's Cut. A sofa. *On white India paper.* From the original Block in my possession.

(4720.) 48. Upholsterer's Cut. A sofa. *On white India paper.* From the original Block in my possession.

(4721.) 49. Upholsterer's Cut. Furniture. *On white India paper.* From the original Block in my possession.

Walker & Featherston's Cut. No. (2466.).

(4722.) 50. Another impression. *On white India*

paper. From the original Block in my possession. The following is an impression.

(4723.) 51. Waxchandler's Cut. A bee-hive, under a festoon of flowers. *On white India paper.* From the original Block in my possession. An impression follows.

(4724.) 52. Woolstapler's Cut. A Lamb seated on a sack of wool. A ship in the right distance. *On white India paper.* From the original Block in my possession.

Query if by Bewick.

(4725.) 53. A border of palm, foliage, and flowers, for an invoice. *On white India paper.* From the original Block in my possession.

ADDITIONS

TO

TRADESMEN'S NEWSPAPER CUTS.

(4726.) 1. "Dr. Patrick Anderson." On a circular border enclosing a shield, with A. H. above, and between the letters the crest of a man's head. *On white India paper.* From the original Block in my possession.

(4727.) 2. "Dr. Patrick Anderson." Very similar, but smaller, and in an oval border. *On white India paper.* From the original Block in my possession.

William Anderson, Auctioneer. No. (2473.)

(4728.) 3. Another impression. *On white India paper.* From the original Block in my possession. A remarkably spirited production. The following is an impression.

(4729.) 4. Auctioneer's Cut. View of an auction. In a border. *On white India paper.* From the original Block in my possession. Of this also I give an impression.

(4730). 5. Auctioneer's Cut. View of an auction. Very similar, but without the border. *On white India paper.* From the original Block in my possession.

(4731.) 6. Blacking Seller's Cut. A man shaving before a polished boot. *On white India paper.* From the original Block in my possession.

Very similar to No. (2529.).

(4732.) 7. Carrier's Cut. A stage waggon. *On white India paper.* From the original Block in my possession.

(4733.) 8. Chemist's Cut. A man with the gout. *On white India paper.* From the original Block in my possession.

(4734.) 9. Chemist's (?) Cut. A bottle, under a shield. *On white India paper.* From the original Block in my possession.

(4735.) 10. Chemist's Cut. A Phœnix. *On white India paper.* From the original Block in my possession.

(4736.) 11. Chemist's Cut. A Phœnix. *On white India paper.* From the original Block in my possession.

Dr. Cullen's "Scarlet Pills."   No. (2481.).

(4737.) 12. Another impression.

(4738.) 13. Draper's Cut. A cornice inscribed "Cheap Cloths Hats Stockings &c." *On white India paper.* From the original Block in my possession.
Very similar to No. (4755.).

(4739.) 14. Florist's Cut. An orange tree growing in a pot. *On white India paper.* From the original Block in my possession.

(4740.) 15. Gardener's Cut. A gardener at work. *On white India paper.* From the original Block in my possession.

Joseph and John Gibson. No. (2494.).

(4741.) 16. Another impression. *On white India paper.* From the original Block in my possession.

(4742.) 17. 1. Joseph & John Gibson. A lamb suspended by the middle. Very similar to the last. Dated June 8, 1793.

(4743.) 17. 2. Another impression. Dated August, 1793.

(4744.) 17. 3. Another.

John Marshall Mather. No. (2512.).

(4745.) 18. Another impression. *On white India paper.* From the original Block in my possession.

Parsons. No. (2517.).

(4746). 19. Another impression. *On white India paper.* From the original Block in my possession.

(4747.) 20. Piano-forte Maker's Cut. A cottage piano-forte. *On white India paper.* From the original Block in my possession.

(4748.) 21. Philosophical Instrument Maker's Cut. Barometer, etc. *On white India paper.* From the original Block in my possession.

(4749.) 22. "B R" in reversed cypher, in a circular border, inscribed "Smelling Medicine 1 Sh." *On white India paper.* From the original Block in my possession.

Done for Mr. Roddam, of North Shields.

(4750.) 23. "T S" in a circular border, inscribed "Smelling Medicine." *On white India paper.* From the original Block in my possession.

Done for Thomas Saint, printer, of Newcastle.

(4751.) 24. "T S" in reversed cypher. *On white India paper.* From the original Block in my possession.

(4752.) 25. "T S" Similar. *On white India paper.* From the original Block in my possession.

(4753.) 26. "T S" Similar. *On white India paper.* From the original Block in my possession.

Done for Thomas Slack, of Newcastle.

(4754.) 27. Shoemaker's Cut. A foot. *On white India paper.* From the original Block in my possession.

Thompson and Robinson. No. (2524.).

(4755.) 28. Another impression. *On white India paper.* From the original Block in my possession.

"Turner & Akenhead." No. (2527.).

(4756.) 29. Another impression.

"Richard Turner." No. (2529.).

(4757.) 30. Another impression.

(4758.) 31. Upholsterer's Cut. A man with an easy chair. *On white India paper.* From the original Block in my possession.

(4759.) 32. Water Carrier's Cut. Two men carrying a barrel of water. *On white India paper.* From the original Block in my possession.

Edward Wilson. No. (2533.)

(4760.) 33. Another impression. Dated "Newcastle upon Tyne, 21st June, 1799."

(4761.) 34. Woollen Draper's Cut. The fleece. *On white India paper.* From the original Block in my possession.

(4762.) 35. Woollen Draper's Cut. The fleece. *On white India paper.* From the original Block in my possession.

ADDITIONS

TO

BAR BILLS.

(4763.) 1. 1. "Eliz. Bendle, Three Indian Kings, Quay-Side, Newcastle." Dated in MS. 12 Mar. 1804. Good woodcut border.

(4764.) 1. 2. Another.
"Mrs. Eliz. Bendle died 13 April, 1824, aged 71 years." Mr. John Bell.

(4765.) 2. The Blue Boar. *On white India paper.* From the original Block in my possession.

(4766.) 3. 1. "Joseph Boggon, Rose & Crown Inn, Whickham." "Edward Walker, Printer, Newcastle." Good square border.

(4767.) 3. 2. Another.

William Burns, Haltwhistle. No. (2541.)

(4768.) 4. Another impression. *On white India paper.* From the original Block in my possession.

(4769.) 5. The Bush. *On white India paper.* From the original Block in my possession.

(4770.) 6. The Bush. *On white India paper.* From the original Block in my possession.

(4771.) 7. The Cock. *On white India paper.* From the original Block in my possession.

Very similar, so far as the figure, to the celebrated cut, No. (2564.). An impression follows.

(4772.) 8. The Cock. *On white India paper.* From the original Block in my possession.

(4773.) 9. " C. Colbeck, Chancellor's Head, New-gate-Street, Newcastle." " M. Angus and Son, Printers, Newcastle." Dated in MS. Dec. 29, 1806. Good square border.

(4774.) 10. " Crown Inn at Penrith." Border of foliage, etc. A post chaise at the foot. Copperplate.

(4775.) 11. 1. " Cuthbertson Chester Le Street." Lambton Arms. Copperplate.

(4776.) 11. 2. Another impression.

(4777.) 12. " Cuthbertson, White Hart Inn, Ches-ter-le-Street." Clever oval border.

(4778). 13. " J. Dewly, George-Inn, Sunderland."

" Summers & Young, Printers, Sunderland."   Clever scroll border.

(4779.) 14. Green Dragon.   *On white India paper.* From the original Block in my possession.

(4780.) 15. Half Moon.   In an oval, with ornaments of grapes, bottle, glass, punchbowl, lemons, and pipe. *On white India paper.*   From the original Block in my possession.   An impression follows.

(4781.) 16. Hat and Feather.   *On white India paper.*   From the original Block in my possession.

(4782.) 17. Hen and Chickens.   *On white India paper.*   From the original Block in my possession.

(4783.) 18. " J. Herd, King's Head, Appleby." Oval portrait of George III.

(4784.) 19. " Hine, Northumberland-Arms, Felton."   " Davison, Printer, Alnwick."   Clever square chain border.

(4785.) 20. " Mary Hird Old Fleece Darlington " The fleece, in a scroll border.   Copperplate.

(4786.) 21. Horse and Groom. *On white India paper.* From the original Block in my possession. The following is an impression.

(4787.) 22. " John Jackson, Queen's Head, Keswick." " R. Gibson, Print." Queen's Head. Dated in MS. June the 4. 1822.

(4788.) 23. Key. *On white India paper.* From the original Block in my possession.

(4789.) 24. King's Head. In a circular border. *On white India paper.* From the original Block in my possession.

(4790.) 25. The Lamb. In an oval border. *On white India paper.* From the original Block in my possession.

(4791). 26. " James Liddle, Nag's Head, Low Framlington." " Newcastle : Printed by Edward Walker, Pilgrim Street." Good square border.

(4792.) 27. " Macgregor. Wooler." Dated in MS. Feb. 11. 1822. Tankerville Arms.

(4793.) 28. " Margaret Maddocks, Tankerville

Arms, Near Wooler."　"Newcastle: Printed by Edward Walker, Pilgrim Street."　Good square border.

(4794.) 29. "R. Martin. King's Head, Richmond." Oval portrait of George III.

Maxwell.　No. (2589.).

(4795.) 30. Another impression.　*On white satin.*

(4796.) 31. Nag's Head.　In a square border.　*On white India paper.*　From the original Block in my possession.

(4797.) 32. "Pyle, Horse and Jockey, Felton." "Catnach, Printer, Alnwick."　Good square border.

(4798.) 33. Queen's Head.　In a circular border. *On white India paper.*　From the original Block in my possession.

(4799.) 34. Red Lion.　*On white India paper.*　From the original Block in my possession.

(4800.) 35. Red Lion.　Smaller.　*On white India paper.*　From the original Block in my possession.

(4801.) 36. Red Lion.　*On white India paper.*　From the original Block in my possession.

(4802.) 37. Red Lion.　*On white India paper.*　From the original Block in my possession.

R. Robinson's Cut, Black Bull Inn, Gateshead. No. (2602.).

(4803.) 38. Another impression.　From the original Block in my possession.　An impression follows.

(4804.) 39. Royal Oak. *On white India paper.* From the original Block in my possession.

(4805.) 40. "Saml. Salt, Legs of Man Call Lane Leeds." Legs of Man in a circle, with grapes on either side. Copperplate.

(4806.) 41. The Salutation. *On white India paper.* From the original Block in my possession.

(4807.) 42. Saracen's Head. *On white India paper.* From the original Block in my possession.

(4808.) 43. 1. "Wm. Shotton. Framwellgate. Durham." Festoon containing a wheatsheaf at the top, and a post chaise with four horses at the bottom. Copperplate.

(4809.) 43. 2. Another impression.

Perhaps older than Bewick.

(4810.) 44. "John Smith, Star and Garter, Tynemouth." A Star and Garter.

(4811.) 45. Stag. In a square border. *On white India paper.* From the original Block in my possession.

(4812.) 46. The Star. *On white India paper.* From the original Block in my possession.

(4813.) 47. "Ann Stephenson, Black Bull Inn, Morpeth." "Blair, Printer, Morpeth." Clever square chain border. Similar to Hine, No. (4784.).

(4814.) 48. Sun. *On white India paper.* From the original Block in my possession.

Perhaps older than Bewick.

(4815.) 49. Swan. *On white India paper.* From the original Block in my possession.

(4816.) 50. "James Ward, Cross Keys Inn, Lough borough." Cross Keys in a circle, surrounded by grapes, punch-bowl, glasses, etc. Copperplate.

"William West, Chester-le-Street." No. (2623.), etc.

(4817.) 51. Another impression. *On white India paper.* From the original Block in my possession. The following is an impression.

(4818.) 52. 1. "Whitfield, Phœnix New Inn, Morpeth." A clever oval scroll border.

(4819.) 52. 2. Another impression.

" E. Wilson. White Swan Alnwick." No. (2632.).

(4820.) 53. Another impression.

(4821.) 54. " R. Younghusband, Queen's Head, Hesket-New-Market." Queen's Head.

ADDITIONS

TO

COAL CERTIFICATES.

———◆———

(4822.) 1. 1. " Bewicke Main Coal." Tyne Side scene, with arms of Bewicke. Copperplate.

(4823.) 1. 2. Another impression.

(4824.) 2. 1. " Bewicke & Craster's Wallsend Coals." View of a spout. An oak with the arms of Bewicke & Craster in the foreground. Copperplate. Dated in MS. " 22 Jany. 1820."

(4825.) 2. 2. Another impression. Dated in MS. " 25 Jany. 1820."

(4826.) 3. 1. " Bewicke & Craster's Wallsend Coals." An inferior copy of the former. Copperplate. Dated in MS. " Aug'. 31ˢᵗ 1826."

(4827.) 3. 2. Another impression.

(4828.) 3. 3. Another.

(4829.) 3. 4. Another.

(4830.) 4. 1. " Birtley Main Coals." A ship at sea.
Copperplate.

(4831.) 4. 2. Another impression.

(4832.) 4. 3. Another.

" Collingwood Main Coal." No. (2726.).
(4833.) 5. Another impression.

(4834.) 6. 1. " Ducks Main Coals." Arms of
I. D. Nesham, Esq., between two palm branches.
Copperplate.

(4835.) 6. 2. Another impression.

(4836.) 6. 3. Another.

(4837.) 7. 1. " Ellison's Walls End Coals." Map
of the neighbourhood of the mine. Copperplate.

(4838.) 7. 2. Another impression.

(4839.) 7. 3. Another.

(4840.) 7. 4. Another.

" Fawcett Main Coals." No. (2759.).
(4841.) 8. 1. Another impression.

(4842.) 8. 2. Another.

(4843.) 8. 3. Another.

" Garesfield Coals." No. (2771.).
(4844.) 9. Another impression.

(4845.) 10. 1. " Heaton Main Coal." Map of the
neighbourhood of the mine. Copperplate.

(4846.) 10. 2. Another impression.

(4847.) 10. 3. Another.

(4848.) 11. 1. "Heaton Main Coal." A copy of the former. Copperplate.

(4849.) 11. 2. Another impression.

(4850.) 11. 3. Another.

(4851.) 11. 4. Another.

(4852.) 12. 1. "Hetton Wallsend Coals." Ships at sea. On wood.

(4853.) 12. 2. Another impression.

(4854.) 12. 3. Another.

(4855.) 12. 4. Another.

(4856.) 13. "Heworth Main Coals." Map of the neighbourhood of the mine. Copperplate.

(4857.) 14. "Heworth Main Coals." Clever view of ships taking coals from a drop. Copperplate.

"Main Team Coal." No. (2840.).
(4858.) 15. Another impression.

"Manor Walls-end Coals." No. (2841.).
(4859.) 16. 1. Another impression.

(4860.) 16. 2. Another.

(4861.) 16. 3. Another.

(4862.) 16. 4. Another.

(4863.) 16. 5. Another.

(4864.) 17. 1. "Nesham High Main Coals." Arms of I. D. Nesham, Esq., between two palm branches. Copperplate.

(4865.) 17. 2. Another impression.

(4866.) 17. 3. Another.

(4867.) 17. 4. Another.

(4868.) 17. 5. Another.

(4869.) 18. 1. " Nesham's Primrose Main Coals."
Arms of I. D. Nesham, Esq., between two palm
branches. Copperplate.

(4870.) 18. 2. Another impression.

(4871.) 18. 3. Another.

(4872.) 18. 4. Another.

(4873.) 18. 5. Another.

(4874.) 19. 1. " New Tanfield Coals." Map of
the neighbourhood of the mine. Copperplate.

(4875.) 19. 2. Another impression.

(4876.) 19. 3. Another.

(4877.) 20. " Newbottle Burn Moor Coals." Arms
of I. Nesham, Esq., with scrip. Copperplate.

(4878.) 21. " Newbottle Main Coals." Arms of
I. D. Nesham, Esq., between two palm branches.

(4879.) 22. 1. " Newcastle Wallsend Coals." Map
of the neighbourhood of the mine. Copperplate.

(4880.) 22. 2. Another impression.

(4881.) 22. 3. Another.

(4882.) 23. " Old Ducks Main Coal." Arms of
Sir H. V. Tempest, Bart. Copperplate.

Very similar to No. (2871.), but larger and of earlier execution.

(4883.) 24. 1. " Pelaw Main Coals." A ship taking
coals from a drop. Copperplate.

(4884.) 24. 2. Another impression.

(4885.) 24. 3. Another.

(4886.) 24. 4. Another.

(4887.) 24. 5. Another.

(4888.) 25. 1. " Pelaw Main Colliery." Copy of the former, on the head of an invoice. Copperplate.

(4889.) 25. 2. Another.

(4890.) 26. 1. " Primrose Main Coals." Arms of Sir H. V. Tempest, Bart. Copperplate.

(4891.) 26. 2. Another impression.

(4892.) 27. " Primrose Moor Main Coals." Arms of W. H. Lambton, Esq., between two sprays of bay. Copperplate.

"South Moor Main Coals." No. (2914.).

(4893.) 28. Another impression.

"Tanfield Moor Coals." No. (2925.).

(4894.) 29. Another impression.

(4895.) 30. " Team Coals." Arms of Sir Thomas H. Liddell, Bart. Copperplate.

(4896.) 31. " Temple Main Coals." Crest of S. Temple, Esq. Copperplate.

(4897.) 32. 1. " Walls End Coals." Arms of I. D. Nesham, Esq. Copperplate.

(4898.) 32. 2. Another impression.

(4899.) 33. " Wallsend Coals." Arms of Sir H. V. Tempest, Bart. Copperplate.

"Whitefield Coals." No. (2969.).

(4900.) 34. 1. Another impression.

(4901.) 34. 2. Another.

(4902.) 35. 1. —— Coals. Crest of Townley, between two sprays of bay. Copperplate.

(4903.) 35. 2. Another impression.

(4904.) 36. "Cinders manufactured at the S°. Shore. Sᵗ Anthons & Heworth Shore." View of the works. Copperplate.

(4905.) 37. "Sheepfold Lime Shells." Arms of Sir H. Williamson, Bart. On wood.

ADDITIONS

TO

THE ROYAL ARMS, ETC.

The Royal Arms of England.   No. (2992.).

(4906.) 1. Another impression.   Showing that the Block is badly cracked in all directions.

(4907.) 2. The Royal Arms.   Nine and a half inches broad.   Shield supported by an oak tree.   Label, with motto, lying in folds on the ground.   Rose, shamrock, and thistle to the left of the lion.   Signed "T Bewick Sculp^t.", the T and B in a monogram.   Copperplate.

(4908.) 3. 1. The Royal Arms.   Small.   Identical with No. (4591.).   *Proof on paper.*

(4909.) 3. 2. Another impression.   *On white India paper.*   From the original Block in my possession. The following is an impression.

(4910.) 4. The Royal Arms of England.   A series of fourteen impressions. *On white India paper.*   From the original Blocks in my possession.

I do not positively claim an attribution to Bewick for each of these cuts, though some are undoubtedly by him.

(4911.) 5. Prince of Wales's Plume. *On white India paper.*   From the original Block in my possession.

(4912.) 6. Prince of Wales's Plume. *On white India paper.*   From the original Block in my possession.

(4913.) 7. Star and Garter.   *On white India paper.* From the original Block in my possession.

(4914.) 8. Star and Garter.   *On white India paper.* From the original Block in my possession.

ADDITIONS

TO

ARMS OF NEWCASTLE AND GATESHEAD.

ARMS OF NEWCASTLE.

Arms of Newcastle.   No. (3c02.).

(4915.) 1. Another impression, but without the ships.

(4916.) 2. Arms of Newcastle.   Shield and supporters.   No crest, but flowers on the top.

Printed with the former article on an 8vo page of paper without letterpress.

(4917.) 3. Arms of Newcastle.   *On white India paper.* From the original Block in my possession.

ARMS OF GATESHEAD.

(4918.) 1. 1. Arms of Gateshead.

On a title privately printed by Mr. John Bell for a volume of his gatherings.   "Collections relative to the Town and Borough of Gateshead, in the Northern Division of the County of Durham, Comprising the Rectories of Saint Mary, Gateshead, and Saint John, Gateshead Fell. By John Bell, Land Surveyor, Gateshead." Folio. n. d.

(4919.) 1. 2. Another impression. *On white India paper.* From the original Block in my possession.

ADDITIONS

TO

NEWSPAPER CUTS.

———◆———

HEADINGS OF NEWSPAPERS.

(4920.) 1. Heading of the Newcastle Courant Newspaper. No. (3011.). Another impression. *On white India paper.* From the original Block in my possession. An impression follows.

I am indebted for the possession of this unrivalled series to the kindness of Messrs. Blackwell and Rutherford, the proprietors of the Newcastle Courant. See further among the "Wood Blocks."

(4921.) 2. Heading of the Newcastle Courant. No. (3012.)–(3015.). Another impression. *On white India paper.* From the original Block in my possession. An impression follows.

(4922.) 3. Heading of the Newcastle Courant. No. (3016.). *On white India paper.* From the original Block in my possession. The following is an impression.

(4923.) 4. Heading of the Newcastle Courant. No. (3017.)–(3020.). *On white India paper.* From the original Block in my possession.

(4924.) 5. 1. Heading of the Newcastle Courant.

Very similar to the last. No pennon; the motto placed on a rock, above which appear the branches of the tree: the steeple of St. Nicholas and the Castle in the left distance. No windmills.

(4925.) 5. 2. Another old impression.

(4926.) 5. 3. Another.

(4927.) 5. 4. Another. *On white India paper.* From the original Block in my possession. An impression follows.

(4928.) 6. Heading of the Newcastle Courant. A fragment, very similar to the last. *On white India paper.* From the original Block in my possession.

(4929.) 7. Heading of the Newcastle Courant. No pennon; the motto placed on a rock; the steeple of St. Nicholas and the Castle in the left distance. One (?) windmill in the right distance. *On white India paper.* From the original Block in my possession. An impression follows.

(4930.) 8. Heading of the Newcastle Courant. No pennon. Motto on rock. St. Nicholas and Castle in the left distance. *On white India paper.* From the original Block in my possession..

Query, if by Bewick. There are indications of the absence of the Master's hand, which the experienced student of his style will hardly fail to recognize. The cut, however, is extremely beautiful.

(4931.) 9. Heading of the Newcastle Courant. No. (3028.)–(3031.). *On white India paper.* From the original Block in my possession.

Still more probably not by Bewick.

(4932.) 10. Heading of the Newcastle Courant. *On white India paper.* From the original Block in my possession.

Of this there can be no doubt. The Master had passed away.

(4933.) 11. Heading of the Newcastle Advertiser. No. (3043.). *On white India paper.* From the original Block in my possession. An impression follows.

(4934.) 12. Heading of a Newspaper. "The Star and". With a Star and the Prince of Wales' Plume, and the motto "Vespero Surgente." *On white India paper.* From the original Block in my possession.

——— — · — ·—

Cock Fighting Advertisements.

Fighting Cocks.　No. (3155.)–(3160.).

(4935.) 13. Another impression. *On white India paper*. From the original Block in my possession. An impression follows.

"Lost, Stolen, or Strayed."

The Devil and Horseman.　No. (3182.).

(4936.) 14. Another impression. Dated in MS. 1782. From Mr. John Bell.

The Devil and Horseman.　No. (3191.).

(4937.) 15. Another impression. *On white India paper*. From the original Block in my possession, of which the following is an impression.

(4938.) 16. The Devil and Horseman. Very similar to No. (3192.), but not the same.

Various.

(4939.) 17. 1. Figure of Mercury. No. (3202.). *On white India paper*. From the original Block in my possession.

(4940.) 17. 2. Another impression.   An old one.

(4941.) 18. Figure of Mercury.   No. (3206.).   *On white India paper.*   From the original Block in my possession.

(4942.) 19. Figure of Mercury, with his wand in his left hand.   *On white India paper.*   From the original Block in my possession.

(4943.) 20. "Literature."   No. (3213.)   Another impression.

(4944.) 21. Figure of Fame blowing a trumpet. *On white India paper.*   From the original Block in my possession.   It is used in No. (3259.).

(4945.) 22. Figure of Fame. Smaller.   *On white India paper.*   From the original Block in my possession.

(4946.) 23. Figure of Justice, in an oval border. *On white India paper.*   From the original Block in my possession.

(4947.) 24. A Pointer.   For Coursing Advertisements. *On white India paper.* From the original Block in my possession.

(4948.) 25. Five Ships.   For Sailing Advertisements. *On white India paper.* From the original Blocks in my possession.

ADDITIONS

TO

BROADSIDES, ETC.

————◆————

(4949.) 1. A leaf, with six cuts. No. (3233.). Another impression.

(4950.) 2. A leaf, with thirty-four cuts.

Dormouse. Ferret. Hunting Tiger. Boar. Wolf. Stag. Lamb. Lion. Fawn. Indian. Jew. Angel. Dolphin. Bear. Wild Horse. Reynard. Dog. Cat. Ass. Panther. Flying Horse. Squirrel. Cat. Tiger Cat. Goat. Greyhound. A Deer. Goose. Lark. Ostrich. Cock. Dove. Eagle. Stork.

(4951.) 3. A leaf, with six cuts.

Well. Traveller and Shepherd. Man and Ass. Reading. Cow Milking (large). A Gentleman in his Phaeton (large).

(4952.) 4. A leaf, with twenty-seven cuts.

Robin Redbreast. A Linnet. A Jackdaw. A Duck. Crow and Pitcher. A Flower. A Flying Dragon. A Vulture. Birds Billing. A Swallow. A Starling. A Basket of Fruit. A Stork. A Cock. A Wood Pigeon. A Dove. A Rose Linnet. A Thistle. A Hawk. A Bullfinch. A Peacock. A Lark. A Tree. A Wren. A Goldfinch. A Swan. A Bird's Nest.

(4953.) 5. A leaf, with six cuts.

Bison. Puss. Camel. Glaud and Simon. Hay Rick. Bauldy and Glaud (all large).

(4954.) 6. A leaf, with six cuts.

Landscape. Cow Grazing. Ploughing. Cottage. Milk-Maid and Cows (large). Countrymen at Work (large).

(4955.) 7. A leaf, with nineteen cuts.

Boar. Bridge. Crow and Jug. Stag. Duck. Eagle. Deer (large). Goat. Fawn. Bull. Wolf. Lark. Serpent. Kanguroo (large). Bear. Lamb. Giraffe (large). Lion. Hunting Tiger.

(4956.) 8. A leaf, with twelve cuts of ships, etc.

The Nightingale. Channel Fleet. Sea Port. Anchor. The Spitfire. The Rover. The Britannia. The Victory. Crusoe shooting a Savage. Sloop Nancy (large). Saving Goods from a Wreck.

(4957.) 9. A Series of "Lottery Sheets," each containing eight cuts, surrounded with a border. "Published by W. Davison, Bondgate Street, Alnwick."

Many of the cuts are by Thomas Bewick, and were used by Davison in others of his publications. The fourth cut in No. 6 is given at page 429 of 'The Bewick Collector,' and the fifth in the same number at page 127 of the present Supplement.

Family Accommodation Mangle. No. (3257.).

(4958.) 10. Another impression. *On white India paper.* From the original Block in my possession.

View of an Execution. No. (3268.).

(4959.) 11. Another impression. *On white India paper.* From the original Block in my possession.

" Martin's Wonderful Prophecies." No. (3267.).

(4960.) 12. Another old impression, on paper, without letterpress.   From Mr. John Bell.

The Hangman, etc.   No. (3539.).

(4961.) 13. Another impression. *On white India paper.*   From the original Block in my possession.

(4962.) 14. A Series of fifteen Cuts of Ships, for Broadside Notices of Ship Auctions, Voyages, etc. *On white India paper.*   From the original Blocks in my possession.

(4963.) 15. A Series of seven Cuts of Horse and Groom, for Broadsides of Horse Sales, etc.   *On white India paper.*   From the original Blocks in my possession.

(4964.) 16. Portrait of a Clergyman.   *On white India paper.*   From the original Block in my possession.

(4965.) 17. Female Figure and Tombstone.   *On white India paper.*   From the original Block in my possession.

For Monodies and similar Broadsides.

(4966.) 18. " Patent Safe Coach."   A two-horse chariot, with lady and gentleman passengers.

On white paper.   Mounted in the volume described under No. (4496.).

(4967.) 19. The Bald Cavalier.   *On white India paper.*   From the original Block in my possession.

(4968.) 20. The Fight with the Devil.   *On white*

India paper. From the original Block in my possession.

Done in ridicule of a fanatic at Newcastle.

—————————

Songs with Cuts by Thomas Bewick.

Out of an immense collection of Songs printed in the North of England, the following selection should be added to the series already given. I am, however, very far from certain of the claims of some of them :—

(4969.) 21. "A New Song. The Rigs of Newcastle Fair." "G. Angus, Printer, Newcastle."

With cut of The Miller on Horseback. An impression has been given under No. (4283.).

(4970.) 22. "Tom Starboard and Faithful Nancy." London—Printed by J. Catnach, and Sold Wholesale and Retail at No. 60, Wardour-Street, Soho-Square."

With cut of a Ship at sea.

(4971.) 23. "A New Song, called The Rump-Steak Lady." "Catnach, Printer, 2, Monmouth-Court."

With the cut of a Swan swimming, mentioned under No. (2632.). The Block has not been seen for many years, and although I have searched for it long and carefully among the stock of Catnach's office, I have been unable to find it. See the note to No. (4626.).

(4972.) 24. "A Funny Dialogue, Between a Fat Butcher, and a Mackarel, In Newport Market Yesterday." "Catnach, Printer, 2 Monmouth-court."

With the same cut of a Swan swimming.

(4973.) 25. "The Lily of the Valley."	"Catnach,
Printer, 2, Monmouth court, 7 Dials."

> With cut of the Arms of the Duke of Northumberland.   See No.
> (217.), note.   This Block also has been long out of sight, and
> cannot be found.

(4974.) 26. "Nature's Gay Day."	"J. Catnach,
Printer, 2, & 3, Monmouth court Seven Dials."

> With cut of "Lads and their Lasses tripping lightly away."

(4975.) 27. "The Fairy Boy."	"J. Paul & Co.,
Printers, 2 & 3, Monmouth Court, 7 Dials."

> With cut of a Boy reading to a party of children.

(4976.) 28. 1. "The Christmas Goose."	"Printed
by W. S. Fortey, Monmouth Court, Seven Dials."

> With cut of a Duck, of which I have the original Block.

(4977.) 28. 2. Another impression of the cut.	*On
white India paper.*   From the same.

> I am not certain of its correct attribution, but the work is of great
> merit, as the following impression will prove.

(4978.) 29. " Skewball."

With a small Horse-Racing Cut, of which I have the original
Block.   See No. (4642.).

(4979.) 30. " The World on Credit."   " C. Croshaw, Printer, Coppergate, York."

With a clever Horse-Racing cut, of which I possess the original
Block.   See No. (4643.).

(4980.) 31. 1. " Tobacco."   " Printed and sold by
J. W. Procter & Son, 4, Engine-Street, Hull."

With cut of a Man shaking his fist at a Boy in a tree.

(4981.) 31. 2. Another copy.

(4982.) 32. "The Drunkard's Ragged Child."

With cut of the Old Man and Death.

(4983.) 33. " Mother, Don't you Cry."

With cut of a Child relieving two Beggars.

(4984.) 34. " Pat M'Guire."   " Published and Sold
by Robert Rankin, 38, Bottle Bank, Gateshead."

With cut of an Old Beggar.

(4985.) 35. 1. " What's a' the Steer Kimmer."
" Printed and Sold by J. Ross, Arcade, Newcastle-on-
Tyne."

With cut of the Farmer and his Visitors, by Lee (?)

(4986.) 35. 2. Another copy.

(4987.) 36. " Duncan Campbell."   " Printed and
Sold by John Ross, Royal Arcade, Newcastle-on-
Tyne."

With cut of Boys tracking a hare.

(4988.) 37. " The Butcher and Chambermaid."

" Printed and Sold by J. Ross, Arcade, Newcastle-on-Tyne."

> With an excellent copy of the cut in Burns's Poems, vol. I. p. 275.　No. (230.).

(4989.) 38. "The Sheffield Apprentice." " Printed and Sold by John Ross, Arcade, Newcastle-upon-Tyne."

> With cut of the Devil driving a man under the gallows.

(4990.) 39. "Napoleon's Farewell to Paris."　"W. R. Walker, Printer, Arcade, Newcastle."

> With cut of Tyne-side Scene, of which I have the Block.　See No. (4545.).

(4991.) 40. "Woodman, Spare that Tree." " Printed and Sold by W. R. Walker, Royal Arcade, Newcastle-upon-Tyne."

> With cut of a Man felling a Tree, an admirable copy of that in Burns's Poems, vol. II. p. 85.　No. (230.).

(4992.) 41. "Donald's Return to Glencoe." "Printed and Sold by W. R. Walker, 7 Royal Arcade, Newcastle-upon-Tyne."

> With cut of a Wild Cat.

(4993.) 42. "Erin's Lovely Home." "Henry Disley Printer, 57, High Street, St. Giles."

> With cut of Donkey and Monument, a copy of the vignette in the 'British Birds,' First Edition, Vol. I. p. 87.

ADDITIONS

TO

MISCELLANEOUS CUTS.

———➤

VIEWS.

(4994.) 1. Large oval view of Jarrow. *On white India paper.* From the original Block in my posses-- sion.

(4995.) 2. Tynemouth Priory. *On white India paper.* From the original Block in my possession.

(4996.) 3. View of Durham Cathedral from the river. *On white India paper.* From the original Block in my possession.

(4997.) 4. View of Bamborough Castle, 6 inc. by $2\frac{3}{8}$ inc.

(4998.) 5. View of Bamborough Castle, a copy of the preceding. Given me by Mr. Geggie, of Alnwick. Query, if by Bewick.

(4999.) 6. View of Sunderland Bridge. A small oval. *On white India paper.* From the original Block in my possession.

(5000.) 7. View of Sunderland Bridge, 2 inc. by 1½ inc. *On white India paper.* From the original Block in my possession.

(5001.) 8. View of Sunderland Bridge. Three fourths of a circle. *On white India paper.* From the original Block in my possession. An impression follows.

(5002.) 9. View of Sunderland Bridge, 4 inc. by 1½ inc. *On white India paper.* From the original Block in my possession.

(5003.) 10. View of a Manufactory, apparently by the side of Newcastle Old Bridge, on which is the name of Bowes. *On white India paper.* From the original Block in my possession.

(5004.) 11. A Series of Eight Views. *On white India paper.* From the original Blocks in my possession.

(5005.) 12. A House. *On white India paper.* From the original Block in my possession.

(5006.) 13. A House. *On white India paper.* From the original Block in my possession.

ANIMALS.

"The Remarkable Kyloe Ox." No. (3388.), etc.
(5007.) 1. Another impression. *On white India paper.*

"Durham Cow. 5." No. (3410).
(5008.) 2. Another impression. *On coarse blue paper.*

(5009.) 3. "Durham Ox. 8." A reversed copy of that in No. (247.). *On coarse blue paper.*

(5010.) 4. White Pony. A reversed copy of that in Reay's Sportsman's Friend. *On coarse blue paper.*

Above the cut is written " Barton Valuations, 1815."
These were intended for covers of copy and account books.

(5011.) 5. A Stag. Signed "T. Bewick, Newcastle." Copperplate. A copy of that at page 260 of the 'Select Fables' of 1820.

(5012.) 6. A Series of Nine Cuts of Animals, each enclosed in a square border.

Horse, Bear (signed " T B "); Wild Boar, Chamois, Fallow Deer (signed " T Bewick"), Sheep, Otter, Raven, and Wood Pigeon (signed " T. Bwk."). Fine impressions. *On white India paper.*
They are thus noticed in a Catalogue of Mr. E. Pearson :—
" NINE VERY RARE BEWICK WOOD-ENGRAVINGS. TWO BRITISH BIRDS, and SEVEN BRITISH QUADRUPEDS, with Borders. These beautiful cuts are nearly 2½ by 3¼ inches in size, and are exceedingly beautiful. One is signed ' T. Bewicke,' another ' Bwk.' They have been in the possession of the descendants of the Foreman to Wilson and Spence's Printing Offices, York, for the last 50 years. I have not seen impressions of them in

any Bewick Collection. Small 4to, uncut, toy wrappers, £5 5s.,
very interesting and choice impressions.

"WILSON AND SPENCE, YORK, *about* 1789."

Although several of these cuts are, as stated, signed by Bewick,
they are, on the whole, unworthy of him. The Horse and
Otter are singularly indifferent. I cannot, therefore, endorse
the expressions either of admiration of the work, or of the
correctness of the attribution of these cuts to Thomas Bewick.
Several of them, nevertheless, indicate considerable ability in
their author, whom I take to have been a pupil rather than
the great Master himself.

(5013.) 7. A Series of Eleven Cuts of Animals. *On
white India paper.* From the original Blocks in my
possession.

They consist of the Kyloe Ox, Lancashire Bull, Group of Sheep,
Lion, Nondescript Animal in the ' History of Quadrupeds,' Bull
Dog, Greyhound Fox, Hare, Kanguroo, Goldfinch, and Carp.
Impressions of the Lion and the Bull Dog will be found among
the " Wood Blocks."

VARIOUS.

(5014.) 1. A remarkably clever copy of the Vignette " Man watering "; British Birds, First Ed. vol.
i. p. 42. Copperplate. *Proof on a folio page of foolscap
paper.*

From the collection of Mr. Lynch, of Newcastle.

(5015.) 2. A Party of four Smokers, one of them

said to be a portrait of Bewick himself. *Proof on white India paper.*

"Said to be engraved by Thomas Bewick. He used to meet a select few at the 'House of Commons,' Newcastle." MS. note on the paper on which the impression is mounted.

ADDITION

TO

DRAWINGS.

———◆———

(5016.) 1. The Letter "T" in German Text, before a shield bearing the Arms of Newcastle.

On the paper is written, in an old hand, "Drawn by T. Bewick. G. R."

ADDITIONS

TO

WOOD BLOCKS.

THE causes which have led to the goodly Additions described in some of the foregoing Departments have been even more full of beneficial results in this of the Wood Blocks—the most precious and invaluable of all. My thanks, in the first place, are due to the generosity of friends, who have either given me their treasures, the collections of lives, or have afforded me introductions, hardly less valuable, to quarters from whence I have acquired what was otherwise unattainable. Then, in the second, through the inducement offered to numerous printing Firms to contribute their stores by purchase to the aggregate already so comprehensive—added to some fortunate accidents in the course of my varied investigations, as detailed in the Preface—I have been enabled to make most interesting additions to the list already given. I have also, both in person and by correspondence, instituted many and strict inquiries, not only in London and his own locality, Newcastle, Gateshead, Hexham, Alnwick, Durham, Sunderland, North and South Shields, etc., but also in various provincial towns south of his neighbourhood, where some of Bewick's productions were used by the publishers in those places,—as York, Knaresborough, Richmond, Penrith, Ludlow, Gloucester, etc. etc.—and have in a number of instances succeeded in recovering the Blocks, while in others I have satisfied myself that they either cannot be found, or, as in some cases, have unquestionably perished. The reader who is familiar with the list which was given in the previous Volume and connects it with the one which follows, bearing also in mind the facts now stated, will thus be aware that, with the exception of those in the possession of the Bewick family, there can be no considerable number of the original Blocks, especially of those executed when the Artists had arrived at eminence and for works of mark and importance, outside the limits of my own Collection. After those of the 'Quadrupeds,' 'British Birds,' and 'Æsop,' to which I have just alluded, the Blocks of their most celebrated and important Book-Illustrations are here associated; while a very large number of their occasional works, done for private persons and miscellaneous purposes of various kinds, have been traced to their hiding places, the concealment of which has been the sole cause of their escaping the fate of so many of their companions, and are now added to numbers which before seemed but little likely to admit of increase, and preclude the hope of future additions of any extent or importance. It hardly need be said that these results, excepting those for which, as already stated, I have to thank the kindness of friends, have been obtained at a very considerable cost of time, patience, labour, travel, and money. To add, indeed, to the difficulty of acquisition, many of them were estimated at a fabulous value from the fact of their being the sole surviving relics of old and celebrated Firms, and hoarded by their possessors accordingly. But the completeness and value of the product so acquired are most satisfactory, and more than compensate for those necessary expenditures, apart from which the present result was simply impossible.

To enable the reader to judge in some measure of the beauty of many of these acquisitions, I have furnished him throughout the volume with impressions from a selection of the original Blocks. Truth, however, obliges me to add, that the action of the modern rolling-press is but poorly adapted for taking fine impressions from Cuts engraved in Bewick's peculiar style, with the lower and more delicate portions of which the ink never comes in contact. The impressions, therefore, rarely do justice to my Blocks, which in most instances are in as good a condition as when first executed. Hence I think I may reckon on the gratification of the reader, when I inform him that a very beautiful Volume is in preparation, which is intended to contain impressions of some eighteen hundred of my Blocks, taken off by the old process, and thus presenting a worthy counterpart of these lovely works of Art, which, as was said of one of the many series included in the Collection, " will be a monument of fame " to the Artist brothers, " of more celebrity than marble could bestow."

ADDITIONS TO WOOD BLOCKS FOR BOOKS AND PAMPHLETS.

FISHER'S NEW ENGLISH TUTOR.　No. (4029.).

(5017.) 1–10. The entire Series of Ten Cuts.　Obtained from Mr. Hodgson.

Specimens have been given under No. (4029.).

GREY'S EPITOME OF THE ANNALS OF GREAT BRITAIN.
No. (4033.).

(5018.) 11–34. The Twenty-four Figures of the Sovereigns.　Obtained from Mr. Hodgson.

Specimens will be found under No. (4033.).

HASTIE'S READING EASY.　No. (11.), ETC.

(5019.) 35–70. The entire Series of Thirty-six Cuts. From Mr. Dodd, of Newcastle, successor to Mr. Emerson Charnley, to whom they came from the Angus family.

Specimens have been given under Nos. (1619.) and (4428.).

NEW YEAR'S GIFT.　No. (4034.).

(5020.) 71–76. Six Cuts, illustrating the Story of Little Red Riding Hood.

Specimens have been given under No. (4034.).

(5021.) 77–81. The entire Series of Five Cuts. From Mr. Blenkhorn, Hargrove's successor at Knaresborough. The following is an impression from the beautiful Cut of the Arms of Knaresborough Priory, the Cornwall Arms, perhaps the finest cut that Bewick ever executed for a provincial publisher.

I possess a considerable number of Hargrove's Wood Blocks, executed for his various topographical works, but do not attribute them to either Thomas or John Bewick. Many of them are undoubtedly the productions of Green, and some apparently of Anderson.

LOOKING GLASS FOR THE MIND. No. (66.), ETC.

(5022.) 82–100. A Series of Nineteen Cuts, namely, that on the title; the large Cuts at pp. 38, 75, 122, 132, 187, 202, 257, and 263: and the Vignettes at

pp. iv, 37, 53, 117, 174, 201, 223, 241, 256, and
262.

After a very careful search which I have been per-
mitted to make through the more ancient stock of
Messrs. Griffith and Farran, the successors of Newbery and Harris, I have been able to select sixty-one
Blocks, which will be found enumerated under the
various heads to which they are referable. It is understood that at the time of Mr. Harris's decease the
greater part of the old stock was disposed of, some
of which found its way to the North of England, and
was ultimately purchased by myself from a trades-
man long resident in Northumberland. It is from
that purchase that I have been able to furnish the
various specimens of the Illustrations of Newbery and
Harris's publications which have been given in the
earlier pages of this and the previous volume. The
Blocks which remained in their successors' possession
were happily the choicest of the whole, and reserved,
I presume, for that special reason. They constituted,
as will be seen, a perfect series of the cuts done for
the 'Tales for Youth,'—the finest and best examples
of John Bewick's work for juvenile publications,—a
considerable number belonging to his next best
volume—the 'Looking Glass for the Mind,'—and
others of hardly less interest. And the very large
price demanded and paid for them was on account of
their being, in the words of their former owners, "all
the valuable relics of the old Firm."

Specimens have been given under No. (4438.), and at page 199.

SPORTING MAGAZINE. No. (71.).

(5023.) 101. Horse Racing. Used on the cover, and at the head of 'The Racing Calendar.' One of the most celebrated productions of John Bewick, which, although subject to hard usage for a number of years, yet preserves much of its original excellence. Obtained in London.

An impression follows.

TALES FOR YOUTH. No. (72.), ETC.

(5024.) 102–131. The entire Series of Thirty Cuts. They are the finest examples of the skill of John Bewick employed in juvenile publications. Purchased of Messrs. Griffith and Farran, successors to Newbery and Harris, of St. Paul's Churchyard. See note to 'Looking Glass for the Mind' above.

Specimens have been given under No. (4442.).

KINGS OF ENGLAND. No. (4078.).

(5025.) 132, 133. Cut of 'Ancient Britons' on the

title, and Portrait of King George III.   Purchased of
Messrs. Griffith and Farran, Successors to Newbery
and Harris, St. Paul's Churchyard.

THE OECONOMIST.   No. (127.).

(5026.) 134, 135. The Series of Two Cuts.   From
Mr. Dodd, and formerly belonging to the Angus
family.

An impression of the Cut on the titles, Mr. Bigge's well-known
Cut of ' Liberty,' has already been given under No. (1966.).

THE PICTURE BOOK.   No. (4101.).

(5027.) 136–173. A Series of Thirty-eight Cuts.
They were originally in the possession of Messrs.
Christopher and Jennett, of Stockton-on-Tees, and
from them appear to have passed to Cornelius Croshaw, of the Pavement, York, who disposed of them
to the gentleman who sold them to me.

Specimens will be found under No. (4101.), and others follow.

THE NEW SONGSTER.   No. (139.).

(5028.) 174, 175. The Two Cuts on the Frontispiece.   From Soulby's office, Penrith, where the book
was printed.

THE VOCAL MISCELLANY.   No. (141.).

(5029.) 176. Cut on the Title.   From Humble's
office, Newcastle.

THE PLEASING INSTRUCTOR. No. (4103.).

(5030.) 177. Cut on the Title. From Soulby's office, Penrith, where the book was printed.

ELMINA. No. (4108.).

(5031.) 178. The Frontispiece. From Messrs. Griffith and Farran, Successors to Newbery and Harris, St. Paul's Churchyard.

THE FORSAKEN INFANT. Nos. (4111.), (4452.).

(5032.) 179–187. The Series of nine Cuts. Done for Mozley, of Gainsborough and Derby.

A specimen will be found under No. (4452.).

REAY'S SPORTSMAN'S FRIEND. No. (163.).

(5033.) 188. The Bay Pony. I have to offer my grateful thanks to T. H. Wilson, Esq., for the possession of this very beautiful work of art.

An impression has been given at p. 139.

FISHER'S GRAMMAR. No. (4134.).

(5034.) 189. Facsimile of Signature. From Hodgson's office, Newcastle, where the book was printed.

PICTURE OF NEWCASTLE-UPON-TYNE. No. (218.).

(5035.) 190, 191. View of Newcastle on the title, and Figure of a Roman Altar at page 152 of the Second Edition. From Akenhead's office, Newcastle, where the book was printed.

An impression of the former will be found under No. (4458.).

WARDEN'S SPELLING BOOK. No. (4235.).

(5036.) 192–198. The entire Series of seven Cuts.

From Humble's office, Newcastle, where the book was printed.

Specimens have been given under Nos. (4235.), (4817.).

FLOWERS OF BRITISH POETRY. No. (281.).

(5037.) 199. "Meditation by Moonlight." From Sunderland.

An impression will be found at page 209.

DAVISON'S SPECIMENS OF WOOD BLOCKS. No. (298.).
Various Cuts enumerated under other heads.

RHYMES OF NORTHERN BARDS. No. (302.).

(5038.) 200, 201. The Cuts at pp. 149, 174. From Angus, Charnley, and Dodd's office, Newcastle.

These Cuts, and the others similarly described, were successively in the office of the publishers named.

GARLAND OF NOTHUMBERLAND HEROES. No. (303.).

(5039.) 202. Cut on title. From Angus, Charnley, and Dodd's office, Newcastle.

An impression will be found under No. (4284.).

FIGURES IN RHYMES. No. (304.).

(5040.) 203–205. The Series of three Cuts. From Angus, Charnley, and Dodd's Office, Newcastle.

An impression of that on the title is given under No. (4289.).

GARLAND OF BELLS. No. (335.).

(5041.) 206. Cut on title. From Angus, Charnley, and Dodd's office, Newcastle.

An impression is given under No. (4285.).

THE CONTENTED COUCKOULD. No. (336.).

(5042.) 207. Cut on title. From Angus, Charnley, and Dodd's office, Newcastle.

An impression is given under No. (4282.).

GARLAND OF NEW SONGS. No. (4282.).

(5043.) 208–220. A Series of thirteen Cuts. From Angus, Charnley, and Dodd's office, Newcastle.

Impressions have been given under No. (4282.).

COLLECTION OF NEW SONGS. No. (4283.).

(5044.) 221. Cut on title. From Angus, Charnley, and Dodd's office, Newcastle.

An impression will be found under No. (4283.).

ACCOUNT OF THE GREAT FLOOD. No. (345.).

Arms of Newcastle on the title. From Hodgson's office, Newcastle, where the Book was printed. It has been already enumerated under No. (3628.).

An impression will be found under No. (2169.).

BATTLE OF FLODDON FIELD. No. (377.).

(5045.) 222. Facsimile of old Woodcut. From Charnley, and Dodd's office, Newcastle.

An impression has been given under No. (1746.).

MITCHELL ON THE PLEASURE AND UTILITY OF ANGLING. No. (384.).

Cut on the title. From North Shields. Enumerated under Cuts for Various Societies, etc.

An impression will be found under No. (4581.).

TOM THUMB'S PLAY BOOK. No. (456.)

(5046.) 223–246. The entire Series of twenty-four Cuts, not including those enumerated elsewhere. From Angus, Charnley, and Dodd's office, Newcastle.

THE TYNE SIDE MINSTREL. No. (459.).

(5047.) 247. The Frontispiece. From Stephenson's office, Gateshead, where the Book was printed.

An impression has been given under No. (4341.).

STANZAS ON INTENDED NEW ROAD.   No. (466.).

(5048.) 248. Arms of Gateshead on the title. From Stephenson's office, Gateshead.

LIST OF KNIGHTS AND BURGESSES OF DURHAM.   No. (4361.).

(5049.) 249. Cut at p. 28. From Stephenson's office, Gateshead.

An impression will be found under No. (4361.).

THE BISHOPRICK GARLAND.   No. (490.).

(5050.) 250. Cut at p. 84. From Stephenson's office, Gateshead.

An impression is given under No. (4483.).

ALLAN RAMSAY'S GENTLE SHEPHERD.   No. (492.).

The Cuts, enumerated under other heads.

JACKSON AND CHATTO'S HISTORY OF WOOD-ENGRAVING.
No. (4376.).

(5051.) 251. Vignette at p. 634. Given me by T. H. Wilson, Esq.

An impression will be found under No. (4376.).

COLLECTION OF NEWSPAPER EXTRACTS.   No. (503.).

The Cuts, enumerated under other heads.

IMPRESSIONS FROM CHARNLEY'S WOOD BLOCKS.   No. (4406.).

A Series of one hundred and thirty-five Cuts, enumerated under various other heads.

THE HOWDY AND THE UPGETTING.   No. (512.).

Three Cuts, elsewhere enumerated.

DESCRIPTIVE AND CRITICAL CATALOGUE.   No. (518.).

Cuts elsewhere enumerated.

GREAT NEWES FROM NEWCASTLE.   No. (520.).

Cut previously enumerated.

Impressions from Dodd's Wood Blocks.   No. (527.).
Cuts elsewhere enumerated.

Impressions from Hodgson's Wood Blocks.   No. (4408.).
Cuts elsewhere enumerated.

Aristotle's Masterpiece.   No. (4494.).
(5052.) 252–255. Four Cuts.   From Kendal.

History of England.   No. (4495.).
(5053.) 256–282. The Series of twenty-seven large

Portraits of the Sovereigns.   Done for Mozley, of
Gainsborough and Derby.

The foregoing are specimens.

———————————

(5054.) 283, 284. A Set of twenty-four Alphabet
Cuts. On two Blocks. Given me by Mr. Pruddah,
of Hexham.   No. (4498.).

Impressions have been given under No. (4498.).

(5055.) 285. A Set of twenty-four Alphabet Cuts.
On one Block. From Kendal. No. (4499.).

(5056.) 286–309. A Set of twenty-four Alphabet
Cuts. On twenty-four Blocks. From York. No.
(4500.).

(5057.) 310–320. Part of an Alphabet, eighteen
Cuts. On eleven Blocks. From Akenhead's office,
Newcastle. No. (4501.). The following are specimens.

(5058.) 321. "M" for Merchant.   Alphabet Cut.
From Catnach's office.   No. (4502.).

(5059.) 322. Large Cut. Boys gathering Apples. For a 'Reading Easy.' From York. No. (4503.).

(5060.) 323. Large Cut. Boys gathering Apples. For a 'Reading Easy.' From Gloucester. No. (4504.).

(5061.) 324–380. A Series of fifty-seven Cuts in rectangular borders, for Book Illustrations. From Newcastle, Durham, Hexham, North Shields, South Shields, Sunderland, York, Darlington, North Allerton, Penrith, Appleby, Whitehaven, Whitby, etc. etc. etc. Nos. (4505.) and (4514.).

The following are specimens.

(5062.) 381–442. A Series of sixty-two Vignettes, for Book Illustrations. From the same localities. No. (4506.).

The following are specimens.

It may be questioned whether all of them should be attributed to Thomas Bewick, but of the great beauty of many there can, fortunately, be no doubt. Take, for example, the following cut of the Chillingham Bull, and the Fishing Scene introducing the distant view of Durham Cathedral.

Some of them are copies, or possibly the first draughts, of vignettes in the ' Quadrupeds ' and ' British Birds,' and it is difficult to say which are to be preferred.

Another specimen will be found at page 151 of the present Supplement.

(5063.) 443. Robinson Crusoe. From Hodgson's office. No. (4515.).

(5064.) 444, 445. Figures of a Plough and a Pitch-fork. From Hodgson's office. No. (4517.).

(5065.) 446. A Line of Music. From Hodgson's office. No. (4518.).

(5066.) 447, 448. Two Blocks of different kinds of handwriting, used in various Spelling Books. From Hodgson's office. No. (4519.).

(5067.) 449. A Mariner's Compass. From Hodgson's office. No. (4520.)

(5068.) 450–462. A Series of thirteen Plans of Coal Mines, etc., to illustrate the working and ventilation of the same. From Hodgson's office. No. (4521.).

(5069.) 463–512. A Series of fifty Geometrical Diagrams. From Hodgson's office. No. (4522.).

ADDITIONS TO WOOD BLOCKS OF BOOK PLATES.

(5070.) 513. Mr. Affleck's Book Plate. (Copper-plate.) From Mr. Dodd, Newcastle. Nos. (1936.), (4524.).

(5071.) 514. Mr. Matthew Anderson's Book Plate. From Humble's office. No. (4525.).

An impression is given under No. (4525.).

(5072.) 515. Mr. Brockett's Book Plate. No. (4529.).

(5073.) 516. Viscount Galway's Book Plate. From Durham.

(5074.) 517. Mr. Sanders' Book Plate. From Mr. Dodd, Newcastle.

An impression is given under No. (2080.).

(5075.) 518. Initial Letter T, with books. From Gateshead. No. (4542.).

(5076.) 519. A blank oval, in a border of oak, palm, etc. From Mr. Hewitson, South Shields. No. (4544.).

(5077.) 520. Tyne-side Scene, apparently intended for a Book-plate. From Mr. Reid, Newcastle. No. (4545.). An impression follows.

(5078.) 521. A blank Shield suspended in a tree among foliage. From Catnach's office. No. (4546.).

(5079.) 522–525. Four Shields of Arms. From Durham. No. (4547.).
Query if by Bewick.

ADDITIONS TO WOOD BLOCKS FOR VARIOUS SOCIETIES, COMPANIES, ETC.

Where the subject of the Block is not stated, it will be found under the Number annexed to each.

I. CLERK OF THE PEACE, DURHAM.

(5080.) 526. Seal of the Clerk of the Peace, Durham. From South Shields. No. (4553.).

EAGLE INSURANCE COMPANY.

(5081.) 527. An Eagle on a rock, inscribed "Safety." Newspaper Cut. From Akenhead's office.

FORRESTERS' LODGE.

(5082.) 528. Forresters' Arms. From North Shields. No. (4554.).

FREEMASONS' LODGE.

(5083.) 529. Freemasons' Cut. From Hexham. No. (4555.).

PARISH OF GATESHEAD.

(5084.) 530. Gateshead Parish Boundary Token, 1824. From Gateshead. No. (4556.).

(5085.) 531. "Merit", on a medal. From Gateshead. No. (4557.).

LOTTERY OFFICE.

(5086.) 532. Figure of Mercury. From Humble's office. No. (4562.).

250 *The Bewick Collector.*

NEWCASTLE ROYAL EXCHANGE ASSURANCE OFFICE.
(5087.) 533. View of the Royal Exchange. Newspaper Cut. From Humble's office. Nos. (2140.),
(4567.).

NEWCASTLE UPON TYNE FIRE OFFICE.
(5088.) 534. Figure of a Fire Engine. Newspaper
Cut. From Durham. Nos. (2157.), (4579.).

(5089.) 535. Figure of a Fire Engine. Another
very similar. Newspaper Cut. From Newcastle.

(5090.) 536. Figure of a Fire Engine. Another
very similar. From Newcastle.

NEWCASTLE WALTONIAN CLUB.
(5091.) 537. River scene, with Anglers, etc. Nos.
(384.), (2239.), (4581.).
An impression will be found under No. (4581.).

NORTHUMBERLAND LIFE BOAT.
(5092.) 538. View off Tynemouth. No. (4583.).
An impression is given under No. (4583.).

PHŒNIX FIRE OFFICE.
(5093.) 539. A Phœnix. Newspaper Cut. From
Humble's office. Nos. (2194.), (4587.).

(5094.) 540. A Phœnix. Newspaper Cut. From
Durham. No. (4589.).

(5095.) 541. A Phœnix. Newspaper Cut. From
Catnach's office. No. (4590.).

WOOLCOMBERS' COMPANY.
(5096.) 542. Woolcombers' Arms. From Humble's office. No. (4595.).

(5097.) 543. Woolcombers' Arms. From Catnach's office.

Perhaps older than Bewick.

(5098.) 544. Figure of Britannia. From Humble's office. No. (4596.).

(5099.) 545. Figure of Fortune. From Walker's office, Durham. No. (4597.).

(5100.) 546. Figure of Hope. From Humble's office. No. (4598.).

(5101.) 547. Figure of Hope. From Walker's office, Durham. No. (4599.)

(5102.) 548. Cut for some Durham Society. The Mitre and Coronet. From Akenhead's office.

ADDITIONS TO WOOD BLOCKS FOR EXHIBITIONS, ETC.

(5103.) 549. Cut apparently done for some Royal Reception. A throne under a tent, ornamented with the Royal Arms, in a border of laurel, etc. From Angus's office. An impression follows.

(5104.) 550. " Coronation " Balloon. From Catnach's office. No. (4601.).

(5105.) 551. The Cockpit. From Humble's office.
No. (4602.).

(5106.) 552. Fighting Cocks. From Akenhead's
office, Newcastle. No. (4603.).

(5107.) 553. Fighting Cocks. From Walker's office,
Durham. No. (4603.). An impression follows.

(5108.) 554. Fighting Cocks. From Walker's office,
Durham. No. (4603.).

(5109.) 555. Fighting Cocks. From Mr. Robertson, Durham. No. (4603.).

(5110.) 556. Fighting Cocks. From Mr. Atkinson, Monkwearmouth. No. (4603.). An impression
follows.

(5111.) 557. Fighting Cocks. From Mr. Henderson, North Shields. No. (4603.)..

(5112.) 558. Fighting Cocks. From Soulby's office, Penrith. No. (4603.). An impression follows.

(5113.) 559. Fighting Cocks. From York. No. (4603.).

(5114.) 560. Fighting Cocks. From Mr. Hudson, Kendal. No. (4603.).

(5115.) 561. Fighting Cocks. From Mr. Hudson, Kendal. No. (4603.).

[See also ' Newspaper Cuts.']

(5116.) 562. Descent of Sadler's Balloon. From Mr. Reid, Newcastle. No. (4607.).

(5117.) 563. Sadler's Balloon, among clouds. From Walker's office, Durham. No. (4608.).

(5118.) 564. "Theatre, North Shields." From North Shields. No. (4610.).

ADDITIONS TO WOOD BLOCKS OF RACING CUTS.

(5119.) 565. Racing Cut. From Mr. Reid, Newcastle. Nos. (2320.), (4634.).

(5120.) 566. Racing Cut. From Mr. Robertson, Durham. No. (4639.).

(5121.) 567. Racing Cut. From Mr. Ainsley, Durham. No. (4640.)

An impression is given under No. (4640.)

(5122.) 568. Racing Cut. From Mr. Reid, New-castle. No. (4641.).

(5123.) 569. Racing Cut. From Humble's office. No. (4642.).

(5124.) 570. Racing Cut. From York. No. (4643.).

(5125.) 571. Racing Cut. Small. Three horses, to the right. No border. From Newcastle.

(5126.) 572. Racing Cut. From Soulby's office, Penrith. No. (4644.).

Very similar to the vignette at page 346, but with a rectangular border.

(5127.) 573. Racing Cut. No. (4645.).

(5128.) 574. Racing Cut. From Mr. Hewitson, South Shields. No. (4646.).

(5129.) 575. Racing Cut. From Mr. Robertson, Durham. No. (4647.).

An impression is given under No. (4647.).

(5130.) 576. Racing Cut. From Chester-le-Street. No. (4648.).

(5131.) 577. Racing Cut. From Mr. Hall, Sun-derland. No. (4649.).

An impression is given at page 173.

(5132.) 578. Racing Cut. From Mr. Ainsley, Durham. No. (4650.).

An impression is given at page 173, the lower cut.

(5133.) 579. Racing Cut. From Mr. Pruddah, Hexham. No. (4651.).

- - - - - - -

ADDITIONS TO WOOD BLOCKS OF SHOP CARDS.

For the subject of each Block see the No. referred to.

(5134.) 580. " J. Catnach, Printer and Publisher." Said to have been drawn by Thurston and engraved by Thomas Bewick. From Mr. W. S. Fortey, successor to Catnach, who preceded Davison at Alnwick, and employed Bewick for several of his publications. See Nos. (158.), (201.), (217.), (221.), (231.), and (4206.). No. (4653.).

An impression follows.

(5135.) 581. " J. Catnach Printer & Publisher" From the same. No. (4654.).

(5136.) 582. Davidson's Cut. From Angus, Charnley, and Dodd's office, Newcastle.   No. (4655.).
An impression follows.

(5137.) 583. Graham's Cut. From Mr. George Pike, Alnwick. No. (4657.). This very beautiful Cut was done by Thomas Bewick, sometime about the year 1794, for a well-known Alnwick printer. The Block was purchased by Mr. Pike at the sale of the stock of Graham's son and successor. The following is an impression.

(5138.) 584. Mr. Noad's Cut. Done by Thomas Bewick for Mr. W. D. Noad, Gun-maker, of Morpeth, about the year 1810, and obtained from him. No. (4663.).

An impression has been given under No. (4663.).

(5139.) 585. Oval Border, for a Shop Card. From Humble's office. No. (4669.).

(5140.) 586. Border for a Shop Card. From Angus, Charnley, and Dodd's office.

The following is an impression.

(5141.) 587. Border for a Shop Card. From Angus, Charnley, and Dodd's office.

These borders have doubtless served for multitudes of cards of which not a single specimen is now extant.

(5142.) 588. Border for a Shop Card. From Newcastle. No. (4670.).

An impression has been given under No. (4670.).

—————————

ADDITIONS TO WOOD BLOCKS OF INVOICE
HEADS, ETC.

For the subject of each Block see the No. referred to.

(5143.) 589. " J. Blackwell and Co."   No. (2423.).
Given me by Mr. Blackwell.

An impression will be found under No. (4674.).

(5144.) 590. Bookseller's and Stationer's Cut.   From
Humble's office.   No. (4675.).

(5145.) 591. Bookseller's and Stationer's Cut.   From
Humble's office.   No. (4676.).

(5146.) 592. Bray's Cut.   From Humble's office.
No. (4677.).

(5147.) 593. Breeches Maker's Cut.   From Angus,
Charnley, and Dodd's office.   No. (4678.).

(5148.) 594. Chemist's Cut.   From Humble's office.
No. (4680.).

(5149.) 595. Chemist's Cut.   From Humble's office.
No. (4681.).

(5150.) 596. Currier's Cut.   From Stephenson's
office.   No. (4682.).

(5151.) 597. Cutler's Cut.   From Mr. Walker, Durham.   No. (4683.).

(5152.) 598. " Original Daffy's Elixir."   From Humble's office.   No. (4684.).

(5153.) 599. Grocer's Cut.   From Messrs. Griffith
and Farran.   No. (4685.).

(5154.) 600. Harris's Cut. From Messrs. Griffith and Farran, successors to Newbery and Harris. No. (4686.).

(5155.) 601. Harris's Cut. From Messrs. Griffith and Farran. No. (4687.).

An impression follows.

(5156.) 602. Harris's Cut. From Messrs. Griffith and Farran. No. (4688.).

(5157.) 603. Harris's Cut. From Messrs. Griffith and Farran. No. (4689.).

An impression is given under No. (4689.).

(5158.) 604. Harris's Cut. From Messrs. Griffith and Farran. No. (4690.).

(5159.) 605. Ironmonger's Cut. From Humble's office. No. (4691.).

(5160.) 606. Ironmonger's Cut. From Angus, Charnley, and Dodd's office. No. (4692.)

(5161.) 607. Printer's Cut. From Stephenson's office. No. (4696.).

(5162.) 608. Printer's Cut. From Soulby's office, Penrith. No. (4697.).

(5163.) 609. Shipbuilder's Cut. From Mr. Walker, Durham. No. (4698.).

(5164.) 610. Silversmith's Cut. From Catnach's office. No. (4699.).

(5165.) 611. Tea Dealer's Cut. From Catnach's office. No. (4700.).

(5166.) 612. Tea Dealer's Cut. From Mr. Ainsley, Durham. No. (4701.).

(5167.) 613. Tea Dealer's Cut. From Gateshead. No. (4702.).

(5168.) 614. Tea Dealer's Cut. From Humble's office. No. (4703.).

(5169.) 615. Tea Dealer's Cut. From Angus, Charnley, and Dodd's office. No. (4704.).

(5170.) 616. Tea Dealer's Cut. From Hodgson's office. No. (4705.).

(5171.) 617. Tea Dealer's Cut. From Messrs. Vint and Carr, Sunderland. No. (4706.).

(5172.) 618. Tea Dealer's Cut. No. (4707.).

(5173.) 619. Tea Dealer's Cut. From Angus, Charnley, and Dodd's office. No. (4708.).

An impression follows.

(5174.) 620. Tea Dealer's Cut.   No. (4709.).

(5175.) 621. Tea Dealer's Cut.   From Mr. Walker, Durham.   No. (4710.).

(5176.) 622. Tobacco Cut.   From Mr. Howe, Gateshead.   No. (4711.).

(5177.) 623. Tobacco Cut.   From Stephenson's office.   No. (4712.).

(5178.) 624. Tobacco Cut.   From Mr. Reid, Newcastle.   No. (4713.).

(5179.) 625. Tobacco Cut.   From Mr. Ainsley, Durham.   No. (4714.).

(5180.) 626. Tobacco Cut.   From Akenhead's office.   No. (4715.).

The following is an impression.

(5181.) 627. Tobacco Cut. From Mr. Harrison, North Shields. No. (4716.).

(5182.) 628. Tobacco Cut. From Stephenson's office. No. (4717.).

(5183.) 629. Tobacco Cut. From Soulby's office, Penrith. No. (4718.).

(5184.) 630. Upholsterer's Cut. From Humble's office. No. (4719.).

(5185.) 631. Upholsterer's Cut. From Akenhead's office. No. (4720.).

(5186.) 632. Upholsterer's Cut. From Catnach's office. No. (4721.).

(5187.) 633. Walker and Featherston's Cut. From Angus, Charnley, and Dodd's office. Nos. (2466.), (4722.).

An impression is given under No. (4722.).

(5188.) 634. Waxchandler's Cut. From Akenhead's office. No. (4723.).

An impression is given under No. (4723.).

(5189.) 635. Woolstapler's Cut. For this I am indebted to Mr. May, of Taunton. No. (4724.).

Query if by Bewick.

(5190.) 636. A border for an invoice. From South Shields. No. (4725.).

ADDITIONS TO WOOD BLOCKS OF TRADESMEN'S
NEWSPAPER CUTS.

For the subject of each Block see the No. referred to.

(5191.) 637. Dr. Anderson's Cut. From Humble's office. No. (4726.).

(5192.) 638. Dr. Anderson's Cut. From Hodgson's office. No. (4727.).

(5193.) 639. William Anderson's Cut. From Mr. Walker, Durham. No. (4728.).

An impression is given under No. (4728.).

(5194.) 640. Auctioneer's Cut. From Mr. Walker, Durham. No. (4729.).

An impression is given under No. (4729.).

(5195.) 641. Auctioneer's Cut. From Mr. Lackland, South Shields. No. (4730.).

(5196.) 642. Blacking Seller's Cut. From Mr. Robertson, Durham. No. (4731.).

(5197.) 643. Carrier's Cut. From Mr. Walker, Durham. No. (4732.).

(5198.) 644. Chemist's Cut. From Humble's office. No. (4733.).

(5199.) 645. Chemist's Cut. From Akenhead's office. No. (4734.).

(5200.) 646. Chemist's Cut. From Angus, Charnley, and Dodd's office. No. (4735.).

(5201.) 647. Chemist's Cut. From Catnach's office. No. (4736.).

(5202.) 648. Draper's Cut. From Mr. Walker,
Durham.   No. (4738.).

The following is an impression.

(5203.) 649. Florist's Cut.   From Humble's office.
No. (4739.).

(5204.) 650. Gardener's Cut.   From Mr. Reid,
Newcastle.   No. (4740.).

(5205.) 651. Gibson's Cut. From Humble's office.
Nos. (2494.), (4741.).   An impression follows.

(5206.) 652. Ironmonger's Cut.   A kitchen range.
From Knaresborough.

(5207.) 653. Mather's Cut. From Humble's office.
Nos. (2512), (4745.).

The following is an impression is given under No. (4745.).

(5208.) 654. Parsons' Cut. From Humble's office. Nos. (2517.), (4746.).

(5209.) 655. Piano-forte Maker's Cut. From Humble's office. No. (4747.).

(5210.) 656. Philosophical Instrument Maker's Cut. From Humble's office. No. (4748.).

(5211.) 657. B. R's Cut. From Humble's office. No. (4749.).

(5212.) 658. Saint's Cut. From Walker's office. No. (4750.).

(5213.) 659. Slack's Cut. From Hodgson's office. No. (4751.).

(5214.) 660. Slack's Cut. From Hodgson's office. No. (4752.).

(5215.) 661. Slack's Cut. From Hodgson's office. No. (4753.).

(5216.) 662. Shoemaker's Cut. From Angus, Charnley, and Dodd's office. No. (4754.).

(5217.) 663. Upholsterer's Cut. From Humble's office. No. (4758.).

(5218.) 664. Water Carrier's Cut. From Mr. Atkinson, Monkwearmouth. No. (4759.).

(5219.) 665. Woollen Draper's Cut. From Angus, Charnley, and Dodd's office. No. (4761.).

(5220.) 666. Woollen Draper's Cut. From Mr. Hall, Sunderland. No. (4762.).

ADDITIONS TO WOOD BLOCKS FOR BAR BILLS.

(5221.) 667. Blue Boar. From Angus, Charnley, and Dodd's office. No. (4765.).

(5222.) 668. Bush. From Angus, Charnley, and Dodd's office. No. (4769.).

(5223.) 669. Bush. From Humble's office. No. (4770.).

(5224.) 670. Cock. From Mr. Atkinson, Monk-wearmouth. No. (4771.).

An impression has been given under No. (4771.).

(5225.) 671. Cock. From Stephenson's office, Gateshead. No. (4772.).

(5226.) 672. Green Dragon. From Humble's office. No. (4779.).

(5227.) 673. Half Moon. From Humble's office. No. (4780.).

An impression has been given under No. (4780.).

(5228.) 674. Hat and Feather. From Humble's office. No. (4781.).

(5229.) 675. Hen and Chickens. From York. No. (4782.).

Probably older than Bewick.

(5230.) 676. Horse and Groom. From Humble's office. No. (4786.).

Of this also an impression is given under No. (4786.).

(5231.) 677. Key. From Catnach's office. No. (4788.).

(5232.) 678. King's Head. From Humble's office. No. (4789.).

(5233.) 679. The Lamb. From Akenhead's office. No. (4790.).

(5234.) 680. Nag's Head. From Humble's office. No. (4796.).

(5235.) 681. Queen's Head. From Mr. Walker, Durham. No. (4798.). An impression follows.

(5236.) 682. Red Lion. From Angus, Charnley, and Dodd's office. No. (4799.).

(5237.) 683. Red Lion. From Humble's office. No. (4800.).

(5238.) 684. Red Lion. From Mr. Harrison, North Shields. No. (4801.).

(5239.) 685. Red Lion. From Hargrove's office, Knaresborough.

(5240.) 686. Red Lion. From Catnach's office. No. (4802.).

(5241.) 687. R. Robinson's Cut. Black Bull Inn, Gateshead. From Angus, Charnley, and Dodd's office. Nos. (2602.), (4803.).

An impression is given under No. (4803.).

(5242.) 688. Royal Oak.   From Hargrove's office, Knaresborough.

(5243.) 689. Royal Oak.   From Kendal.   No. (4804.).   An impression follows.

(5244.) 690. The Salutation.   From Kendal.   No. (4806.).

(5245.) 691. Saracen's Head.   From Akenhead's office.   No. (4807.).

(5246.) 692. Stag.   From Humble's office.   No. (4811.).

(5247.) 693. Star.   From Akenhead's office.   No. (4812.).

(5248.) 694. Sun.   From Humble's office.   No. (4814.).

(5249.) 695. Swan.   From Kendal.   No. (4815.).

(5250.) 696. William West's Cut, White Hart, Chester - le - Street.   From Humble's office.   Nos. (2623.), (4817.).

Used also in Warden's Spelling Book, No. (4235.).   An impression has been given under No. (4817.).

Additions to Royal Arms, etc.

(5251.) 697. Royal Arms. From Mr. Reid, Newcastle. No. (4909.).

An impression is given under No. (4909.).

(5252.) 698. Royal Arms. From Angus, Charnley, and Dodd's office. No. (4910.).

(5253.) 699. Royal Arms. From Angus, Charnley, and Dodd's office. No. (4910.).

(5254.) 700. Royal Arms. From Humble's office.

Perhaps older than Bewick.

(5255.) 701. Royal Arms. From Humble's office.

(5256.) 702. Royal Arms. From Humble's office.

(5257.) 703. Royal Arms. From Humble's office.

(5258.) 704. Royal Arms. From Humble's office.

(5259.) 705. Royal Arms. From Mr. Atkinson, Monkwearmouth. No. (4910.).

(5260.) 706. Royal Arms. From Mr. Hewitson, South Shields. No. (4910.).

(5261.) 707. Royal Arms. From Mr. Hewitson, South Shields. No. (4910.).

(5262.) 708. Royal Arms. From Mr. Pruddah, Hexham. No. (4910.).

(5263.) 709. Royal Arms. From Mr. Walker, Durham. No. (4910.).

(5264.) 710. Royal Arms. From Catnach's office. No. (4910.).

(5265.) 711. Prince of Wales' Plume. From Akenhead's office.   No. (4911.).

(5266.) 712. Prince of Wales' Plume. From Akenhead's office.   No. (4912.).

(5267.) 713. Star and Garter.   From Akenhead's office.   No. (4913.).

(5268.) 714. Star and Garter.   From Akenhead's office.   No. (4914.).

ADDITIONS TO ARMS OF NEWCASTLE AND GATESHEAD.

(5269.) 715. Arms of Newcastle.   From Humble's office.   No. (4917.).

(5270.) 716. Arms of Gateshead. From Mr. Howe, Gateshead.   No. (4919.).

ADDITIONS TO WOOD BLOCKS FOR NEWSPAPER CUTS.

(5271.) 717. Heading of the Newcastle Courant Newspaper.   No. (3011.).

An impression has been given under No. (4920.).

I am indebted for the possession of this most noble series of Blocks to the kindness of my friends the Messrs. Blackwell and Rutherford, proprietors of the Newcastle Courant. They were executed, as required, for the celebrated Newspaper of that name, and for the gratification, as the Artist was well-aware, of his friends and neighbours. By singularly good fortune these interesting relics were preserved in the office, when they might at any moment have been destroyed as useless, until, after upwards of sixty years, they have been allowed to enrich my Collection, and to take their place by the side of so many other treasures similarly rescued from accident, and transferred to what may be hoped to be a safe asylum.

(5272.) 718. Heading of the Newcastle Courant. No. (3012.)–(3015.).

An impression has been given under No. (4921.).

(5273.) 719. Heading of the Newcastle Courant. No. (3016.).

An impression has been given under No. (4922.).

(5274.) 720. Heading of the Newcastle Courant. No. (3017.)–(3020.).

An impression follows.

(5275.) 721. Heading of the Newcastle Courant. No. (4924.)–(4927.).

An impression has been given under No. (4927.).

(5276.) 722. Heading of the Newcastle Courant. A fragment. Generally similar to the last, but with the steeple of St. Nicholas on the right instead of the left of the Castle, and on the other side of the shields a tree instead of a windmill. From impressions in various numbers of the Courant, I find that it was used during the autumn of 1809, but was then cracked as the fragment indicates. No. (4928.).

An impression follows.

(5277.) 723. Heading of the Newcastle Courant. No. (4929.).

An impression will be found under No. (4929.).

(5278.) 724. Heading of the Newcastle Courant. No. (4930.).

(5279.) 725. Heading of the Newcastle Courant. Nos. (3028.)–(3031.), (4931.).

(5280.) 726. Heading of the Newcastle Courant. No. (4932.).

(5281.) 727. Heading of the Newcastle Advertiser. No. (3043.). From Humble's office. No. (4933.).

An impression is given under No. (4933.).

(5282.) 728. Heading of a Newspaper. From Mr. Hodgson. No. (4934.).

(5283.) 729. Fighting Cocks. No. (3155.)–(3160.). From Akenhead's office. No. (4935.).

An impression will be found under No. (4935.).

(5284.) 730. The Devil and Horseman. No. (3191.). From Humble's office. No. (4937.).

An impression is given under No. (4937.).

(5285.) 731. Figure of Mercury. No. (3202.). From North Shields. No. (4939.).

(5286.) 732. Figure of Mercury. No. (3206.). From North Shields. No. (4941.).

(5287.) 733. Figure of Mercury. No. (3205.). From North Shields. No. (4942.).

(5288.) 734. Figure of Fame. From Mr. Walker, Durham. No. (4944.).

(5289.) 735. Figure of Fame. From Mr. Walker, Durham. No. (4945.).

(5290.) 736. Figure of Justice. In an oval. From Angus's office. No. (4946.).

(5291.) 737. A Pointer. From Humble's office. No. (4947.).

(5292.) 738. A Ship. From Akenhead's office. No. (4948.).

(5293.) 739. A Ship. From Hodgson's office. No. (4948.).

An impression follows.

(5294.) 740. A Ship. From Walker's office. No. (4948.).

T

(5295.) 741. A Ship.   From Walker's office.   No. (4948.)

(5296.) 742. A Ship.   From Walker's office.   No. (4948.)

ADDITIONS TO CUTS FOR BROADSIDES.

(5297.) 743. Family Accommodation Mangle. No. (3257.).   From Blair's office, Morpeth.   No. (4958.).

(5298.) 744. Portrait of Dr. "Willm Markham." From Akenhead's office.

(5299.) 745. Portrait of Dr. Markham (?)   From Akenhead's office.

Not improbably done for a Frontispiece to Spelling Books.

(5300.) 746. Portrait of a Clergyman.   From Kendal.   No. (4964.).

(5301.) 747. Female Figure and Tombstone.   From Gateshead.   No. (4965.).

(5302.) 748. The Tame Duck.   From Catnach's office.   No. (4975.).

An impression has been given under No. (4975.).

(5303.) 749. The Bald Cavallier.   From Mr. Reid, Newcastle.   No. (4966.).

(5304.) 750. The Fight with the Devil.   From Mr. Reid, Newcastle.   No. (4967.).

(5305.) 751. View of an Execution.   No. (3268.). From Mr. Ainsley, Durham.   No. (4959.).

(5306.) 752. The Hangman, etc. No. (3539.). From Angus's office. No. (4961.).

(5307.) 753. A Ship. From Angus's office. No. (4962.).

An impression follows.

This and the following were done for Broadside Notices of Ship Auctions, Voyages, etc.

(5308.) 754. A Ship. From Angus's office. No. (4962.).

(5309.) 755. A Ship. From Angus's office. No. (4962.).

(5310.) 756. A Ship. From Angus's office. No. (4962.).

(5311.) 757. A Ship. From Humble's office. No. (4962.).

(5312.) 758. A Ship. From Akenhead's office. No. (4962.).

(5313.) 759. A Ship.   From Akenhead's office.
No. (4962.)

(5314.) 760. A Ship.   From Akenhead's office.

(5315.) 761. A Ship.   From Mr. Walker, Durham.   No. (4962.).

(5316.) 762. A Ship.   From Mr. Walker, Durham.   No. (4962.).

(5317.) 763. A Ship.   From Mr. Hall, Sunderland.
No. (4962.).

(5318.) 764. A Ship.   From Mr. Hall, Sunderland.
No. (4962.).

(5319.) 765. A Ship. From Mr. Henderson, North
Shields.   No. (4692.).

(5320.) 766. A Ship.   From Mr. Hewitson, South
Shields.   No. (4962.).

(5321.) 767. A Ship.   From Mr. Lackland, South
Shields.   No. (4962.).

(5322.) 768. A Ship. From Blair's office, Morpeth.
No. (4962.).

(5323.) 769. Horse and Groom.   From Humble's
office.   No. (4963.).

> This and the following were done for Broadside Notices of Horse
> Sales, etc.

(5324.) 770. Horse and Groom.   From Humble's
office.   No. (4963.).

(5325.) 771. Horse and Groom.   From Akenhead's
office.   No. (4963.).

> An impression follows.

(5326.) 772. Horse and Groom. From Mr. Walker, Durham. No. (4963.).

(5327.) 773. Horse and Groom. From Mr. Hewitson, South Shields. No. (4963.).

(5328.) 774. Horse and Groom. From Gateshead. No. (4963.).

(5329.) 775. Horse and Groom. From Gateshead. No. (4963.).

ADDITIONS TO BLOCKS OF MISCELLANEOUS CUTS.

VIEWS.

(5330.) 776. View of Jarrow. From Mr. Reid, Newcastle. No. (4994.).

(5331.) 777. View of Tynemouth Priory. From Catnach's office. No. (4995.).

(5332.) 778. View of Durham Cathedral, from the river. From Akenhead's office. No. (4996.).

(5333.) 779. View of York Minster. From Akenhead's office.

(5334.) 780. View of Sunderland Bridge. From
Humble's office. No. (4999.).

> Probably, as the following Views of the Bridge, done for some
> Sunderland tradesman.

(5335.) 781. View of Sunderland Bridge. From
Mr. Hall, Sunderland. No. (5000.).

(5336.) 782. View of Sunderland Bridge. From
Mr. Walker, Durham. No. (5001.).

> An impression has been given under No. (5001.).

(5337.) 783. View of Sunderland Bridge. From
Mr. Walker, Durham. No. (5002.).

(5338.) 784. View of a Manufactory. From North
Shields. No. (5003.).

> Perhaps for the head of an invoice.

(5339.) 785. View of ———? From Soulby's
office, Penrith. No. (5004.).

> An impression follows.

(5340.) 786–791. A Series of six Views. From Catnach's office. No. (5004.).

Two specimens follow.

(5341.) 792. A House. From Mr. Henderson, North Shields. No. (5005.).

(5342.) 793. A House. From Mr. Henderson, North Shields. No. (5006.).

Perhaps done for Sale Announcements.

ANIMALS.

(5343.) 794. Kyloe Ox. From Mr. Walker, Durham. No. (5013.).

(5344.) 795. Lancashire Bull. From Stephenson's office, Gateshead. No. (5013.).

(5345.) 796. Group of Sheep. From Catnach's office. No. (5013.).

(5346.) 797. Lion. From Messrs. Griffith and Farran. No. (5013.).

The following is an impression.

(5347.) 798. The Nondescript Animal of the History of Quadrupeds, Ed. 1820, p. 293. From Humble's office. No. (5013.).

(5348.) 799. Greyhound Fox. From Catnach's office. No. (5013.).

(5349.) 800. Bull Dog. From Catnach's office. No. (5013.).

The following is an impression.

(5350.) 801. Hare. From Stephenson's office. No. (5013.).

(5351.) 802. Kangaroo. From Mr. Harrison, North Shields. No. (5013.).

An impression follows.

(5352.) 803. Goldfinch. From Catnach's office. No. (5013.).

(5353.) 804. Mackerel. From Akenhead's office.

(5354.) 805. Carp. From Stephenson's office. No. (5013.).

ADDITIONS

TO

APPENDIX.

——◆——

PORTRAITS OF THOMAS BEWICK.

Thomas Bewick. Meyer after Ramsay. No. (3879.).
(5355.) 1. Another impression. *On vellum.*

> Only seven printed. An error occurs in my description of this
> portrait under the No. cited. It is on copper, and not on
> steel. The artist, who was a nephew of John Hoppner, R.A.,
> died soon after the completion of the work.
> Given me by Mr. E. Pearson.

(5356.) 2. 1. Thomas Bewick. Meyer after Ramsay. A photographic reduced copy. From Mr. E. Pearson.

(5357.) 2. 2. Another.

MISCELLANIES.

(5358.) 1. Cover for the Mourning at Thomas Bewick's Funeral.

" Mr. James Burnett Mourner for the Funeral of the late Mr. Thos. Bewick. Mr. Burnett is requested to join the Funeral Procession at Ovingham on Thursday the 13th Novr. Inst. about 1 o'clock."

(5359.) 2. Autograph Letter of W. C. Trevelyan, Esq. dated " Wallington October 29th [1820] to " Mr. Bewick, St. Nicholas Ch. Yd. Newcastle on Tyne ", containing various orders, and communicating an extract from a letter from Norfolk on the Kestrel's hawking after cockchafers.

Mr. Brand's Bookplate. No. (3949.).

(5360.) 3. 1. Another impression.

(5361.) 3. 2. Another.

(5362.) 4. Letter of Mr. J. T. W. Bell, with cuttings from the Newcastle Newspapers, announcing the sudden death, and giving a sketch of the life of Mr. W. Garret.

(5363.) 5. Portrait of E. H. Baily, sculptor.

(5364.) 6. 1. " A Book Of Wood-Cuts. Cut & Printed by Wm Garret Newcastle."

8vo. A pamphlet consisting of a title and fifteen leaves, each of the latter containing a rough woodcut.

Given me by Mr. Garret.

(5365.) 6. 2. Another copy.

Purchased of Mr. Rutland, Newcastle.

(5366.) 7. On Illicit Love. Written among the Ruins of Godstow Nunnery, near Oxford. By John Brand, A.B. Of Lincoln College, Oxford.

Newcastle Upon Tyne: Printed by T. Saint, for J. Wilkie, No. 71, St. Paul's Church-yard, London; J. Fletcher, Oxford: and W. Charnley, Newcastle. MDCCLXXV.

> 4to. Pp. 20. With a view, on the title, of Godstow Nunnery, engraved on copper by Ralph Beilby.
> Fine copy, half bound in green morocco.

(5367.) 8. An Address To the Subscribers For the History and Antiquities Of the County Palatine Of Durham: With a Sketch of the Materials from whence The intended Publication is compiled. By William Hutchinson, F.A.S. 1784.

> 4to. Pp. 10. With an engraving on copper of a seal, said to be by Ralph Beilby, Bewick's master.
> Good copy, in its original cover.

(5368.) 9. Mr. E. Pearson's Book Catalogues. On large 4to paper.

> Several of these are embellished with impressions from the original Blocks, lent to the publisher for the purpose of illustration. Among them are those of "The Foolish Stag," Mr. Bigge's cut of "Liberty," and two of Saint's woodcuts. All of these Blocks are now in my possession.

WORKS OF PUPILS.

View of St. Nicholas' Church, Newcastle. By Charlton Nesbit. No. (3975.)

(5369.) 1. Another very beautiful impression. From Mr. Robert Robinson, of Newcastle.

(5370.) 2. A Bacchanalian Scene.

" And long may the sons of Anacreon, etc."

Said to be by Luke Clennell.

INSERENDA.

——◆——

Books and Pamphlets.

(5371.) 1. "The Newcastle Journal" Newspaper [for 1776.].

It contains, besides the cuts mentioned in No. (3032.), some clever advertisement cuts of Fighting Cocks, Stolen or Strayed, etc.

(5372.) 2. The History Of the Castle, Town, and Forest Of Knaresborough, With Harrogate, And its Medicinal Waters. [etc.] The Third Edition, Improved. By E. Hargrove.

York: Printed by W. Blanchard and Co. for the Author. M.DCC.LXXXII.

18mo. Pp. iv, 144. With cut of the Cornwall Arms, the Arms of the Priory of Knaresborough, at p. 51. The Cut is now in my possession, and an impression will be found under No. (5021.).

Good copy, in old calf.

(5373.) 3. The Honours of the Table, Or, Rules for Behaviour during Meals; [etc.] The Second Edition.

London. Printed for the Author, at the Literary-Press, No. 62, Wardour-street, Soho; and all Booksellers in Town and Country. M,DCC,XCI.

> 12mo. Pp. 120. With various engravings of joints, poultry, fish, etc. At the back of the title is the Trusler Coat of Arms, mentioned in his Memoir, No. (210.), pp. 12, 13.
> Very fine copy, in its original cover.

(5374.) 4. On the Conduct of Man to Inferior Animals, &c. No. (97.).

> Another very fine copy, in old calf.

(5375.) 5. A Father's Legacy to His Daughters. By the late Dr. John Gregory, of Edinburgh.

Manchester, Printed and sold at the Office of G. Nicholson, 9, Spring-gardens. Sold also by T. Knott, 47, Lombard-street; and Champante & Whitrow, Jewry-street, London. Anno 1797.

> 18mo. Pp. 38. With cut on the title.
> Fine copy, in old calf.

(5376.) 6. Moral Philosophy, &c. On the Duties of the Young, by Dr. Hugh Blair. [etc.]

Manchester, Printed at the Office of G. Nicholson, No. 9, Spring-gardens. Sold by T. Knott, No. 47, Lombard-street; and Champante & Whitrow, Jewry-street, London. Anno 1798.

> 18mo. Pp. 27. With cut on the title.
> Fine copy, in old calf.
> (See the note to No. (4095.).)

(5377.) 7. Moral Philosophy, &c. On Human Pursuits. [etc.]

Manchester, Printed at the Office of G. Nicholson,

No. 9, Spring-gardens. Sold by T. Knott, No. 47, Lombard-street ; and Champante & Whitrow, Jewry-street, London.   Anno 1798.

18mo.   Pp. 28.   With cut on the title.

Fine copy, in old calf.

(5378.) 8. The Economy of Human Life. By Robert Dodsley.

Manchester, Printed at the Office of G. Nicholson, No. 9, Spring-gardens. Sold by T. Knott, No. 47, Lombard-street ; and Champante & Whitrow, Jewry-street, London.   Anno 1798.

18mo. Pp. 40. With cut on the title, "W. M. Craig, del. T. Bewick, sculp."

Fine copy, in old calf.

(5379.) 9. Ancient Ballads, Songs, and Poems. No. (135.). .

Another copy.

(5380.) 10. Ballads & Songs.   Scotish.

Printed and sold by G. Nicholson, Poughnill, near Ludlow.   Sold also, in London, by H. D. Symonds, Paternoster-row ; Champante & Whitrow, Aldgate ; [etc.]   [n. d.]

18mo.   Pp. 56.   With an " Emblematic Vignette in the Title-page, designed by Mr. W. M. Craig and engraved by Mr. T. Bewick."

Good copy, half bound.

This together with the foregoing article forms a volume which belonged to " Elizabeth Pigot, 1808."   The lady was a friend of Lord Byron, and is given as the authority for some verses on the flyleaf being in the poet's autograph.

(5381.) 11. Miscellaneous Poems.

Manchester Printed at the Office of W. Shelmer-
dine and Co. No. 5, Hanging-Ditch.   [n. d.]

> 12mo.   Pp. xii, 145.   With a few insignificant cuts, the authen-
> ticity of which is very doubtful.
>
> Good copy, in its original boards.

(5382.) 12. Wood Engravings From Tommy Trip.
No. (4037.).

> A doubt has been expressed of the genuineness of these impres-
> sions, but, as it appears to me, without any foundation.   They
> were purchased of Mr. Lynch of Newcastle, and were in the
> old stock of his predecessor Mr. Farren.
>
> Another fine copy, in old calf.

(5383.) 13. Songs, Comic and Satyrical.   By George
Alexander Stevens.   A New Edition, Corrected.

London: Printed for G. Kearsley, at Johnson's-
Head, No. 46, Fleet-Street, [etc.]   M,DCC,LXXXVIII.

> 12mo.   A reprint of No. (7.).   With the cut of the ' Poculum
> Poculorum,' at p. 7.
>
> Good copy, in old calf.

(5384.) 14. Captain Cook's Voyages Round the
World. [etc.]

Newcastle: Printed by M. Brown, At the Bible, in
the Flesh-Market.   M.DCC.XC.

> 8vo.   2 vols.   Vol. I. pp. xxvi, 1022.   Vol. II. pp. 796.   With
> many copper-plates, among which are some with the inscrip-
> tion " Beilby & Bewick Sculp."
>
> Good copy, in old calf.

(5385.) 15. A Compendious History of England,
[etc.]

London: Printed for G. G. and J. Robinson, W.
Bent, and J. Scatcherd.   1794.

12mo. Pp. xii, 249. With full length portraits of the Sovereigns, which appear to be the work of John Bewick. They
are improved copies of those used in Carnan's publications.
Good copy, in old calf.

(5386.) 16. Fables By the late Mr. Gay.   In One
Volume Complete.

London : Printed for T. Longman, B. Law, [etc.]
E. Newbery, and J. Walker.   1796.

12mo.   Pp. viii, 232.   A reprint of Nos. (4056.), (63.), etc.
Fair copy, in old calf.

(5387.) 17. The British Champion; Or, Honour
Rewarded. [etc.]

York : Printed for Wilson, Spence, & Mawman.
[Price Fourpence.]   [n. d.]

18mo.   Pp. 95.   With a frontispiece and forty-two cuts, several
of which are repeated.   Very similar to No. (4091.).
Fine copy, in its original Dutch paper boards.

(5388.) 18. The Hermit : Or, The Unparalleled
Sufferings and Surprising Adventures Of Philip Quarll,
[etc.] With a Curious Frontispiece. The Tenth
Edition.

London : Printed for the Booksellers. M,DCC,XCVII.

12mo. Pp. 240. With a frontispiece attributed to John Bewick,
but in my opinion with little or no proof.
Good copy, in old calf.

(5389.) 19. The History Of the Castle, Town, and
Forest Of Knaresbrough, [etc.] The Fifth Edition.

York : Printed by Wilson, Spence, and Mawman,
[etc.]   1798.

12mo. Pp. 4, 382. With the cut of the Cornwall Arms at p. 82.
Good copy, half-bound.

(5390.) 20. The New Harrogate Guide: [etc.]
Knaresbrough: Printed at Hargrove's Office: And
Sold by J. Hargrove, Harrogate, and Knaresbrough;
Longman, Hurst and Co. London; And by the Book-
sellers of York, Leeds, &c. &c.   [n. d.]

> 12mo. Pp. 135. With several Cuts said to be by Thomas
> Bewick, of which I possess the original Blocks.
> Good copy, in its original paper cover.

(5391.) 21. The Oracles: Containing Some Par-
ticulars of the History Of Billy and Kitty Wilson;
[etc.]
London: Printed for E. Newbery, at the Corner of
St. Paul's Church-Yard, By E. Rider, No. 36, Little-
Britain.   [Price Sixpence.]   [n. d.]

> 18mo. Pp. 124. With thirteen cuts to which I give the benefit
> of a doubt. They are exactly similar in style to those of No.
> (4108.), of which a specimen is given at p. 31, and are I be-
> lieve the work of Lee, to whom without doubt the great
> majority of the cuts in Newbery's publications, ordinarily
> attributed to John Bewick, are to be referred.
> Very fine copy, in its original Dutch boards. It belonged to
> " Mary Burchell, Feby. 15th. 1803."

(5392.) 22. Poems and Ballads.
Huddersfield: Printed by Brook and Lancashire,
for J. Todd, York; [etc.]   [n. d.]

> 12mo. Pp. 63. With cuts used by the same publishers in Mel-
> moth's Beauties of British Poetry, No. (174.), whose claim to
> be the work of Thomas Bewick is very doubtful.
> Good copy, in old calf.

(5393.) 23. An Excellent Collection of Popular
Songs: viz. 1. The Gypsie Laddie. [etc.]   [n. d.]

Edinburgh : Printed for the Booksellers in Town
and Country.

> 12mo.   Pp. 8.   With cut on the title of the Piper, occurring at
>   page 26 of Crosby's Caledonian Musical Repository, No. (144.).
> Good copy, as published.

(5394.) 24. Fables Of Æsop And Others : [etc.]
By Samuel Croxall, D.D. [etc.]   A New Edition.
London : Printed for J. Brambles, A. Meggitt,
and J. Waters, By H. Mozley, Market-Place, Gainsborough.   1804.

> 12mo.   Pp. xxiv, 336.   With cut on the title, said to be by
>   Thomas Bewick.
> Good copy, in old calf.

(5395.) 25. Scarronides, Or Virgil Travestie, [etc.]
By Charles Cotton, Esq.   The Thirteenth Edition.
London : Printed by J. Galton, Little Eastcheap ;
And Sold by The Booksellers in Town and Country.
1804.

> 12mo.   Pp. 122.   With the four large cuts.
> Good copy, in its original boards.

(5396.) 26. The Waes o' War; Or, The Upshot O'
the History o' Will and Jean.   In Four Parts. [etc.]
Newcastle upon Tyne : Printed by J. Mitchell,
Dean-Street.   1804.

> 12mo.   Pp. 23.   With a cut at p. 19, used by J. Mitchell in
>   others of his publications.
> Good copy, in its original paper cover.

(5397.) 27. Impressions of Wood Blocks in the
possession of J. Mitchell of Newcastle.   [n. d. but
about 1805.]

8vo. Consisting of seventy-six leaves, with two hundred and twenty-nine cuts, printed on one page only of each leaf, without title or pagination. It contains the cuts of Relph's Poems, the 'Charms of Literature,' and other publications of Mitchell's Press. Many of the original Blocks of this most rare book are now in my possession.

Fine copy, in its original cover. It formerly belonged to Mr. Thomas Bell, and has his book-plate.

(5398.) 28. The York Herald [for 1805].

This Newspaper contains several cuts of Fighting Cocks, similar in character to Nos. (3138.), (3143.), (3149.), [etc.].

(5399.) 29. A Modern Delineation Of the Town & Port Of Kingston Upon Hull: [etc.]

Hull: Printed by and for W. Turner, Silver street; And sold by all the Booksellers in Hull, & the County of York. 1805.

12mo. Pp. ii, vi, 114, vi, xiv. With a few insignificant cuts. Good copy, in its original boards.

(5400.) 30. The Economy Of Human Life. By Robert Dodsley.

Printed and sold by G. Nicholson, Poughnill, near Ludlow. [etc.] 1805.

18mo. Pp. 39. With a cut on the title, "designed by Mr. W. M. Craig, and engraved on wood by Mr. T. Bewick." Good copy, in its original wrapper.

(5401.) 31. The Child's Monitor, [etc.] By John Hornsey, [etc.]

York: Printed by T. Wilson and R. Spence, High-Ousegate: [etc.] 1806.

12mo. Pp. xxiv, 240. With a few insignificant vignettes, used

in Gay's Fables, No. (14.), Select Fables, No. (24.), etc.
etc.

Good copy, in old sheep.

(5402.) 32. Fables By the late Mr. Gay. [etc.]
London : Printed by Savage and Easingwood, For
J. Johnson ; [etc.] and J. Harris.　1806.

18mo.　Pp. vi, 224.　A reprint of No. (4056.), etc.
Good copy, in old calf.

(5403.) 33. Flowers of British Poetry.　No. (281.).
Another very fine copy, in its original boards.

(5404.) 34. The Leeds Intelligencer [for 1807, etc.].

This Newspaper has the Arms of Leeds for a Heading, probably
　by Bewick.　Among the various Cuts for Advertisements, in
　the rest of which it would appear that he had no hand, is one
　for the Newcastle Fire Office, similar to those described under
　Nos. (2151.), (2154.), (2157.), etc., which is doubtless his
　work.

(5405.) 35. A Compendious History of England,
[etc.]
London : Printed for J. Johnson, [etc.]　1807.

12mo.　Pp. xii, 274.　A reprint of No. (5385.).
Good copy, in old calf.

(5406.) 36. Scarronides : Or, Virgil Travestie. [etc.]
By Charles Cotton, Esq.　Compared with former Edi-
tions.
Durham : Printed and sold by G. Walker, Sold also
By all the Booksellers in Town and Country.　1807.

12mo.　Pp. 144.　With vignettes at pp. 61 and 144.
Good copy, in its original boards.

(5407.) 37. Furnass' Practical Surveyor. No. (236.).

Another very fine copy, in its original boards and uncut, as it left
the publisher.

(5408.) 38. A History Of the Earth And Animated
Nature: [etc.]   Embellished with upwards of One
Hundred Elegant Copper-Plates Engraved on Purpose
Representing some Hundreds of Figures.   In Two
Volumes.

Alnwick: Printed at the Apollo Press, By and for
W. Davison.   And Sold by all the Booksellers in
England and Scotland.   1810.

12mo.   Vol. I. pp. viii, 278.   Vol. II. pp. vi, 272.   The engravings on copper are not by Bewick, but the volumes contain four vignettes, used in the Poems of Burns and others of
Davison's publications, of which I possess the original Blocks.
Fine copy, in old sheep.

(5409.) 39. British Picture Book, Of Beasts, [etc.]
Alnwick: Printed by and for William Davison.

12mo.   This and the two following contain a selection of the
copperplate engravings of the previous article, and the covers
are embellished with various cuts from Davison s Natural Histories and other works.
Good copy, as published.

(5410.) 40. British Picture Book, Of Birds, [etc.]
Alnwick: Printed by and for William Davison.

12mo.   With Bewick's cuts on the cover.
Good copy, as published.

(5411.) 41. Alnwick Picture Book, [etc.]   Consisting of Beasts, Birds, &c. [etc.]

Alnwick: Printed by and for William Davison.

12mo.   With Bewick's cuts on the cover.
Good copy, as published.

(5412.) 42. Fables By the late Mr. Gay. [etc.]
London: Printed by J. M'Creery, Black Horse-
Court; For J. C. and J. Rivington; [etc.] J. Harris;
[etc.]   1810.

18mo.   Pp. 224.   A reprint of No. (4056.), etc.
Good copy, in old calf.

(5413.) 43. The Caledonian Musical Repository:
A Choice Selection Of Esteemed Scottish Songs,
Adapted for The Voice, Violin, and German Flute.
Edinburgh: Published by Oliver & Boyd, Cale-
donian Press, Netherbow.   1811.

Large 12mo.   Pp. 286.   Apparently the same as No. (144.),
with a different title.
Very fine copy, on large paper, in its original boards, and uncut.

(5414.) 44. Dr. Goldsmith's Abridgment Of his
History of England, [etc.]
Gainsborough: Printed by and for Henry Mozley.
1812.

12mo.   With the large Heads of the Sovereigns, as in Nos.
(299.), (3797.), and (4302.).
The original Blocks, which are in my possession, are those enumerated under Nos. (4495.), (5053.), but the oval line borders
have been removed.
Good copy, half-bound.

(5415.) 45. The Poetical Works Of Oliver Goldsmith.   No. (271.).

Another fine copy, in its original paper cover.

(5416.) 46. Divine Songs, Attempted in Easy Language, For the Use of Children.   By I. Watts, D.D.
[etc.]   Adorned with appropriate Wood Cuts, by T.

Bewick, of Newcastle, to impress more lasting ideas of each Subject on the Mind, than can be attained by those in common Use.

York: Printed by and for Thomas Wilson and Son, High-Ousegate. 1812.

18mo. Pp. vi, 72. With thirty-eight cuts.

A very beautiful copy of this rare little book, a reprint of No. (4112.), in purple morocco, gilt.

(5417.) 47. Fables Of Æsop And Others: [etc.] By Samuel Croxall, D.D. [etc.]   A New Edition.

Gainsborough: Printed by and for H. Mozley. 1814.

12mo. Pp. xxiv, 336. With frontispiece and cut on the title, attributed to Thomas Bewick.

Good copy, in old calf.

(5418.) 48. A New Garland Of Excellent Songs, [etc.]

South Shields: Printed by J. Paxton, Market Place. [n. d.]

12mo. Pp. 8. With cut of a Ship, thought to be by Thomas Bewick, on the title.

Good copy, uncut.

(5419.) 49. Charnley's Book Catalogues.

Newcastle: 1816–1824.   Nos. (349.), (3804.)– (3806.), (4318.).

8vo. With various cuts by Thomas Bewick.

Fine copies, bound in one volume, half-morocco.

(5420.) 50. Dialogues Consisting of Words of One Syllable only; [etc.]

London : Printed for J. Harris, Corner of St. Paul's
Church Yard, 1816.

 18mo. Pp. 136. With a number of cuts, of which those at
  pp. 84 and 93 are by John Bewick.
 Fine copy, in its original half-binding.

(5421.) 51. Newcastle Remembrancer, And Free-
man's Pocket Companion, [etc.] By J. C.
Printed at the Newcastle Press, By and for J. Clark,
Bookseller, Newgate Street, And may be had of all
other Booksellers. 1817.

 8vo. Pp. viii, 136. With frontispiece portrait of Clark, and his
  cut " J. C." on the title.
 Good copy, in old calf.

(5422.) 52. Fables Of Esop And Others : Trans-
lated into English, [etc.] By Samuel Croxall, D.D.
Late Archdeacon of Hereford.
Derby : Printed by and for Henry Mozley. 1819.

 12mo. Pp. xxiv, 329, vii. With many cuts, all of which are
  older than Thomas Bewick except the frontispiece and a cut on
  the title, which are used in No. (5417.), and are possibly by him.
 Fair copy, in its original binding.

(5423.) 53. The Shipwreck, A Poem : By William
Falconer. With The Life of the Author, &c. [etc.]
North Shields : Printed and Sold by T. Appleby.
1819.

 18mo. Pp. vii, 120. With a very fine frontispiece of the Shipwreck, and a vignette of a ship at sea at p. v, of the latter of
  which the original Block is in my possession.
 Good copy, half-bound.

(5424.) 54. The Caledonian Muse : No. (434.).

Another very fine copy, in its original boards, and uncut.

(5425.) 55. Thomas Curry, [etc.]   No. (444.).

Another copy, in its original paper cover.

" M". Fawcett, Cockermouth, With the respects of the Author."

(5426.) 56. Declaration Of the Objects of The Newcastle Upon Tyne Society For Promoting the Gradual Abolition of Slavery Throughout the British Dominions.

Newcastle upon Tyne : Printed by W. A. Mitchell, St. Nicholas' Church-Yard.   1823.

8vo.   Pp. 11.   With cut of the Kneeling Negro, No. (3446.), on the title.

Good copy, in its original cover.

(5427.) 57. Fables By the late Mr. Gay. [etc.]
London : Printed for C. and J. Rivington ; [etc.] J. Harris and Son ; [etc.]   1823.

18mo.   Pp. 224.   A reprint of No. (4056.), etc.

Good copy, in half-calf.

(5428.) 58. Local Records ; Or, Historical Register Of Remarkable Events, [etc.]   By John Sykes.
Newcastle : Printed for, and sold by, John Sykes, Bookseller.   MDCCCXXIV.

Imp. 8vo.   Pp. xiv, 372.

Fine copy, on large drawing paper, of which only twenty copies were done, and in its original boards.   It formerly belonged to Mr. Fenwick, and has his book-plate.

(5429.) 59. First Report Of The Committee Of the Newcastle upon Tyne Society for the Gradual Abolition of Slavery, [etc.]

Newcastle on Tyne : Printed at the Mercury Press
By W. A. Mitchell.   1825.

> 8vo.   Pp. 28.   With cut of the Kneeling Negro, No. (3446.),
> on the title.
>
> Good copy, in its original cover.

(5430.) 60. The Comical History Of the King and
the Cobler. [etc.]
Edinburgh : Printed for the Booksellers in Town
and Country.   [n. d.]

> 18mo.   Pp. 24.   With a cut on the title, exactly similar in style
> to that in No. (4338.), and which I am willing to believe to
> be by Thomas Bewick.
>
> Good copy, as published.

(5431.) 61. The New Robinson Crusoe; An Instructive and Entertaining History.
Dublin : Printed by B. Smith, 46, Mary-Street.
1827.

> 18mo.   Pp. 180.   With the frontispiece of No. (19.), etc., which
> has the appearance of having been inserted as an additional
> illustration, for imparting a value to an otherwise worthless
> book ; but, as I have never seen another copy, I am unable to
> speak to this point with certainty.
>
> Good copy, half-bound.

(5432.) 62. Time's Telescope For 1829; [etc.]
London : Printed for the Assignees of Sherwood and
Co. 20, Paternoster Row.   1829.

> 12mo.   Pp. xviii, 428.   With various cuts then belonging to the
> publishers, among which are several from Scott's British Field
> Sports, No. (410.), at pp. 92, 147, 195, 289, 368, 417, etc., of
> which I now possess the original Blocks.
>
> Good copy, in its original boards.

(5433.) 63. The Modern Farrier; [etc.] By A. Lawson. Fourteenth Edition. Illustrated with numerous Engravings.

Newcastle upon Tyne: Printed and Published by Mackenzie and Dent, St. Nicholas' Church-Yard. 1830.

8vo. Pp. iv, 616. With a vignette at page 292, thought to be by Thomas Bewick.
Good copy, in old calf.

(5434.) 64. A Concise View Of Colonial Slavery. [etc.]

Newcastle: Printed by T. and J. Hodgson, For the Newcastle Ladies Anti-slavery Association. 1830.

8vo. Pp. 20. With cut of the Kneeling Negro, No. (3441.), on the title.
Good copy, in its original cover.

(5435.) 65. Declaration And Address Of the Durham Society For the Universal Abolition of Slavery.

Durham: Fewster and James, Sadler-street. 1836.

8vo. Pp. 11. With the cut of the Kneeling Negro, No. (3446.), on the title.
Good copy, in its original cover.

(5436.) 66. The Entertaining Naturalist, [etc.] Illustrated by upwards of Three Hundred and Fifty Accurately Drawn Figures, Finely Engraved in Wood by Bewick, Harvey, Whimper, And others. [etc.] By Mrs. Loudon.

London: Henry G. Bohn, York Street, Covent Garden. 1843.

12mo. Pp. xliii, 532. With many cuts by Thomas Bewick, of which I possess the original Blocks.

Fair copy, in cloth. It formerly belonged to the printer of the volume, Mr. Rickerby, and has his autograph on the title.

(5437.) 67. The British Angler's Manual, [etc.] By T. C. Hofland, Esq. New Edition, Revised and Enlarged By E. Jesse, Esq. [etc.]

London : H. G. Bohn, York Street, Covent Garden. 1848.

12mo. Pp. xxxii, 448. With three cuts attributed to Thomas Bewick, two of which were used in the Fisher's Garlands.

Good copy, in its original cloth boards.

(5438.) 68. Adelaide ; Or, The Shepherdess of the Alps.

Newcastle-on-Tyne : W. R. Walker, Royal Arcade. [n. d.]

18mo. Pp. 24. With cut on the last page, given under No. (5077.), from the original Block in my possession.

Good copy, as published.

(5439.) 69. The Complete Angler, [etc.] Of Izaac Walton and Charles Cotton. [etc.]

London : Henry G. Bohn, York Street, Covent Garden. MDCCCLVI.

12mo. Pp. xxi, 498. With seven cuts attributed to Thomas Bewick, three of which were used in No. (5437.).

Good copy, in its original cloth boards.

(5440.) 70. Local Records ; [etc.] By John Latimer.

Newcastle : Published at the Chronicle Office, 42, Grey Street. 1857.

8vo. Pp. iv, 420. With cut used in the 'Reedwater Minstrel,'
No. (243.), etc., and others also used in other publications.
Good copy, in cloth boards.

**(5441.) 71. A Collection Of Right Merrie Gar-
lands For North Country Anglers. [etc.] No. (530.).**

Another and very beautiful copy on large paper, of which very
few were done. Each copy was numbered, and the present is
No. 3.

4to. Half-bound in green morocco, top edge gilt, others uncut,
as issued by the publisher, from whom it was purchased.

**(5442.) 72. A Pretty Book of Pictures. No.
(4412.).**

Another very beautiful copy, in red morocco.

**(5443.) 73. 1. Mr. Edwin Pearson's Catalogue of
Books and Wood Engravings By or Relating to Thomas & John Bewick, To be Sold by Messrs. Sotheby,
Wilkinson & Hodge, on Wednesday, 10th of June,
1868, & following day.**

8vo. Pp. v, 67.

(5444.) 73. 2. Another copy.

Imp. 8vo. One of a few copies taken off on large paper. It
contains several engravings by Thomas Bewick, as well as
others not by him, together with a fresh title and the imprint
" London. Printed by J. Davy & Sons, 137, Long Acre. 1868."

--- --- --- --- ---

PROOFS OF CUTS IN MISCELLANEOUS BOOKS.

**(5445.) 1. A Large Folio Volume, thus described
in pp. 10 and 11 of the last Article :—**

" BEWICK'S (T. AND J.) EARLIEST AND RAREST
WOOD ENGRAVINGS. TWELVE HUNDRED
WOOD ENGRAVINGS by Thomas and John Bewick,

engraved for Thomas Saint of Newcastle, and Wilson and Spence of York, previous to the years 1784 and 1810, including all the beautiful Cuts used in New Lottery Book of Beasts and Birds, 1771, Child's Horn Book, 1770, Moral Instructions, 1772, Select Fables, 1776, Youth's Instructive and Entertaining Story Teller, 1778, A Pretty Book of Pictures, or Tommy Trip's History of Beasts and Birds, 1779, Gay's Fables, 1779, Select Fables, 1784, *with the borders to each cut* (a most beautiful series of cuts), Philip Quarll, Robinson Crusoe, Little Jack, Cock Robin, Red Riding Hood, Cries of London and York, Robin Hood's Garland, Poetical Fabulator, Holy Bible in miniature, Full-length Kings and Queens of England, with heraldic shields, Fairing or Golden Toy, the Picture Book, Goody Two Shoes, Death of Abel, Watts' Divine and Moral Songs, Happy Family, Tommy Tagg's Poems, Patty Primrose, several editions of Æsop's Fables, Dodsley in Miniature, The Happy Family, Lessons of Truth, Morning Amusements or Tales of Quadrupeds, Afternoon Amusements or Tales of Birds, Christmas Tales, York Toy, Peter Painter's Pretty Picture Book, and a whole host of Juvenile Toy Books now almost extinct; "and though many of these publications were of an extremely trivial nature, the Wood Engravings with which they were embellished caused them at this early period (1770 to 1810) to have an extensive sale," they have delighted thousands of "Little Masters and Misses" in years gone by, and are *nearly unknown* to the "Bewick Collector" of the present day, but will be instantly recognized and admired on examination as the early handy-work and designs of these great Masters.

1200 beautiful Cuts, the earliest designs and handy-work (unaided by pupils) of these great artists. "Set No. 1" of only seven sets printed (*see vellum guarantee on title*), portrait and cuts, neatly mounted in handsome folio volume, EXCESSIVELY RARE."

Purchased at Mr. E. Pearson's Sale, 10th June, 1868.

TRADESMEN'S NEWSPAPER CUTS.

(5446.) 1. John Craike, Woollen Draper. A curtain. Dated Newcastle, June 2. 1801.

(5447.) 2. J. and W. Middleton, Linen Drapers. A cornice and curtain. Dated Sunderland, Nov. 18. 1801.

BAR BILLS.

(5448.) 1. Henry Sunderland, Turk's Head Inn, Bigg-Market, Newcastle. A Turk's Head in a circle within a square, the corners black.

NEWSPAPER CUTS.

(5449.) 1. Heading of the Newcastle Courant. A cutting. Dated August 8. 1801.

This is the cut given under No. (4674.), and should have been placed among the series of headings. It was used in the Courant in the year 1801, as well as by Mr. Blackwell for his invoices.

(5450.) 2. Heading of the Newcastle Courant. No. (4929.). A cutting. Dated Feb. 13. 1830.

(5451.) 3. 1. Heading of the Newcastle Advertiser. Arms of Newcastle. A cutting. Dated March 21. 1801.

(5452.) 3. 2. Another impression. A cutting. Dated June 6. 1801.

(5453.) 4. Blank oval for the insertion of a letter. In a tree by a river-side, on the bank of which is inscribed " Tyne."

X

NOTE

On the variations in individual copies of the same Editions of the ' Quadrupeds' and 'British Birds.'

There are several variations observable in individual copies of the ' Quadrupeds' and 'British Birds.' For example, in the 1st vol. of the 1st Ed. of the latter work, 1797, the back of the last leaf, as I have stated in the B. C., p. 47, is sometimes blank, sometimes with an advertisement of the Third. and sometimes with one of the Fourth Ed. of the ' Quadrupeds.' In some copies also of the same volume, the Sea Eagle is with, and in others without, " Wycliffe 1791 ". Other instances are known to Collectors.

The late Mr. W. Garret furnished me with the explanation of this difficulty. He was the foreman, it will be remembered, of the House from which the work was published, and was an eyewitness of Bewick's frequent practice of altering the forms when his volumes were in press, whenever he thought that some alteration was desirable, or had some later information to communicate. As related in Mr. Chatto's sketch of him in Jackson's ' Hist. of Wood Engraving,' p. 600, " When any of his works were in the press, the first thing Bewick did each morning, after calling at his own shop, was to proceed to the printers to see what progress they were making, and to give directions to the pressmen about printing the cuts." It was during these visits that the alterations were made. The discovery, therefore, of the variations referred to does not militate against the genuineness of any volume in which they are found to occur.

The most direct proof of the actual issue of the copies of the 1st vol. of the ' Birds,' 1st Ed., is the un-inked state of the cut at p. 285. Three days after that of publication, all the copies remaining unsold were daubed with ink at the page referred to, in the endeavour to obliterate an offensive vignette.

APPENDIX I.

BOOKS PRINTED FOR T. CARNAN, SUCCESSOR TO J. NEWBERY, IN ST. PAUL'S CHURCHYARD.

[For some remarks on these Books see the Preface].

The Fairing: or, Golden Toy for Children.   Price *6d.*

A Little Pretty Pocket-Book, intended for the Instruction of Little Master Tommy and Pretty Miss Polly.   Price *6d.*

The Infant Tutor; or an Easy Spelling-Book for Little Masters and Misses.   Price *6d.*

Juvenile Trials for Robbing Orchards, [etc.]   Price *6d.*

Be Merry and Wise: or, The Cream of the Jests, and Marrow of Maxims.   Price *6d.*

The Holy Bible Abridged: or, The History of the Old and New Testament.   Price *6d.*

The History of Little Goody Two-Shoes.   Price *6d.*

The Lilliputian Magazine: or, The Young Gentleman and Lady's Golden Library.   Price One Shilling.

A Collection of Pretty Poems.   Price *1s.*

Short Histories for the Improvement of the Mind.   Price *1s.*

The Museum for Young Gentlemen and Ladies.   Price *1s.*

The Newtonian System of Philosophy.   Price *1s.*

A Spelling Dictionary of the English Language.   Price *1s.*

The New Testament adapted to the Capacities of Children. Price *1s.*

The History of the Life, Actions, Sufferings, and Death of our Blessed Saviour.   Price *1s.*

An History of the Lives of the Apostles and Evangelists.　Price 1*s.*

An History of the Lives of the Fathers of the Church.　Price 1*s.*

A plain and concise Exposition of the Book of Common Prayer. Price 1*s.*

The Twelfth Day Gift.　Price 1*s.*

The Important Pocket Book.　Price 1*s.*

The Circuit of Human Life.　Price 1*s.*

Fables for Youth.　Price 2*s.*

The Adventures of Telemachus.

APPENDIX II.

BOOKS PRINTED FOR E. NEWBERY, THE CORNER OF ST. PAUL'S CHURCHYARD, LONDON.

(The same Series, with few exceptions, was issued by J. HARRIS, *Successor to* E. NEWBERY).

[For some remarks on these Books see the Preface.]

PRICE ONE PENNY EACH.

Holiday Entertainments, or The Good Child's Fairing.

History of The Little Boy found under a Hay-cock.

Hermit of the Forest, and The Wandering Infants.

The Foundling, or The History of Lucius Stanhope.

Rural Felicity, or The History of Thomas and Sally.

Lovechild's Golden Present to all Little Masters and Misses.

The Royal Alphabet, or Child's Best Instructor.

The Father's Gift, or The Way to be Wise and Happy.

The Sister's Gift, or The Naughty Boy Reformed.

The Brother's Gift, or The Naughty Girl Reformed:

History of Tommy Careless, or The Misfortunes of a Week.

History of a Doll.

The Holiday Spy.

PRICE TWO PENCE.

Elmina, or The Flower that Never Fades.

The Visits of Tommy Lovebook to his Young Friends.
The History of Jacky Idle and Dicky Diligent.
History of Tommy Titmouse.
The Flights of a Lady Bird.
The Village Tatlers, or Anecdotes of The Rural Assembly.
The Fortune Teller, by the Renowned Dr. Hurlothrumbo.
The History of Little King Pippin, to which is added, The Story of The Children in the Wood.
Virtue and Vice.
The Entertaining Traveller.
Tom Thumb's Exhibition.
The Hobby Horse; or Christmas Companion.
Robin Goodfellow, A Fairy Tale, written by a Fairy.
Little Tales for Little People.

PRICE THREE PENCE.

Three Instructive Tales.
Little Moralists, or The History of Amintor and Florella.
Little Wanderers.
The Mountain Piper.
False Alarms.
The Adventures of Master Headstrong and Miss Patient.
The Juvenile Biographer.
A Bag of Nuts ready Cracked, by Thomas Thumb, Esq.
The Puzzling Cap; being a Choice Collection of Riddles, in Familiar Verse; with a Curious Cut to each.
Royal Primer.

PRICE SIX PENCE.

Juvenile Rambles through the Paths of Nature.
The Oracles, containing Some Particulars of the History of Billy and Kitty Wilson, &c.
The New Robinson Crusoe.
The History of the Family at Smiledale.
Youthful Recreations, or The Amusements of a Day.
Sinbad the Sailor.
Life and Adventures of a Fly.

Triumph of Good Nature.

The Youthful Jester, or Repository of Wit.

Adventures of a Silver Penny.

Adventures of a Silver Three Pence.

The Toy Shop, or Sentimental Preceptor.

The Adventures of Peter Wilkins.

The History of Tommy Play-love and Jacky Love-book.

The First Book for Children, or Reading made Easy.

The Royal Guide.

The Ladder to Learning.　Step I. II. III.

The Cries of London.

The Sugar Plumb.

Vice in its Proper Shape.

The Adventures of Captain Gulliver.

Gulliver's Instructive Lessons.

The Lilliputian Library; or Gulliver's Museum.

The Poetical Flower Basket.

Mr. Winlove's Collection of Entertaining Stories.

Mr. Winlove's Lectures on Moral Subjects.

Mr. Telltruth's Natural History of Four-footed Beasts.

Mr. Telltruth's Natural History of Birds.

A Short Introduction to Geography.

The Pocket Bible.

The History of the Enchanted Castle.

Little Robin Redbreast, A Collection of Songs.

A Description of The Tower of London.

A Description of Guildhall, with The History of the Giants.

An Accurate and Historical Account of St. Paul's Cathedral.

A Description of Westminster Abbey.

Spiritual Lessons for Children to Read and Learn to be Wise.

Pilgrim's Progress.　Part I. II. III.

Fables of the Wise Æsop.

History of the White Cat.

PRICE EIGHT PENCE.

The Infant's Friend, Part I.　A Spelling Book, by Mrs. Lovechild.

PRICE NINE PENCE.

Mother Goose's Tales.
Parsing Lessons for Young Children.   By Mrs. Lovechild.
Mother Bunch's Fairy Tales.
Pilgrim's Progress, Parts I. II. III.

PRICE ONE SHILLING.

The History of the Davenport Family.
The Life and Adventures of Joe Thomson, abridged.
The Bible in Miniature.
A New Spelling Dictionary.
The History of Joseph Andrews, abridged.
The History of Tom Jones, abridged.
Pamela, or Virtue Rewarded, abridged.
Clarissa, or the History of a Young Lady, abridged.
Choice Collection of Riddles, by P. Puzzlewell.   Parts I. II. III.
The Florist or Poetical Nosegay.
Museum for Young Gentlemen and Ladies.
The History of a Pin.
The History of Young Edwin and Little Jessy.
Reading Lessons, by Mrs. Lovechild, being Part II of the Infant's Friend.
A Short Introduction to English Grammar, by Mr. Davis.
The Village Matron.
Choice Scraps, Historical and Biographical.
The Sunday Miscellany.
Moral Sketches for Young Minds.
Polite Academy.
Filial Duty Recommended and Enforced.
Lives of the Admirals, Part I. and II.
The Crested Wren.   By Edward Augustus Kendall.
Sir Charles Grandison, abridged.
The Adventures of Gil Blas, abridged.
Anecdotes of a Little Family.

PRICE ONE SHILLING AND THREE PENCE.

Parsing Lessons for Elder Pupils.   By Mrs. Lovechild.

Price One Shilling and Six Pence.

Geography for Children.

A New History of France, by the Rev. Mr. Cooper.

A New History of the Grecian States, by the same.

A New History of England, by the same.

The same in French.

A New Roman History, by the same.

The History of North America, by the same.

The History of South America, by the same.

The Tutor, or Epistolary Guide.

Jeu des Fautes.　Par Gaultier.

The Faithful Contrast.　By Mrs. Hurry.

The Paternal Present.

History of Prince Lee Boo.

The Paths of Virtue.

Poetical Blossoms, by the Rev. Mr. Cooper.

Lord Chesterfield's Maxims.

Newbery's Familiar Letter Writer.

Constantio and Selima, a Fairy Tale.

The New Children's Friend.

Keeper's Travels in Search of his Master.

Moral Amusement.

Youthful Portraits.

Newtonian System of Philosophy by Tom Telescope.

Memoirs of a Sparrow.

Price Two Shillings.

The Amusing Instructor.

Choice Emblems, Natural, Historical, Fabulous, and Moral.

The Fables of Flowers.

Life of Henry IV of France.

Chronicle of the Kings of England.

Characters of the Kings of England.

Pity's Gift.

Historical Beauties.　By Mrs. Pilkington.

The History of England on Cards.

A Geographical Description of England on Cards.

A Geographical Description of the World on Cards.
Tales for Youth.
The Looking Glass for the Mind, or Intellectual Mirror.
The Blossoms of Morality.

APPENDIX III.

Books Printed and Sold by John Marshall, No. 17, Queen Street, Cheapside, and No. 4, Aldermary Church Yard, Bow-Lane, London.

[For some remarks on these Books see the Preface].

The Happy Family; or, Memoirs of Mr. and Mrs. Norton. Price 6*d*.

The Life and Perambulation of a Mouse. By M. P. 2 vols. Price 1*s*.

The Village School; or, A Collection of Entertaining Histories. By M. P. 2 vols. Price 1*s*.

Jemima Placid. By S. S. Price 6*d*.

The Holiday Present. Containing Anecdotes of Mr. and Mrs. Jennet and their Little Family. By M. P. Price 6*d*.

Memoirs of a Peg-Top. By S. S. Price 6*d*.

The Adventures of a Pincushion. By S. S. 2 vols. Price 1*s*.

First Principles of Religion. By M. P. 2 vols. Price 1*s*.

Sermons to Children. Price 6*d*.

Mrs. Norton's Story Book. Price 6*d*.

The Renowned History of Primrose Prettyface. Price 6*d*.

The Orphan; or, The Entertaining History of Little Goody Goosecap. By Toby Teachem. Price 6*d*.

Christmas Tales for the Amusement and Instruction of Young Ladies and Gentlemen in Winter Evenings. By Solomon Sobersides. Price 6*d*.

History of England, in Verse. Price 2*d*.

The English Hermit; or the Life and Adventures of Philip Quarll.　Price 6*d.*

Little Timothy Ticklepitcher's Tales and Fables.　Price 6*d.*

The Imperial Spelling-Book, by C. Bolton.　Price 9*d.*

Lilliputian Spectacle de la Nature.　By Mrs. Teachwell.　3 vols. Price 2*s.* 3*d.*

The Fairy Spectator; or, The Invisible Monitor.　By Mrs. Teachwell and Her Family.　Embellished with a Frontispiece. Price 1*s.*

The Juvenile Tatler.　By a Society of Young Ladies under the Tuition of Mrs. Teachwell.　Embellished with a Frontispiece. Price 1*s.*

Moral and Instructive Tales.　With an Engraved Title and Frontispiece.　Price 1*s.*

La Bagatelle.　2 vols.　Price 3*s.*

Letters from a Mother to Her Children.　By M. P.　Price 2*s.*

Dialogues and Letters on Morality, Oeconomy, and Politeness. By M. P.　3 vols.　Price 3*s.*

Poems on Various Subjects.　Price 1*s.*

Anecdotes of a Boarding School; or, An Antidote to the Vices of those Useful Seminaries.　By M. P.　2 vols.　Price 2*s.*

School Occurrences.　Supposed to have arisen among a Set of Young Ladies under the Tuition of Mrs. Teachwell, and to be recorded by one of them.　Price 1*s.*

The Infant Lawyer.　Price 1*s.*

William Sedley; or, The Evil Day Deferred.　By S. S.　Price 2*s.* 6*d.*

A Father's Advice to His Children.　By M. P.　Price 2*s.*

A Course of Lectures for Sunday Evenings.　By S. S.　2 vols. Price 3*s.*

A Clear and Concise Account of the Origin and Design of Christianity.　By M. P.　2 vols.　Price 2*s.*

The Good Child's Delight.　By M. P.　Price 4*d.*

The Histories of More Children than One; or, Goodness better than Beauty.　By M. P.　Price 4*d.*

Short Conversations; or, An Easy Road to the Temple of Fame. By M. P.　Price 4*d.*

The History of a Great Many Little Boys and Girls, Four and Five Years of Age. By M. P. Price 4*d.*

Familiar Dialogues for the Instruction and Amusement of Children Four and Five Years of Age. By S. S. Price 4*d.*

Dramatic Pieces. By P. I. 3 vols. Price 6*s.*

Fables in Monosyllables, by Mrs. Teachwell. Price 2*s.*

A Father's Advice to his Son. By M. P. Price 2*s.*

The Conversations of Emily. Translated from the French by Madame la Comtesse d'Epignay. 2 vols. Price 7*s.*

The Birth Day Present; or, Nine Days' Conversation between a Mother and a Daughter. Price 1*s.*

Midsummer Holidays; or, a Long Story. Price 1*s.*

May Day; an Anecdote of Miss Lydia Lively. Price 1*s.*

Cobwebs to Catch Flies. 2 vols. Price 2*s.*

Rational Sports. In Dialogues passing among the Children of a Family. Price 1*s.*

The Rational Dame; or, Hints towards supplying Prattle for Children. Price 1*s.* 6*d.*

The Rotchfords; or, The Friendly Counsellor. By M. P. 2 vols. Price 3*s.*

The Footstep to Mrs. Trimmer's Sacred History. By A. C. Price 1*s.* 6*d.*

The Female Guardian. By Mrs. Teachwell. Price 1*s.* 6*d.*

Fables, by Mrs. Teachwell. Price 1*s.*

Juvenile Correspondence. By Mrs. Teachwell. Price 1*s.* 6*d.*

School Dialogues for Boys. By Mrs. Teachwell. 2 vols. Price 4*s.*

Little Stories for Little Folks, in Easy Lessons of One, Two, and Three Syllables. By M. P. Price 4*d.*

APPENDIX IV.

BOOKS OF THE VALUE OF ONE SHILLING AND UNDER,
PRINTED AND PUBLISHED BY T. WILSON AND R.
SPENCE, HIGH OUSEGATE, YORK.

(Many of them were subsequently reprinted by WILSON & SON,
Successors of WILSON & SPENCE, *also of High Ousegate, York).*

[For some remarks on these Books see the Preface].

TWELVEPENNY BOOKS :—

    Happy Family.
    Anecdotes for Children.
    Visible World.
    History of Pamela.
    Letter Writer.
    Æsop's Fables.
    Lessons of Truth.
    Hymns and Moral Songs.
    Morning's Amusement.
    Afternoon's Amusement.
    Mother Goose's Tales.
    Christmas Tales,
    Robin Hood's Garland.
    Dodsley in Miniature.
    Moore's Female Fables.
    Mental Instruction.
    Thomas Lovechild's Reading Easy.
    Thomson's Seasons.
    Anecdotes of the Clairville Family.
    Indian Cottage.
    Gregory's Legacy.
    Gay's Fables.
    Whole Duty of Woman.

Dictionary of Love.
Death of Abel.
Economy of Life.
Rochefoucault's Maxims.
Wisdom in Miniature.
Tommy Tagg's Poems.
Queen Mab.
The Mirror.

SIXPENNY BOOKS :—

Pretty Poems.
Prettiest Book for Children.
Primrose Prettyface.
Memoirs of a Peg Top.
Pleasing Moralist.
Be Merry and Wise.
Enchanted Castle.
Holy Bible abridged.
History of the Bible.
Children's Manual of Prayers.
Tom Trip's History of Birds and Beasts.
Food for the Mind.
Gulliver's Travels.
Robinson Crusoe.
Sleeping Beauty in the Wood.
Picture Exhibition.
Goody Goosecap.
Sandford and Merton.
History of the Goodville Family.
The Fairing, or Golden Toy.
Canary Bird.
The Sugar Plum.
Mrs. Pleasant's Story Book.
Holiday Present.
Pleasing Fabulist.
Tales of Past Times, by Mother Goose.

Goody Two Shoes.
Babes in the Wood.
Philip Quarll.
Valentine Gift.

FOURPENNY BOOKS:—

Charms for Children.
Primrose Bank.
Memoirs of Little Personages.
Mother Shipton's Legacy.
Chronicle of the Kings of England.
The British Champion.

THREEPENNY BOOKS:—

Child's First Book.
Tom Thumb's Play Book.
Mother's Gift.
Looking Glass.
Instructive Miscellany.
New Royal Primer.

TWOPENNY BOOKS:—

Lilliputian Masquerade.
King Skilful.
Golden Present.
Master Charles and Miss Kitty.
Fables for the Instruction of Youth.
Child's Delight.
The New Year's Gift.
Easter Offering.
Easter Gift.
Winter's Amusement.
Honey Jug.

PENNY BOOKS:—

Golden Plaything.
History of Little Francis.

Tom Thumb.
Tom Thumb's Toy.
Picture Gift.
Picture Alphabet.
Golden Alphabet.
Whittington and his Cat.
Goody Two Shoes.
Tommy Two Shoes.
Riddle-Book.
Robinson Crusoe.
Babes in the Wood.
Robin Hood.
Cock Robin.
Cinderella.
House that Jack Built.
Parent's Best Gift.
Sister's Gift.
Fables.
The Looking Glass.
Enchanted Castle.
Giant Grumbo.
London Cries.
Serious Address and Catechisms.

Many of these, as already remarked, were subsequently reprinted by Wilson and Son, with the addition of the following Shilling Books :—

The Holy Bible in Miniature.
The Poetical Fabulator.
Ellinor ; or the Young Governess.

APPENDIX V.

A Century of Books and Pamphlets, the Illustrations of which have been incorrectly attributed to Thomas or John Bewick.

[As stated in the Preface, the articles in the following list are not given with any view of exhausting the subject, but are merely selected from some thousands of volumes for their plausible appearance, and that the Bewick Collector may be instructed as to the kind of books to which, how interesting soever in other ways, he would do well to refuse a place in his Collection.]

1. Choice Emblems, Natural, Historical, Fabulous, Moral and Divine, [etc.]
London: Printed for George Riley, in Curzon Street, May Fair. MD,CC,LXXII.

    12mo. Pp. xii, 192. The first edition of a celebrated book, to the third edition of which I believe that John Bewick contributed some cuts. See the note to No. (13.).

2. Introductory Grammatical Remarks On the Persian Language [etc.] By George Hadley, Esq.; [etc.]
Bath: Printed by R. Crutwell, for the Author; [etc.] MDCCLXXVI.

    4to. Pp. 216. With a vignette, containing the " R. C." of the printer, at p. 42.

3. The Adventures of Telemachus, [etc.]
London: Printed for T. Carnan, in St. Paul's Church Yard. MDCCLXXXI.

    18mo. Pp. xviii, 305. With oval cuts, by the engraver of those in 'Choice Emblems' noticed above.

4. The Circuit of Human Life: A Vision. The Second Edition, Corrected.

London : Printed for T. Carnan, at Number 65, in St. Paul's Church-Yard. (Price One Shilling.) [n. d. about 1783.]

18mo. Pp. 116. With a frontispiece.

5. The History of Little Goody Two-Shoes; [etc.]
London : Printed for T. Carnan, Successor to Mr. J. Newbery, in St. Paul's Church-Yard. M DCC LXXXIII. Price Six-Pence, bound.

24mo. Pp. 158. With a frontispiece and many cuts, by Carnan's usual artist.

6. Fables of Æsop, and others : Translated into English. [etc.] By Samuel Croxall, D.D. Late Archdeacon of Hereford. The Thirteenth Edition.
London : Printed for J. F. and C. Rivington, [etc.] 1786.

12mo. Pp. xxxiiii, 329, 7.

7. Juvenile Trials For Robbing Orchards, [etc.]
London : Printed for T. Carnan, In St. Paul's Church-Yard. M DCC LXXXVI. (Price Sixpence.)

Sm. 18mo. Pp. xxii, 124. With a frontispiece and sixteen cuts, by the artist who executed the engravings in others of Carnan's publications.

8. The Testament Of the Twelve Patriarchs, The Sons of Jacob. [etc.]
Sold by the Booksellers in Great Britain, Ireland and America. 1787.

12mo. Pp. 96. With a frontispiece of "The Tewlve (*sic*) Sons of Jacob."

9. The History of Pamela; or, Virtue Rewarded. [etc.]
London : Printed for E. Newbery, at the Corner of St. Paul's Church-Yard. Price 1s. [n. d. but about 1792.]

Small 18mo. Pp. 168. With a frontispiece.

10. The Death of Abel. In Five Books. [etc.]
Printed, and Sold, by Brodbelt, Knaresborough. MDCCXCIII.

Square 18mo. Pp. iv, 160. With twelve oval cuts.

11. Belisarius.   By M. Marmontel.   A New Edition.
London : Printed for Vernor and Hood, Birchin-Lane, Cornhill ; and Ogilvy and Speare, Middle Row, Holborn.   MDCCXCIV.

12mo.   Pp. viii, 259.   With a cut on the title, and others at pp. viii and 289, by Vernor and Hood's usual artist.

12. The Journey of Joseph Jolly : [etc.]   By Nick Nightcap.
London : Printed and sold by R. Carpenter, No. 16, Aldgate High-Street ; [etc.]   M.DCC.XCIV.

18mo.   2 vols.   Vol. I. pp. 135.   Vol. II. pp. 136.   With a frontispiece to each volume.

13. Junius.
London : Printed for R. Floyer, Strand.   1795.

18mo.   In two vols.   With cut at the end of the Index.

14. Lessons For Youth, Selected For the Use of Ackworth, And Other Schools.
London : Printed and Sold by Darton and Harvey, No. 55, Gracechurch-Street.   M,DCC,XCV.

18mo.   Pp. 204.   With a few insignificant cuts.

15. The British Miscellany For Youth ; [etc.]
London : Printed for R. Snagg, No. 13, Brunswick Street, near New Surry Street, [etc.]   [n. d. but about 1795 ?]

12mo.   With six cuts.

16. The Village Orphan ; [etc.]
London : Printed by C. Whittingham, For Longman and Rees, Paternoster Row.   Price 2s. 6d.   [n. d.]

18mo.   Pp. 140.   With cuts in the style of those in Mrs. Pilkington's ' Historical Beauties.'   (See the Preface to this volume.)

17. Sermons By Laurence Sterne, [etc.]
London : Printed for J. Rivington.   1796.
Berwick, Printed by John Taylor.

18mo.   Pp. vi, 284.   With cuts on the title, and at pp. 47, 118, and 147.

18. Jeu des Fautes [etc.]   Par M. L'Abbé Gaultier.
A Londres : Chez P. Elmsley, dans le Strand ; & chez E. Newbery, St. Paul's Church-yard.   M.DCC.XCVI.

   18mo.   Pp. xii, 106.   With a frontispiece in the style of the
   cuts in ' Joseph Jolly,' ' Pamela,' ' Circuit of Human Life,'
   etc., already mentioned.

19. An Easy Introduction To the Arts and Sciences : [etc.]   By
R. Turner, Jun. LL.D. [etc.]   The Sixth Edition, [etc.]
London : Printed for C. Dilly, J. Johnson, [etc.]   1797.

   18mo.   Pp. xi, 252.   With rough figures of Beasts and Birds,
   hardly worthy of a place even in this Appendix.

20. Solitude ; [etc.]   Written Originally By M. Zimmerman.
London : Printed for the Associated Booksellers, Vernor & Hood,
J. Cuthell, J. Walker, Lackington, Allen & Co. J. Nunn, and Dar-
ton & Harvey.   1797.

   12mo.   In two vols., the second printed in 1799.   Vol. I. pp.
   xi, 303.   Vol. II. pp. 338, 26.   With cuts by Vernor and
   Hood's usual artist.   (See the Preface to this volume.)

21. The Letters of Junius.   In Two Volumes.   A New Edition.
London : Printed for Vernor and Hood in the Poultry.   1798.

   18mo.   With cuts by Vernor and Hood's usual artist.   (See the
   Preface to this volume.)

22. Discourses on a Sober and Temperate Life.   By Lewis Cor-
naro, [etc.]
London : Printed for Cadell and Davies, J. Scatcherd, and Vernor and Hood.   1798.

   18mo.   Pp. xii, 166.   With two cuts by the engraver of those in
   Mrs. Pilkington's ' Historical Beauties,' etc.   (See the Preface
   to this volume.)

23. Anomaliae.   Being Desultory Essays On Miscellaneous Subjects.
Whitby.   Printed by T. Webster.   1798.

   12mo.   Pp. vi, 272.   With a cut on the title.

24. The Dramatic Works Of David Garrick, [etc.] In Three Volumes.

London : Printed for A. Millar, Strand.   M,DCC,XCVIII.

12mo.   With cuts by the same artist, and similar to those in the works of Foote, issued by the same publisher.

25. Visions in Verse, [etc.]

London, Printed for Vernor and Hood. J. Cuthill; [etc.]   1798.

Small 8vo.   Pp. 144.   With cuts at pp. 70 and 144, by Vernor and Hood's artist before referred to.

26. The Scotish Gallery; or, Portraits of Eminent Persons of Scotland : [etc.]   By John Pinkerton.

London : Printed for E. Harding, No. 98, Pall-Mall.   1799.

Imp. 8vo, unpaged.   With a few vignettes at the end of some of the Memoirs.

27. Solitude; Written originally by J. G. Zimmerman.

London : Printed by T. Maiden, Sherbourne-Lane, For Vernor and Hood, J. Cuthell, [etc.]   1799.

Small 8vo.   With cuts by the artist of the "Associated Publishers."

28. Beauties of Saint Pierre : By Edward Augustus Kendall.

London : Printed for Vernor and Hood ; No. 31, Poultry. [etc.] 1799.

12mo.   Pp. xxxiii, 203.   With a cut on the title by Vernor and Hood's artist.

29. Studies Of Nature.   By M. de St. Pierre.   Abridged from the Translation Of Henry Hunter, D.D.   Third Edition.

London : Printed for C. Dilly, in the Poultry.   M DCC XCIX.

12mo.   Pp. viii, 424.   With a cut on the last page.

30. The Entertaining and Affecting History Of Prince Lee Boo : [etc.]

London : Printed for the Proprietors; [etc.]   [n. d. but about 1799.]

18mo.   Pp. 127.

31. An English Spelling Book, [etc.]   By Arthur Masson, A.M., Teacher of Languages.   The Seventeenth Edition, [etc.]

Air: Printed by J. & P. Wilson, 1800.

12mo. Pp. xiv, 168. With twelve Fable cuts.

32. Solitude, Written Originally by J. G. Zimmerman. [etc.]

London: Printed by Thomas Maiden, Sherbourne-Lane, For Vernor and Hood; J. Cuthell, [etc.] 1800.

Small 8vo. Pp. xlviii, 310, 20. With nine vignettes.

33. Aphorisms And Reflections [etc.] Translated from MSS. of J. G. Zimmerman. [etc.]

London: Printed by Thomas Maiden, Sherbourne-Lane, For Vernor and Hood, J. Cuthell, [etc.] 1800.

12mo. Pp. 356. With a few small vignettes.

34. Instructive Lessons Conveyed to the Youthful Mind. [etc.] By Lilliputius Gulliver.

London: Printed for E. Newbery, at the Corner of St. Paul's Church-Yard. 1800.

18mo. Pp. 128. With cuts by the engraver of those in 'Jemima Placid.'

35. A Collection Of The Most Approved Entertaining Stories, By Solomon Winlove, Esq. A New Edition.

London: Printed for E. Newbery, Corner of St. Paul's Church-Yard; By J. Cundee, Ivy-Lane. (Price Sixpence.) [n. d.]

18mo. Pp. ii, 121. With cuts by the same artist.

36. The Adventures Of A Silver Penny.

London: Printed for E. Newbery, Corner of St. Paul's Church-Yard; [etc.] [n. d.]

18mo. Pp. 126.

37. The Adventures Of Master Headstrong, And Miss Patient, [etc.]

London: Printed for E. Newbery, at the Corner of St. Paul's Church-Yard; [etc. n. d.]

24mo. Pp. 94.

38. A Bag of Nuts ready Cracked, By Thomas Thumb, Esq.

London: Printed for E. Newbery, Corner of St. Paul's Church-Yard; [etc. n. d.]

24mo. Pp. xv, 94.

39. The Adventures Of A Silver Three-Pence. [etc.]   Written
by Mr. Truelove.

London : Printed by J. Cundee, Ivy Lane, Newgate Street ; For
E. Newbery, Corner of St. Paul's Church-Yard.   (Price Sixpence.)
[n. d.]

18mo.   Pp. 119.   With cuts of the ' Jemima Placid ' type.

40. The Nurse, A Poem.   Translated from the Italian of Luigi
Tansillo.   By William Roscoe.   The Second Edition.

Liverpool, Printed by J. M'Creery, For Cadell and Davies,
Strand, London.   1800.

18mo.   With cuts which are doubtless by Henry Hole.

41. Persian Lyrics, [etc.]   [By John Haddon Hindley.]

London, Printed, at the Oriental Press, by Wilson & Co. Wild-
Court ; For E. Harding, Pall-Mall ; [etc.]   1800.

4to.   Pp. 98, x, 54.   With a vignette on the title.

42. The Stranger.   A Drama. [etc.]   Translated from the German of Augustus Von Kotzebue, By Benjamin Thompson, Esq.

London : Printed by T. Maiden, Sherbourn-Lane, For Vernor
and Hood, No. 31, Poultry.   1800.

8vo.   Pp. x, 71.   With several charming vignettes by Vernor
    and Hood's artist.

43. Pizarro ; A Romantic Tragedy.   In Five Acts.   Translated
from the German of Augustus Von Kotzebue, By Benjamin Thompson, Esq.

London : Printed by T. Maiden, Sherbourn-Lane, For Vernor
and Hood, No. 31, Poultry.   1800.

8vo.   Pp. 92.   With a cut used in the previous article.

44. The Farmer's Son ; An Entertaining History For Young
Masters and Mistrefses. [etc.]   Interspersed with fine Cuts.

London : Printed by R. Bafsam, No. 53, St. John's Street, West
Smithfield.   (Price Three-pence.)   [n. d.]

24mo.   Pp. 79.   With a frontispiece and twenty cuts.

45. The Effects Of Tyranny & Disobedience ! Or The History
Of Hamet, Prince of Persia. [etc.]

Printed by R. Bafsam, No. 53, St. John's Street, West Smith-field.   (Price Sixpence.)   [n. d.]

24mo.   Pp. 80.   With a frontispiece and thirteen cuts, most of which occupy the entire page.

46. The Blossoms Of Morality; [etc.]   With Forty-two Cuts, Designed by J. Bewick, and engraved by T. Kelly.

Dublin, Printed by J. Jones, 90, Bride-Street.   1801.

12mo.   Pp. xii, 239.   With copies of the original cuts.

I introduce this volume into the present series with the view of suggesting to some, who are in the habit of referring to either Thomas or John Bewick the very indifferent cuts which ac-company a multitude of volumes published during the last hun-dred years, the untenable nature of such attribution.   In the present case, there was no endeavour to deceive.   The cuts are expressly stated to be the work of a " young Irishman, a native of Dublin;" and the publisher avows his intention, if the present attempt should meet with encouragement, to reprint a number of other London publications.   Let Collec-tors be assured that hundreds of volumes offered to them as " with cuts by Bewick " have really no more connection with him than the volume now described.

47. Melancholy; As it proceeds from The Disposition and Habit, [etc.]

London : Printed by T. Maiden, Sherbourne-Lane, For Vernor and Hood, J. Cuthell, [etc.]   1801.

12mo.   Pp. xii, 420.   With a few tailpieces by Vernor and Hood's artist.

48. The Beautiful And Interesting History Of Emilius & Sophia; In Two Parts.

Burslem : Printed by J. Tregortha.   1801.

24mo.   Pp. 114.   With a frontispiece and twenty-one cuts, some of the most important of which bear the name of Lee.

49. Zion's Pilgrim.   By Robert Hawker, D.D. Vicar of Charles, Plymouth.   Second Edition.

London : Printed for the Author; And Published by T. Williams, Stationers' Court, Ludgate Street.　1802.
Small 8vo.　Pp. 180.　With cut on the title.

50. Zion's Warrior; Or, The Christian Soldier's Manual. [etc.]
London : Printed for the Author; And Published by T. Wil-
liams, Stationer's Court, Ludgate Street.　1802.
Small 8vo.　Pp. 52.　With cut on the title.

51. Moral Tales And Poetic Essays, By Mrs. Crowther.
Huddersfield : Printed by Brook and Lancashire, For the Sub-
scribers.　1802.
Large 12mo.　Pp. ix, 136.　With thirteen cuts.

52. The Adventures Of Gil Blas, [etc.]
London : Printed for Vernor and Hood, Poultry, [etc.]　1802.
8vo.　3 vols.

53. False Alarms, [etc.] as in No. (3779.)
London : Printed by J. D. Dewick, Aldersgate Street, For I.
Harris, Successor to E. Newbery, Corner of St. Paul's Church-Yard.
1802.　Price Three Pence.
24mo.　Pp. 96.　With a frontispiece and ten cuts.

54. Virtue and Vice ; Or The History Of Charles Careful, And
Harry Heedless. [etc.]
London : Printed for J. Harris, Successor to E. Newbery, the
Corner of St. Paul's Church-yard.　Printed by E. Hemsted, Great
New street.　[n. d.]
24mo.　Pp. 57.　With a frontispiece and seventeen cuts.

55. Gradus Ad Cantabrigiam : [etc.]
London : Printed by Thomas Maiden, Sherbourne-Lane, For
W. J. and J. Richardson, Royal Exchange.　1803.
12mo.　Pp. viii, 140.　With a clever cut at the end of the Dedi-
cation, by the engraver of those which usually adorn the works
of Maiden's press.

56. An Efsay on Man. [etc.]
Gainsborough : Printed by H. Mozley, Market-Place.　1803.
18mo.　Pp. 49.　With a few trifling cuts.

57. The Grave; A Poem: By Robert Blair. [etc.]
Gainsborough: Printed by H. Mozley, Market-Place. [n. d.]
18mo. Pp. 37. With a few trifling cuts.

58. The Traveller: [etc.] By Oliver Goldsmith.
Gainsborough: Printed by H. Mozley, Market-Place. (n. d.]
18mo. Pp. 16. With cut on title.

59. The English Spelling Book, [etc.] By William Mavor, LL.D. [etc.]
London: Printed for Richard Phillips, No. 71, St. Paul's Church-yard. 1804.
12mo. Pp. 166. With Alphabet, Animal, and Fable cuts.

60. The Faithful Contrast; [etc.] By Mrs. Hurry, [etc.]
London: Printed for J. Harris, Successor to E. Newbery, at The Original Juvenile Library, Corner of St. Paul's Church Yard. 1804.
12mo. Pp. 215. With engravings similar in style to those in Mrs. Pilkington's ' Historical Beauties,' ' Pity's Gift,' etc. (See the Preface to this volume.)

61. A Town Eclogue.
Edinburgh: Printed for the Author, By Oliver and Co. Sold by John Buchanan, North Bridge. 1804.
8vo. Pp. 33. With three vignettes, in imitation of those by Thomas Bewick.

62. The Naturalist's Cabinet: [etc.] By the Rev. Thomas Smith.
Albion Press Printed: Published by J. and J. Cundee, Ivy-Lane, Paternoster Row. [n. d. but 1805.]
12mo. 6 vols. With cuts by the publishers' usual artist.

63. The Moralist: A Selection of Tales, From Various Authors.
Huddersfield: Printed and Sold by Brook and Lancashire. Sold also by Vernor and Hood, Crosby and Letterman, London. [n. d. but about 1805 ?]
18mo. Pp. 95. With a number of cuts, used by the same printers in others of their publications.

64. Effusions of Love From Chatelar To Mary Queen of Scotland. [etc.]

London : Printed for C. Chapple, Pall-Mall, and Southampton-Row, Bloomsbury.   1805.

18mo.   Pp. vi, 151.   With seven vignettes.

65. Miscellaneous Poems, Some of which are in the Cumberland Dialect.   By John Stagg.   Second Edition.

Workington : Printed by W. Borrowdale, In the Market Place.   1805.

12mo.   Pp. xii, 237.   With a few insignificant tailpieces.

66. Letters on Natural History : [etc.]   By John Bigland [etc.]

London : Printed for Longman, Hurst, Rees and Orme, Paternoster-Row ; and James Cundee, Ivy-Lane.   1806.

Sm. 8vo.   Pp. xviij, 448.   With a few vignettes.

67. The Cottage Library of Christian Knowledge.

London : Printed by W. Nicholson, Warner-street, For Williams & Smith, 10, Stationers' Court, Ludgate Hill.   1807.

12mo.   4 vols.   With a cut to each tract, many of which bear the name of Lee.

68. The Pilgrim's Progress, By John Bunyan.

Printed for James Cundee, London.   1808.

12mo.   Pp. xxxii, 463.   With a tailpiece at p. 236, used in various publications of the same press.

69. The History of The Irish Rebellion, in the year 1798, &c.

Alston, Cumberland : Printed by John Harrop.   1808.

12mo.   2 vols.   With a few tailpieces.

70. The Adventures of Captain Gulliver, In a Voyage to Lilliput.

Edinburgh : Published by Oliver & Boyd.   1808.

32mo.   Pp. 47.   With a frontispiece and eleven cuts.

71. A Tour through Cornwall, in the Autumn of 1808.   By The Rev^d. Richard Warner, of Bath.

Printed by Richard Cruttwell, St. James's Street, Bath ; [etc.]   1809.

8vo. Pp. iv, 363. With a cut on the title, by the engraver of other cuts in Cruttwell's various publications.

72. The Foundling; or, The History of Lucius Stanhope. Embellished with Cuts.

London: Printed for J. Harris, Successor to E. Newbery, at the Corner of St. Paul's Church-Yard; by J. Crowder, Warwick-square. 1809. (Price One Penny.)

24mo. Pp. 31. With a frontispiece and seven cuts, which bear no resemblance to those of the genuine edition, No. (3788.).

73. Mamma's Token Of Tender Love.

Coventry: Printed by Luckman & Suffield, Broadgate. (Price Two Pence.) [n. d.]

24mo. Pp. vi, 63. With a frontispiece and five cuts. The former bears the name of " Lee," to whom, as I have already remarked, is to be referred the great majority of the cuts for children's books which within the last few years have been attributed to John Bewick.

74. A Winter Season: [etc.] By James Fisher, Author of The Spring-Day.

Edinburgh: Printed for the Author, By John Moir, Royal Bank Close. [etc.] 1810.

8vo. Pp. viii, 204. With four full-page cuts.

75. The Wren; Or, the Fairy of the Green-House; [etc.]

Dublin: Printed by Graisberry and Campbell, 10, Back-Lane. Price, 1s. 1d. [n. d. but about 1810?]

Square 12mo. Pp. 63. With a frontispiece and twelve cuts.

76. Memoirs of a Peg-Top. By the Author of Adventures of a Pincushion. [etc.]

London: Printed and Sold by John Marshall, No. 4, Aldermary Church-Yard, Watling-Street. Price One Shilling. [n. d. but about 1810.]

18mo. Pp. iv, 82.

77. Harrison's Amusing Picture & Poetry Book, Containing nearly One Hundred Engravings.

Devizes: printed by J. Harrison; And Sold by The London Booksellers and Stationers. Price One Shilling.

12mo. Pp. 48. With ninety-five cuts, most of which are said to be the work of Harrison himself.

78. Harrison's Amusing Picture and Poetry Book, Containing Seventy Engravings.

Printed by J. Harrison, Devizes, And sold by the London Booksellers and Stationers. Price Sixpence. [n. d.]

18mo. Pp. 36. With seventy cuts, most of which also are said to be the productions of the printer himself. It is entirely different from the foregoing article, and from No. (64.).

79. Dorastus and Fawnia: Or the Life and Adventures of a German Princess.

Darlington, Printed by W. Appleton. 1812.

12mo. Pp. 24. With cut on the title, which is a copy of Bewick's cut of the Habit of an Englishman, in the History of All Nations, No. (3762.).

80. The Adventures Of a Silver Three-Pence. [etc.]

London: Printed for J. Harris, Successor to E. Newbery, the Corner of St. Paul's Church-Yard. Price Six-pence. [n. d. but about 1813 ?]

24mo. With a frontispiece and sixteen cuts, similar in style of execution to those in 'Jemima Placid' and 'Memoirs of a Peg-Top.' (See the Preface to this volume.)

81. The Life and Perambulation of a Mouse. In Two Volumes.

London: Printed & sold by John Marshall, No. 4, Aldermary Church-Yard [etc.] [n. d.]

18mo. Vol. I. pp. 91. Vol. II. pp. 84. With cuts by the engraver of those in 'Jemima Placid,' etc.

82. The Orphan; or, The Entertaining History of Little Goody Goosecap. [etc.] By Toby Teachem.

London, Printed and sold by John Marshall and Co. No. 4, Aldermary Church-Yard, [etc.] [n. d.]

18mo. Pp. 99. With a frontispiece and numerous cuts, in the manner of those in 'Jemima Placid,' etc.

83. The Life and Adventures of Robinson Crusoe. [Imperfect.]
18mo. With cuts at pp. 8, 17, 48, 55, 70, 76, 85, 91, and 104,
which are very similar in execution to those in ' Jemima
Placid,' etc. (See the Preface to this volume.)

84. The Happy Family; Or, Memoirs Of Mr. & Mrs. Norton.
[etc.]
London : Printed & sold by J. Marshall & Cᵒ. Nᵒ. 4, Aldermary
Church Yard, in Bow Lane. & Nᵒ. 17 Queen Street, Cheapside.
[n. d.]
24mo. Pp. x, 89. With cuts by the artist of those in ' Jemima
Placid,' etc. (See the Preface to this volume.)

85. Illustrations Of the School-Virgil, In Copper-Plates, And
Wood-Cuts; [etc.] By Robert John Thornton, M.D. [etc.]
London : Published by F. C. and J. Rivington ; J. Johnson ; and
Newbery, St. Paul's Church-yard ; [etc.] 1814.
12mo. With many cuts, the best of which bear the name of
Thompson.

86. The Galloping Guide To the A B C, [etc.]
Banbury : Printed and Sold by J. G. Rusher, Bridge-Street.
Price One Penny. [n. d. but about 1815.]
24mo. Pp. 14. With a frontispiece and twenty-six cuts, including two on the cover.

87. The Ladder to Learning : [etc.] By Mrs. Trimmer.
London : Printed for J. Harris, Successor to E. Newbery, at the
Juvenile Library, Corner of St. Paul's Churchyard. 1817.
18mo. Pp. vi, 223.

88. A Guide To the English Tongue. In Two Parts, [etc.]
By The Rev. Thomas Dyche. A New Edition, Carefully Revised
and Improved, By The Rev. Thomas Smith.
London : Printed for Scatcherd and Letterman ; G. Wilkie,
Baldwin, Cradock, and Joy ; [etc.] 1818.
12mo. Pp. viii, 156. With a frontispiece portrait of Dyche,
two pages of Copies for Writers, and fifteen Fable cuts.

89. A Collection of Armorial Bearings, Inscriptions, &c. In the
Parochial Chapel of Saint Andrew, Newcastle upon Tyne.

Newcastle : Printed by Edward Walker.   MDCCCXVIII.

8vo.   Pp. viii, 32.   The plates are by Armstrong and Walker.

90. The Cries of London : Or, Picture Exhibition. [etc.]
York : Printed and Sold by E. Peck, Lower-Ousegate.   (Price
One Penny.)   [n. d.]
24mo.   With a frontispiece and twenty-two cuts.

91. Ballads of Archery, Sonnets, etc.   By the Rev. James William Todd.
London : Printed for R. H. Evans, Pall Mall ; And W. Ginger,
College Street, Westminster.   1818.
12mo.   Pp. xxxii, 175, 33.

92. The Natural History of Quadrupeds. [Birds, Fishes, and In-
sects.]   For the Entertainment and Instruction of Children.   With
Numerous Cuts.
London : Printed for Baldwin, Cradock, and Joy. Paternoster
Row.   1819.   Price 2s. 6d.

The ' Fishes ' have, in addition to the foregoing imprint, ' and
     N. Hailes, Piccadilly.'
18mo.   In four vols.   Four of the cuts of the Quadrupeds,—
     the Horse, Bull, Urus, and Thibet Musk,—have the name of
     J. Bewick, but I do not believe that they are by him.   The
     second is palpably a forgery, and I have no doubt that all are
     so.   Some of the best are copies of Bewick's Quadrupeds and
     Birds.

93. The Life and Perambulations of a Mouse.   By M. P.   In
Two Volumes.
London : Printed for Baldwin, Cradock & Joy, Paternoster-Row ;
[etc.]   1819.
18mo.   Pp. 59.

94. A Collection Of Armorial Bearings, Inscriptions, &c. In the
Church of St. Nicholas, Newcastle on Tyne, [etc.]
Newcastle : Printed by Edward Walker.   MDCCCXX.
8vo.   2 vols.   Vol. I. pp. xxvii, 90.   Vol. II. pp. 84.   The
     illustrations are by Richardson, Armstrong, and Walker.

95. An Abridgment of Natural History.   By Dr. Goldsmith.
London : C. Cradock and W. Joy, Paternoster Row. [n. d. but 1820?]
12mo. Pp. xvi, 376. With figures of Animals, copied from Bewick's cuts.

96. A Picture of Whitby And its Environs. By the Rev. Geo. Young, A.M. [etc.]
Whitby : Printed and sold by R. Rodgers : [etc.] 1824.
12mo. Pp. viii, 310. With cuts by Green and others.

97. The Cries of York. (In Two Parts.) For the Amusement Of Young Children. Decorated with Cuts from Life.
York : Printed by J. Kendrew, Colliergate. [n. d.]
Square 18mo. Pp. 15. With a frontispiece and twelve cuts.

98. The Cries of York, For the Amusement Of Young Children. Decorated with Cuts.
York : Printed by J. Kendrew, Colliergate. [n. d.]
24mo. Pp. 31. With a frontispiece and twenty-six cuts, several of which are those of the former edition, but the borders have been removed.

99. The Cries of London. For the Amusement And Instruction of Good Children. Decorated with Cuts from Life.
York : Printed by J. Kendrew, Colliergate. [n. d.]
Pp. 23. With twenty-one cuts.
Of all the cuts in Kendrew's publications, of which I have a very large number, none are attributable to Bewick. Those of the three little books above noticed are the best, but Bewick had no hand in them.

100. Fables of Æsop, And Others : [etc.] By Samuel Croxall, D.D. The Twenty-Third Edition.
London : Printed for C. J. G. and F. Rivington ; Longman and Co.; [etc.] 1831.
Sm. 8vo. Pp. xxiii, 336. Many of the old cuts have been re-touched by Charlton Nesbit, who engraved the frontispiece.

JAMES the II.

INDEX

TO

BOOKS AND PAMPHLETS DESCRIBED OR MENTIONED IN THIS SUPPLEMENT.

——◆——

Z

J. E. TAYLOR AND CO., PRINTERS,
LITTLE QUEEN STREET, LINCOLN'S INN FIELDS.

ANNOUNCEMENT.

Messrs. L. REEVE & Co. *have the pleasure of announcing that they have made arrangements to issue, by Subscription, a series of Impressions of about Two Thousand Wood Blocks engraved for the most part by* THOMAS *and* JOHN BEWICK. *Among them will be found the engravings of a large number of the most celebrated works illustrated by these Artists, and an unique assemblage of Cuts for Private Gentlemen, Public Societies, and Companies, Amusements, Newspapers, Shop Cards, Invoices, Bar Bills, and other miscellaneous purposes. The volumes referred to are in general rare and costly, while of most of the miscellaneous engravings, very few impressions are known to exist.*

An Introduction, including a Descriptive Catalogue of the Blocks, will be furnished by the Rev. T. HUGO, *the possessor of the Collection.*

The Work, of which a very limited number will be printed, will be executed in the best possible style, and will form a very handsome volume in Royal Quarto.

— — - —

L. REEVE & Co., 5, HENRIETTA ST., COVENT GARDEN.